SLATER'S WAY

"Hey, boy! What the hell do you think you're doin'?"

He turned to find Arlen Tucker walking up behind him. Tucker, a blacksmith and a prominent member of the vigilance committee, was no doubt instrumental in the hanging of Jace's father. "I'm takin' my pa for buryin'," Jace answered.

"The hell you are," Tucker said. "Nobody told you you could cut that murderer down. Now you can help me haul him back up that pole. I oughta give you a good whippin' for pullin' a stunt like that."

Jace gave no thought to his response to Tucker's threat. Tucker was just beside his father's horse, and his face was no more than a foot from the butt of the Henry rifle riding in the saddle sling. Following his natural instincts, Jace pulled the weapon from the scabbard, cocking it as he brought it to bear on the surprised blacksmith.

"I wouldn't advise you to try it," Jace said. "You look like a pretty stout feller, so I reckon you oughta be able to lift my pa up across that saddle."

"The hell I will," Tucker responded. "Boy, you'd better put that rifle down! If I have to take it away from you, I'm gonna break it across your backside." He threatened, but he made no move toward the determined boy.

"I reckon you could try," Jace said calmly, "if you think it's worth gettin' shot over."

SLATER'S WAY

Charles G. West

A SIGNET BOOK

SIGNET
Published by the Penguin Group
Penguin Group (USA) LLC, 375 Hudson Street,
New York, New York 10014

USA | Canada | UK | Ireland | Australia | New Zealand | India | South Africa | China
penguin. com
A Penguin Random House Company

First published by Signet, an imprint of New American Library,
a division of Penguin Group (USA) LLC

First Printing, July 2015

 REGISTERED TRADEMARK—MARCA REGISTRADA

ISBN 978-0-451-47199-4

Printed in the United States of America
10 9 8 7 6 5 4 3 2 1

For Ronda

Chapter I

It was altogether fitting on this spring day in 1864 that the muddy streets of Virginia City were awash with a flood of water from a violent thunderstorm.

Nothing good can come of a day as dreary as this, Leona Engels thought.

The heavy dark clouds hovering over Alder Gulch erupted again late in the afternoon and threatened to continue their assault of thunder and lightning into the evening. The disagreeable weather had not been sufficient to keep John Slater Engels and his longtime friend and partner, Henry Weed, from their usual visit to the Miners Saloon. It was a ritual that John's wife loathed, since the little bit of pay dirt her husband and Henry were able to pull from their claim in Daylight Gulch went straight into Gil Mobley's pockets at his saloon, but she was too fearful to complain about it.

As darkness began to gather in the gulch, Leona became more concerned, for it was well past time when the two men usually came home for supper. She walked to the door of the rough cabin once again to peer out into the rain. There was still no sign of her husband and his partner. Finally she turned and called to her fifteen-year-old son, "Jace, come here, boy."

John Slater Engels Jr. was originally called J.S. by his parents, but in a short time the initials evolved into the nickname of Jace, since the sounds were not that far apart. The boy carefully put the shotgun he had been cleaning aside and came from the kitchen.

"Ma'am?" he replied.

"I'm startin' to worry about your pa," Leona said. "Him and Henry are usually through with their drinkin' and card playin' by now. I want you to go down to Virginia City and tell them I'm gonna throw their supper out the door if they don't get theirselves home."

"Yes'um," the stoic young boy replied.

With no sign of emotion, he turned and went to the front corner of the cabin, where he slept on a bedroll, and picked up his hat. It was not the first time he had been sent to find his father and his hard-drinking friend, and it was a chore that he didn't much care for. It would be a year this month since they had come to the gulch in search of gold. And so far, it seemed the main thing his father had accomplished was to garner a reputation for himself as a drunk and a brawler.

There wasn't much law enforcement in most parts of Alder Gulch. Outlaws and hell-raisers were ultimately dealt with by the vigilance committee, and Jace felt sure they were keeping an eye on Weed and his father. He was disappointed that his father lacked the backbone to resist the temptations of the lawless crowd. The family had fled Kansas after his father and Weed were identified by witnesses as the men involved in a bank holdup. That holdup had been Weed's idea, and he had talked Jace's father into it. It seemed as though every scrape his father found himself in could be traced back to some illegal scheme that Henry Weed had come up with. Mostly Jace was ashamed for his mother, and the abuse she sometimes suffered when his drunken father came home after a night of gambling and dallying with the *fancy ladies* at the saloon.

On this day, the rain had started in the morning and his father had said it was too wet to work their claim. But he and Weed decided it was not too wet to ride over to Alder Gulch for a drink of whiskey and maybe a hand or two of poker. When Jace had asked how the rain could hurt the gold they were looking for in the water, he received a backhand for his sarcasm. And then off they went, riding to Alder Gulch in the rain after a casual promise to be back by suppertime.

With his hat pulled low to help shield him from the rain, Jace plodded along the trail that led to Virginia City. His coat was soon soaked through, but he ignored the discomfort, concentrating more on what he would say to convince his father to come home.

When he reached the point where the trail ended at the main street that traced the length of Alder Gulch, he was immediately aware of an event going on beside the Miners Saloon. A sizable crowd had gathered to stand in the rain, ignoring the occasional flash of lightning and rumble of thunder. And when he came closer, he realized they were there to witness a hanging. As curious as anyone, he edged up through the noisy circle of spectators to see for himself. There was no tree next to the saloon, but it was not the first hanging that had taken place there. One single pole served as a gallows. Approximately fifteen feet tall, the pole had been notched near the top so that a rope could be tied and secured to support the unfortunate victim as he dangled at the noose end of the rope. With his hands tied behind his back and his feet bound together, the victim hung motionless, his head cocked to the side by the heavy noose around his neck. In the darkness, it was hard to see the man's face, but from the excited conversation he overheard around him, he learned that the man had been hanged because he killed a fellow he had argued with in the saloon.

Since he didn't see him in the crowd of spectators, Jace decided he'd best look for his father instead of gawking at a dead man. So he had started to turn away and head for the saloon when he was startled by a sudden bright flash, followed almost immediately by a loud clap of thunder. In those few seconds, he was stunned to see the grotesque features of his father's face, in the flash of lightning.

"That's the good Lord saying thank you for riddin' this world of troublemakers like John Engels," he heard someone say. It was followed by a hardy chuckle from someone else.

Jace felt his body go numb, and his legs threatened to deny him support as he pushed blindly through the crowd of men standing around the pole. Confused and horrified by the terrible scene he had just witnessed, he didn't know what to do. After making his way through the mob, he leaned against the wall of the saloon until he could think clearly once again. His father was dead, and that was the only thing he knew for sure.

Weed, he thought then. *Where is Henry Weed?*

He decided he should find him, so he left the side of the building and started searching through the crowd again. But Weed was nowhere to be found, so he went inside the saloon to look for him there, but to no avail. He was left with no choice but to return home as fast as he could to take the terrible news to his mother.

Running almost all of the two miles back to the camp, Jace was surprised to find Weed's and his father's horse standing beside the cabin. Weed had evidently started for home shortly before the boy arrived at the scene of the hanging, and had somehow circled back on the trail Jace had walked. Perhaps Jace would have seen him if he had not been walking with his head down in the driving rain.

So Ma already knows about Pa, he thought as he opened the door.

He walked into the cabin to find his mother sobbing in Henry Weed's arms. When she heard Jace come in, she turned and beckoned to him. He went at once to comfort her. She put her arm around him and pulled him close to Weed and herself.

"Oh, Jace," she wailed. "Did you see your pa?" When he answered yes, she sobbed again. "You poor boy," she cried. "I'm so sorry you had to see him like that, hung on a post."

"There warn't nothin' I could do to help him," Henry Weed said. "He got into a tussle with some feller we was playin' cards with, and before I knowed it, they was goin' at each other with their guns. John was faster'n that feller, and shot him through the chest before he ever cleared the table with his six-shooter. Then a bunch of fellers that had been standin' at the bar, drinkin', took your pa down before he could get off another shot. They said they was on the vigilance committee, and they was fixin' to put a stop to all the lawlessness in town. I got back here as fast as I could. You don't have to worry, I'm gonna take care of your ma."

"I reckon I can take care of my ma," Jace said.

"Why, sure you can," Weed said, "but I expect I'd best be the one to take care of both of you."

Leona stopped crying then. "Henry's right, Jace. He's offered to stay with us and take care of us now that your pa's gone. We'll talk some more about it later on tonight."

"What about Pa?" Jace wanted to know. "We've got to go get him down from that pole and bury him proper." He looked at Weed, waiting for his answer.

"I don't know if we can do that," Leona said.

"Why not?" Jace asked.

Weed answered for her. "They ain't likely to let us take John down from there for a while yet. They'll most likely want him to hang there to let other folks know what happens to troublemakers in Virginia City."

Jace couldn't believe the indifference on the part of his father's wife and his supposed best friend. "How can you just not care what happens to Pa's body?" he charged. He turned to look into his mother's eyes. "We've got to take care of Pa."

"We can't," Leona said. "It's best to just do what we can to carry on now without him. I knew it was gonna come to this. It was just a matter of time."

"The hell we will!" Jace exclaimed.

"Now, don't be gettin' yourself riled up about this," Weed said. "It's over and done with. Your pa's gone, and I reckon it was bound to happen—the way things were goin' and all."

Jace made no response other than the angry glare he cast in Weed's direction. His pa wouldn't be dead if he had never crossed paths with Henry Weed. After a moment, Jace shifted an accusing gaze at his mother, who was no longer crying, but stood wringing her hands in apparent distress. It infuriated the boy that Henry Weed was acting as if John Engels was the wild, hard-drinking troublemaker, and he was no more than an innocent bystander.

Some friend, he thought, glaring at Weed again.

He made up his mind then that he was going to cut his father down from that pole, no matter what his mother or Weed said. He had never had a particularly close relationship with his father, but he was his father, and he didn't intend to leave him hanging as an amusement for the miners in Virginia City.

"I'll put the horses away," he volunteered, and headed for the door.

"That's a good idea," Weed said. "There're some things I wanna talk to your mama about while you're doin' that."

Outside the cabin, Jace paused to study the night-time sky. The rain had slackened considerably as the thunderstorm moved across the gulch, though the clouds were as dark and thick as before. He led the two horses behind the cabin to the simple shelter that served as a stable for them and the two mules. Having already decided what he was going to do, he left the saddles on the horses, then tied a shovel to the saddle on Weed's horse. Next, he checked the Henry rifle riding in the sling on his father's saddle to make sure it was still there and had not suffered any from the rain. Satisfied that Weed would not likely take the trouble to check on the horses, he returned to the cabin.

When he walked in the door, he found the two of them standing before the fireplace, facing the door as if waiting for him. "We need to tell you somethin',"

Weed said. "We decided that the way things are, the best thing is for me and your mama to live together as man and wife."

Jace recoiled sharply. Seeing his reaction, his mother tried to soften the shock. "Henry has been kind enough to offer to take care of us, now that your father's gone. I know it's kind of sudden, but I think John would approve of it. He and Henry were such close friends."

Unable to speak for a moment while his brain spun wildly, Jace finally blurted, "Pa ain't even in the ground yet! It didn't take you long to jump into the bed together!"

"Jace!" Leona scolded. "You watch your mouth! It ain't like that at all."

"Your mama's right," Weed said. "It's just the best thing to do. I've always had a fondness for your mama, and I intend to make it right when we can stand up before a preacher. We'll make a new start. Me and John had been talkin' about movin' on anyway. We ain't found much of anythin' in the sluice box for a while now, so I think it's best to leave our claim and head up to Helena. There's a new strike at Last Chance Gulch and we can make a fresh start there—might have a little better luck. There ain't no reason me and you can't get along, as long as you mind your ma and me. Whaddaya say?"

"Sounds to me like it don't make no difference what I think," Jace replied. "You and Ma have already decided what you're gonna do."

Tired of trying to solicit the boy's cooperation, Weed smirked and said, "That's about the size of it, boy, so you might as well get used to it."

Anxious to avoid a conflict between Weed and her son, Leona spoke up then. "Let's sit down and eat the supper getting cold on the table. No matter what's happened, we need to eat."

Jace still found it hard to believe his mother's apparent acceptance of his father's death and her immediate acceptance of Weed's proposal—not much different from changing one horse to ride another when the first one gets tired. But he said nothing more. He sat down at the table with them and ate the supper she had cooked. When he was finished, he excused himself to make a final check on the livestock before going to his bedroll in the front corner of the cabin. "We'll start a new day in the morning," his mother said to him as he pulled the quilt that served as his bedroom wall across his little corner.

"Yes, ma'am," he mumbled.

He lay there on the thin pallet for what seemed hours, listening to the whispered conversation between his mother and Henry Weed. Finally the talking stopped. Even then he continued to lie there until he felt certain they were both asleep. As quietly as he could, he pulled the edge of the quilt back far enough to peek into the main room. Weed was sprawled on the pallet he had been using before, snoring lustily, the alcohol he had apparently consumed earlier finally rendering him unconscious. Jace slipped outside the quilt and paused to watch the sleeping man. There was no sound from the bedroom.

At least he ain't already jumped in bed with my mother, he thought, and tiptoed to the door.

Outside, he went quickly to the stable and led the horses out, walking them up the path until certain he was away from the cabin without anyone aware of his departure. Stepping up into the saddle then, he headed back to Virginia City, his father's cartridge belt around his waist, and his Henry rifle riding in the saddle sling.

The storm had spent its energy and moved on, leaving a dark and damp night. He had no watch to tell the time, but he knew the hour was late when he reached the ridge overlooking the gulch and the lusty town that never slept.

Nudging his father's sorrel gelding, he descended to the noisy street below, riding along unnoticed by the drunks coming and going from the saloons. He pulled the horses up when he got to the harness shop next to the Miners Saloon, thinking he was prepared to see the grisly sight of his father's lifeless body dangling from the solitary pole again. He was wrong, however, for the sight of his late father jolted him as before. The crowd that had been there had dispersed, returning to the saloons of their choice to talk about the shooting and the hanging that had followed. At present, there were only two spectators standing at the foot of the pole, gazing up at the late John Slater Engels. Jace remained in the saddle and waited until the novel sight of the dead man yielded to the craving for another drink of whiskey and the two men walked back toward the Miners Saloon.

Jace nudged the sorrel, anxious to do what he had come to do before someone else showed up to gawk at the hanged man. He felt the blood in his veins go cold as ice when he pulled up beside the corpse. Seated as he was in the saddle, his eyes were even with his father's belt. With his heart pounding inside his chest, he forced himself to remain calm and do what he had to do.

"Easy, boy," he said softly to the horse. "Steady, now," he repeated as he pulled his feet from the stirrups and carefully placed one foot on the saddle. Then, using his father's body to steady himself, he stood up on the saddle. As he pulled himself up, he almost lost his footing when he brushed against his father's face and looked into the sightless eyes staring grotesquely at him as if already suffering the fiery coals of hell. Forcing himself to look away from the cruel face, he pulled the skinning knife from the cartridge belt and sawed furiously at the rope above his father's head. It seemed the rope was never going to part, but finally the last strands were severed and the corpse dropped to the ground. Rigor mortis having already set in, the body landed feetfirst and, rigid as a pole, fell face forward in the trampled mud.

Jace dismounted and stood staring at the body for a long moment. It would be no easy task to get the corpse across the saddle. He was still contemplating the job when he was startled by a voice behind him. "Hey, boy! What the hell do you think you're doin'?"

He turned to find Arlen Tucker walking up behind him. Tucker, a blacksmith and a prominent member of the vigilance committee, was no doubt instrumental in the hanging of Jace's father. "I'm takin' my pa for buryin'," Jace answered.

"The hell you are," Tucker said. "Nobody told you you could cut that murderer down. Now you can help me haul him back up that pole. I oughta give you a good whippin' for pullin' a stunt like that."

Jace gave no thought to his response to Tucker's threat. Tucker was just beside his father's horse, his face was no more than a foot from the butt of the Henry rifle riding in the saddle sling. Following his natural instincts, Jace pulled the weapon from the scabbard, cocking it as he brought it to bear on the surprised blacksmith.

"I wouldn't advise you to try it," Jace said. "You

look like a pretty stout feller, so I reckon you oughta be able to lift my pa up across that saddle."

"The hell I will," Tucker responded. "Boy, you'd better put that rifle down! If I have to take it away from you, I'm gonna break it across your backside." He threatened, but he made no move toward the determined boy.

"I reckon you could try," Jace said calmly, "if you think it's worth gettin' shot over."

Tucker hesitated, measuring the cold ominous look in Jace's eyes. He decided it not worth the risk to test the boy's resolve. "You're makin' a helluva mistake," he said. "You're gonna wind up with the same reputation your pa had."

"Pick him up and lay him across that saddle," Jace said, motioning with his rifle. "I ain't waitin' around here all night."

"All right, all right," Tucker replied, "just don't get careless with that damn rifle."

He took hold of John Engels' shoulders and stood him up. Then he bent down, put his arms around his knees, and lifted him up as though hoisting a log. Henry Weed's roan was not sure it wanted the body across its back, and it sidestepped nervously when the corpse landed on the saddle. The sudden motion caused Jace to quickly grab his father's shoulder to keep the body from sliding off the saddle. Tucker saw it as his chance to act. He pulled the .44 he wore, to his instant regret. Because of the stiffness of the body, John Engels' feet kicked up to spoil Tucker's aim when Jace pulled on his father's shoulder, causing his shot to miss. Jace took no time to think. Holding the nine-pound Henry in one hand, he pulled the trigger and cut Tucker down with a slug in his belly.

Staring in disbelief, the blacksmith sat down heavily

in the mud, clutching his stomach. Equally surprised, Jace paused only a moment to consider what had just happened. Someone was bound to have heard the shots, so, in a panic, he grabbed the horses' reins and turned to discover a witness staring at him, seemingly in a drunken stupor. Until that moment, he had not noticed the man slumped against the side door of the saloon, obviously having gotten no farther after leaving the saloon. Although he continued to gape openly at the boy, the drunk didn't move, and he said not a word. Jace paused for only a moment before leading the horses around behind the saloon to secure his father's body across the saddle. Working as quickly as he could, he bound the body with a rope, hearing voices from the side of the saloon. Thinking the man sitting against the side door was no doubt telling them what had happened, he climbed up into the saddle as fast as he could and rode down the alley behind the stores, leading the roan behind him. When he came to the first trail that led up from the gulch, he followed it out of Virginia City and into the hills beyond. His only quest now was to find a place to dig a grave. It didn't matter where, as long as it was not easily seen. The burial itself was not as important to him as the removal of his father's body from public display. So when he came to a grassy ravine with one solitary spruce tree standing as a grave marker, he decided to bury his father there instead of taking him back to Daylight Gulch.

When the grave was done, and his father's body was in the ground, Jace stood looking at it for a long moment. It was customary to say something about a person when he was buried, talk about all the good things he had done before he died. He continued to stand there while he thought back over his short life and the relationship he had had with his father.

Finally he said, "I can't think of a damn thing he ever did for me and my ma except make life hard for both of us. Amen."

It was in the wee hours of the morning when Jace rode back into the camp at Daylight Gulch, but there was a glow from a lamp in the window of the cabin. Hearing him ride in, Henry Weed burst out the door to confront him. Jace's mother stood in the doorway behind Weed.

"Where the hell have you been with those horses?" Weed demanded.

"Buryin' Pa," was Jace's stoic reply. He dismounted and led the horses to the makeshift stable with Weed following right behind him.

"You dumb little shit!" Weed blurted. "I reckon you led a posse of vigilantes right back here, too."

"I might have," Jace calmly allowed. "So I expect I'd best get my things together and be gone when they get here." He had already decided that he was not going to live with Henry Weed. He pulled the saddle off Weed's roan but left the sorrel saddled. "I don't reckon you and Ma have to worry. It'll be me they're lookin' for."

"Maybe they won't be lookin' for you," his mother said, just then joining them. "Did anyone see you?"

"Just one man, but I don't know if he'll tell or not," Jace replied.

"Why wouldn't he, if he saw you?" Weed demanded.

"He was fallin'-down drunk. I'm hopin' he don't know what he saw," Jace said.

"Nobody tried to stop you from takin' John down?" Weed asked.

"One man and I don't know if he'll tell, either."

Exasperated with the boy's lack of distress, Weed demanded, "Well, why in the hell wouldn't he?"

"Because I shot him," Jace replied. "And I don't know if I killed him or not."

"My Lord!" his mother gasped, and clutched the corner post for support. It was almost more than she could comprehend, coming as it did on top of her husband's death.

"I'm sorry, Ma," Jace said. "I wouldn'ta done it if he hadn't tried to shoot me. He didn't give me no choice."

She was too distressed to think clearly, but Weed was quick to advise, "He's right, Leona. He needs to get packed up and get the hell away from here. They'll be comin' lookin' for him, sure as shootin'."

"But he's just a boy," Leona protested. "He said the man was going to shoot him. Maybe if he tells them that—"

"That won't make no difference to that posse," Weed insisted. "They'll string him up, just like they did John. It's best he gets away from here. If he's old enough to shoot a man, he's old enough to look out for himself."

"I can take care of myself," Jace assured her. "I'll be all right." He was well aware of Weed's preference that he should leave, even before this happened. "I can tell you where I buried Pa if you want to visit his grave."

"She don't wanna visit his grave," Weed quickly declared. "That's over and done with."

Jace ignored the remark and addressed his mother. "Like I said, I can draw you a little map to show you where Pa's buried."

She glanced nervously at Weed before answering, "I guess it's not necessary. I don't need to see the

grave." Concerned for herself, she realized that it was
in her best interest to concede to Weed's wishes. He
clearly wanted Jace out of the picture, and her son had
conveniently accommodated him by shooting a man.
"Henry's right," she said to her son. "It's best for you
to leave before they come here looking for you."

Jace nodded solemnly, glancing at the scowling
Weed, then back at his worried mother.

"Yes, ma'am," he said. "I'm leavin' just as soon as I
get some things together." He went back to the cabin
then to gather what clothes he had, his blanket roll,
and some of his late father's things. Most of what he
might need was already in the saddlebags on his
father's horse. "I don't reckon you mind if I take this,"
he said to his mother as he pulled a rain slicker out
from under her bed.

She shook her head, but Weed saw fit to comment,
"I reckon it's fittin' for you to take some of your dad-
dy's stuff, but I don't know about his horse and rifle.
They might better be left with your mama and me."

"I expect I could just walk off in the hills with
nothin' except what I was born with," Jace replied sarcastically. "But I ain't gonna. I reckon Pa would druther they was left with me, instead of you."

Weed bristled a bit at the remark. "I might have
more to say about that than you. I ain't sure I'm gonna
let you leave with that sorrel and that Henry rifle. I
don't see as how you've earned a damn thing that
belonged to your pa."

Jace dropped his hand to rest on the handle of his
father's single-action Colt .44 he still had strapped to
his side. "You and me ain't ever really got along too
good," he said solemnly. "And right now ain't a good
time to mess with me unless you wanna make my ma
a widow for the second time."

"Jace!" Leona cried out, shocked by the threat from her son. She looked at Weed then and pleaded, "Let him take what he wants, Henry. Just let him go!"

Weed was caught in an uncertain position. This was not the boastful bluster of an immature boy. There was a lethal quality in his tone that promised this was no idle threat. Although smarting mentally at the thought of being faced down by a fifteen-year-old boy, he found himself at a distinct disadvantage, since he was not wearing a gun. And the stony-eyed boy had already shot one man that night.

"All right," he said. "I'll do it for you, Leona." Back at Jace then, he blurted, "Just get the hell on outta here."

"With pleasure," Jace replied calmly.

Chapter 2

With no destination in mind, Jace pointed the sorrel's head toward the north and made his way down through the hills in the dark, being careful to avoid the deep cuts and gravel slides that might cause the horse to stumble. Once out of the higher hills, he continued north across an open plain that stretched seven or eight miles before encountering the foothills of a dark mountain range.

He rode on, and as first light approached, he could see that the range he was entering boasted snow-covered peaks extending up from pine-clad slopes. It looked like the perfect country he needed to escape to from those who might be searching for him. He felt sure he could find a place to hide from a lynch mob in those mountains, thinking the drunken bunch of volunteers would soon weary and go back to the saloons. Montana had been made a territory for less than a year, and Bannack was named the capital. So maybe there was a U.S. Marshal there already; Jace had no idea. But had there been, he might have considered telling his version of the shooting to a deputy marshal.

A line of trees running about halfway across the plain told him there was a fair-sized creek between him and the mountains. As he rode, he considered the occurrence of this unexpected turn in his life, and the sobering thought that at his young age, he had shot a man and probably killed him. He thought about his father, lying dead in a shallow grave, and realized that he did not feel the grief that should come with the loss of one's parent. He could not recall any happy times spent with his father, only occasions of drunken abuse at worst and almost total indifference at best.

Jace had never been an emotional child. His father had often remarked that the boy had the disposition of a hanging judge, never smiling, never laughing. Maybe he was right. There wasn't a brother or sister to compare himself to, and no friends his age, so he didn't bother to care about his stoic nature.

He was not without compassion, however, for those who deserved it—like his mother. He hoped for her sake that she would have a decent life with Henry Weed. But he felt no regret that he would not be there to share that life, for he could not forget how quickly she had agreed to become Weed's wife, and how she had urged him to leave. The two deserved each other, he decided, and resolved to think of it no further. It was time to consider the rest of his life, and at present, that meant finding a place to camp and rest his horse.

When he reached the creek, he stopped to let his horse drink. It would have been a good place to camp had he not been concerned about a posse riding to catch up with him. So he decided he'd better not stop until he gained the safety of the mountains. With that in mind, he pushed on, following the creek until he came upon a small stream. The stream appeared to come from high up the slope, flowing down a narrow ravine to reach the creek. This, he decided, was more like what he was looking for, so he began to follow the stream back up the mountain.

The higher up he climbed, the harder it became to follow the stream, until he finally determined it was safer to dismount and lead the horse. The trees, mostly pine with patches of firs, grew thick on the mountainside and so close to the stream that it became necessary to walk in the water in many places. About a third of the way up the slope, he came to a grassy meadow, where the stream split in two. This was the spot he picked for his camp.

He pulled the saddle off the sorrel and unrolled his blanket, succumbing to a deep feeling of weariness from not having slept all night. He took the precaution to hobble the horse, however, before crawling into his blanket roll.

It was past noon when he woke to find the sorrel gelding nibbling the meadow grass near his feet. An empty feeling in his stomach told him that he was hungry as well, but it also reminded him that he had no food. It did not cause him undue concern. He had been a skillful hunter for as long as he could remember, and he felt sure game was readily available in these mountains. There remained the question, however, that someone might be close enough behind him to hear the distinctive report of the Henry rifle. He rolled out of his blanket and got to his feet.

Addressing the sorrel, he said, "Well, I'm gonna have to find something pretty soon, or learn to eat grass like you."

There were other things to think about for a man on his own, and regardless of his age, he was a man on his own. And he was smart enough to know that he couldn't live forever on nothing more than what he could kill. But that was going to be his diet for the foreseeable future, so he counted the cartridges in his cartridge belt. There were twenty-two left. In addition to those, there were six in the rifle's magazine, plus five shots in his handgun, the hammer resting on an empty chamber for safety's sake. He would have to be very conservative with his cartridges, for he had no money to buy new ones. That thought caused him to remember that he had no money to buy basic supplies to live on, either.

"I'll have to think of something," he said to the sorrel. "I reckon I'll have to take up my pa's trade, if I can't find some way of makin' honest money." He was not inclined to follow in his father's lawless footsteps, but he didn't rule out the possibility if it was his only recourse.

Ignoring the gnawing in his stomach, he saddled his horse and pushed on farther into the rugged mountains, his eyes constantly searching for signs of game. The stream led him to a small lake high up the mountain that bore evidence of numerous visits by deer as well as elk and grizzlies. This was the place, he decided, where he would acquire his meat supply. So he dismounted, pulled the saddle off his horse, and left it to graze near the edge of the lake while he picked a good place to hide and wait for a potential target to come for water. As he had suspected, judging by the many tracks, he didn't have to wait long before supper showed up in the form of half a dozen deer that suddenly appeared in the pines above the lake. Showing no concern for the horse grazing near the lower side of the lake, they filed down to the water's edge to drink.

Shifting slightly in the gully he had selected for his ambush, he swung his rifle around to sight upon a doe that offered an inviting target as she drank next to a ten-point buck that was obviously the leader of the harem. Jace squeezed the trigger slowly until the Henry suddenly spoke and the doe jumped backward before falling helplessly to the ground. The other deer immediately bolted back into the trees as the echo of the shot rang out from the mountainside.

Jace did not move from his position for a few minutes while he watched the fallen deer from the cover of the gully. He told himself that it was unlikely a posse following him would be close enough to have heard the shot, but it had seemed unusually loud when it broke the silence of the mountains. When all seemed as peaceful as it had been before, he left the gully and hurried down to the edge of the lake. Mortally wounded, the deer tried to get to her feet when he approached, so he drew his knife and ended her suffering as quickly as he could. It was not the first deer he had butchered, so he wasted no time starting the skinning.

It was late in the afternoon by the time he had a good fire going with strips of flesh roasting over the flames. He ate the freshly cooked meat while he continued butchering the carcass, planning to smoke a good supply to last him for a while. His methods were decidedly primitive, since he had not had the foresight to take cooking utensils with him when he left his father's cabin. Still, he did not let that discourage him. With his belly filled, he started smoking the rest of the meat over the fire. Although it was comfortably cool in the mountains, he knew that the meat would not keep long if it was not prepared properly.

It was then that he had a feeling that he was being watched. There was no reason to suspect it. It was more a sensing that he was not alone. He looked toward his horse, but the sorrel gave no indication that it had heard anything. Having learned to trust his instincts, he became immediately alert while careful not to show any sign of being aware of a visitor. He picked up his rifle as casually as he could and moved unhurriedly out of the firelight.

As soon as he was out of the fire's light, however, he hurried to circle around toward his horse. Without knowing if his visitor was Indian, grizzly, or a posse man, he knew that his horse would be the primary target for any of the three. When he got in position behind the sorrel, he knelt beside a clump of chokecherry bushes, where he had a good view of his campfire and bedroll, and waited. He was about to conclude that his senses were spooked and he was just being overcautious when he heard the voice behind him.

"What the hell are you doin' here?"

Startled, but reacting instantly, Jace dropped to the ground, rolling over on his back as he did to end up with his rifle pointed straight at the surprised intruder. "Whoa! Whoa!" the man exclaimed. "Don't shoot! Just hold on a minute. If I meant you any harm, I'da shot you instead of sayin' something."

Jace hesitated, not sure if he could trust the stranger. Finally he said, "Well, you sure coulda sung out instead of sneakin' up on a man's camp."

"I warn't sure who you were and what you was up to," the man said. "I heard your shot a couple of hours back, so I figured I'd come over and see who was messin' around in my huntin' spot."

"Your huntin' spot?" Jace repeated. "Well, I reckon I oughta be proud to get a chance to meet God, 'cause I figure that's who owns these mountains."

In the darkness of the trees, it was difficult to make out the features of the man, other than the fact that he looked to be sizable. Jace couldn't see that his impertinent response had caused a smile to appear on his visitor's whiskered face.

"God lets me look after it for him," he said with half a chuckle. "I could smell that meat cookin' a mile away. Maybe I could help you eat a little of it. Looks like you've got a plenty."

"I reckon," Jace said, and got to his feet, being careful to keep his rifle in front of him. "Come on over by the fire and you can help yourself to some meat."

"Much obliged," the man said, and walked out of the shadow of the trees. "Why, you ain't much more'n a boy. I couldn't tell from back yonder. You're kinda tall and stringy."

"This Henry rifle don't know how old I am," Jace informed him, still cautious, as his visitor was dressed in animal skins, looking much like an Indian.

The man laughed. "Nah, I reckon it don't. But you ain't got no reason to worry about me. Like I said, if I was figurin' on doin' you any harm, I'da already done it. I was just a little curious about you; that's all. Anyway, I appreciate your hospitality. My name's Teddy Lightfoot. What's your'n?"

When Teddy walked out closer to the light of the fire, Jace could see that he was a white man, although he wore his hair Indian-style in two long braids. He seemed friendly enough, so Jace let his rifle drop by his side.

About to state his name, Jace hesitated. As far as he knew, he was most likely wanted by the law. Maybe it was not a good idea to use his real name. It was not a name his father had brought much honor to, anyway. With no time to think about it, he responded with the first name that came to mind. "Slater," he said, giving his middle name.

"Slater," Teddy repeated. "Slater what, or what Slater?"

"Just Slater," the boy answered. "That's all."

Teddy shrugged. "All right, Slater," he said, figuring the boy had a reason to use only one name, but he was indifferent as to that reason. "Let's see how good you are at roastin' deer meat. A little coffee wouldn't be bad to go with it." Without waiting for Jace, he strode eagerly over to the fire.

"I ain't got no coffee," Jace said

"Dang! No coffee?" He glanced at the fire as if unable to believe it. When he saw no coffeepot, he took a closer look around the boy's camp. "I swear, you ain't got much of anything, have you?" He turned to Jace again and looked him in the eye. "Looks to me like you musta left somewhere in a hurry."

"I've got this rifle and flint and steel to make a fire, so I reckon I won't go hungry," Jace stated.

"Until your cartridges run out," Teddy said, sizing up the situation fairly easily. "Even an Injun don't live on nothin' but meat. You've got to have some beans and biscuits from time to time. You live on nothin' but meat and pretty soon your belly will draw up in a knot. And you've got to have coffee," he stated emphatically. "I know I do. Hell, the first thing I cried for after my ma popped me outta the oven was a cup of coffee." He paused to study Jace's reactions before concluding. "The way I see it, you musta had to run for it in a helluva hurry, and you didn't have time to grab everything you need. That about right?"

"Maybe," Jace replied stoically, seeing no reason to deny it.

"You don't talk much, do you? Well, don't matter, I can talk enough for both of us." He paused then while he continued to study the young man he had happened upon. Although sober and dispassionate, he showed no reluctance to look a man straight in the eye. Teddy decided there was no evil in the steady gaze. "Tell you what," he decided. "Why don't we pack your little mess up here and ride on down the mountain a piece? I've got a camp in a canyon about two miles from here. We'll have us some coffee then." He didn't wait for Jace's answer. "I'll go fetch my horses and we'll load that meat up."

Jace watched the huge man as he walked away, and wondered if he was as friendly as he appeared to be. He decided to be cautious until he was sure.

Teddy disappeared into the trees again, but reappeared a short time later leading two horses, one of them loaded with what looked to be a good supply of meat. "You ain't the only one that's been doin' some huntin'," he announced cheerfully as he led the horses up to the fire. "I got me an elk on the other side of this mountain, and I was on my way back to my camp when I heard you shoot that deer. I'll be dryin' the meat for jerky. If you want, I'll help you smoke that deer."

Jace took only a moment to consider, not realizing at the time that he was about to make a decision that would set the pattern for his life.

"I reckon," he said, deciding that he could trust Teddy Lightfoot. The thought of a cup of hot coffee to help choke down his venison seemed too good to pass up and might have had the most influence upon that decision.

I hope to hell I ain't gonna be sorry for this, Teddy thought as he led the strange boy down the far side of the mountain. Going solely on his instincts, he had decided there was no real evil in the boy's intentions. He was in trouble. That was easy enough to see. He was running from someone, and since Teddy couldn't be sure whether or not that someone was hot on his trail, he thought it best to assume that they were. Consequently, he made sure he didn't leave an easy trail to follow when they descended the mountain.

Jace had a good sense of direction, so he had to wonder if Teddy had forgotten the way to his camp, considering the many changes in directions, even doubling back to ride up the mountain again, climbing up the middle of a stream when there was a usable game trail right beside it.

In time, it occurred to him that Teddy was making sure no one followed them, and the thought occurred to him then, *I hope I ain't making a mistake.* Without thinking about it, he dropped his hand to rest on the butt of his rifle.

Finally they rode over a ridge and down into a secluded ravine lined with aspen and pines. Teddy rode to the lower end and dismounted in a small clearing. Almost hidden from view was a small shelter formed by several young pines bent over and tied together, with a portion of buffalo hide serving as a roof. Jace stepped down and looked around him at the ashes of a fire, but little else. And he wondered about the offer Teddy had made of hot coffee when he saw nothing in the camp in the way of utensils or supplies. He had looked at his host, about to ask, when Teddy said, "Let's take care of the horses first, and then we'll get us some coffee started."

"How we gonna do that?" Jace wondered aloud.

His question caused Teddy to chuckle. "We're gonna get my coffeepot and the rest of my possibles outta that tree yonder," he said, pointing to a pine on the side of the ravine. Jace turned to see a sack hanging from a length of rope tied to a slender branch halfway up the tree. "I've seen plenty of bear sign near here, so I had to find me a limb too thin to hold a bear. I'da had that sack with me if I'd knowed I was gonna be ridin' up to where I found you. Didn't know I'd be gone that long, but it looks like I lucked out. Don't look like no critters found it."

What a strange man, Jace thought as he released the cinch and pulled his saddle off.

In a short time, they had a fire going and coffee boiling. Teddy even had an extra cup he had brought along in case he lost the other one. With fresh-killed meat to roast over the fire, they sat back to enjoy their repast.

Teddy reached for the coffeepot and refilled Jace's cup, suddenly asking, "So, just who are you runnin' from, Slater?" When the boy hesitated, Teddy asked, "Is it the law? What did you do, steal somethin'?"

"I shot a man," Jace blurted before taking more time to think about the consequences of his answer.

"Is that a fact?" Teddy responded, not seeming to be especially shocked. "How'd you come to do that?" He kept prodding until Jace finally told him the circumstances that had led him to shoot the blacksmith in Virginia City. "And you don't know if you killed him or not," Teddy repeated to himself. "Well, hell, you say he took a shot at you? And all you was tryin' to do was bury your daddy?" Jace nodded. Teddy went on. "I can't say as how I might notta done the same thing in your shoes. Least you didn't steal nothin'. I can't abide a man that's a thief."

He finished his coffee and sat back against a tree to relax for a few minutes before starting the process of smoking the meat.

They remained there two more days, preparing Jace's deer, the elk that Teddy had shot, and another deer that was misfortunate enough to wander through the ravine. During that time the crusty mountain man and the solemn boy became comfortable in each other's company. When the work was done, and they decided they had run all the game away from the valley, Teddy announced that he was going to head for home. "Why don't you come along, Slater?" he asked, taking the boy somewhat by surprise.

"I don't know," he replied. "You ain't ever said where home is."

"Four or five days southeast of here, on the other side of the Yellowstone, in the Absaroka Mountains," Teddy said. "God's country," he went on, "best huntin' there is—elk, mule deer, moose, bears—damn near every critter a man wants to hunt. You can even find sheep and goats, especially in the Beartooth Mountains right next to the Absarokas."

Slater thought about that for a moment before asking, "If there's all that game there, what are you doin' huntin' elk in these mountains?"

Teddy shrugged. "I reckon even ol' Adam wanted to get outta paradise once in a while. That's kinda the way it is with me. I live with a small village of Crow Injuns, back in a narrow canyon where a waterfall makes a deep lake that not many folks know about. There ain't but seven tipis, but many years ago those valleys were the homeland of a lot of Crows. It's pretty rugged country, but it suits me fine, and I don't know no place that beats it. But like I said, every now and again I feel the itch to get off by myself for a spell. So I'll ride off like I used to do when I was a young man, free and easy, and never mind tomorrow." He paused to chuckle. "I told Red Basket—that's my woman—I was goin' to look for a medicine elk, and there warn't none in the Absarokas or the Beartooths. Truth be known, she most likely is as glad to get rid of me for a little spell, too." He beamed at the thought. "Make no mistake, though, she's mighty glad to see ol' Teddy come home."

"So you've got a family," Slater said. "I didn't figure you to be married."

"Well, why not?" Teddy replied grandly. "A distinguished-lookin' gent like myself? It's more of a miracle that I stayed single as long as I did." He drew himself up in a stately pose that caused Slater to grunt derisively.

"You have any children?" Slater asked.

"No, thank heaven for that. I'm a little past the child-raisin' age and so is Red Basket." He became serious for a moment then. "If you're worried about the law, or a lynch mob lookin' for you, there ain't a better place to hide out than those mountains. I guarantee you that." He waited for Slater to think it over. "Whaddaya say?"

After a moment, Slater decided. "All right, if you're sure the rest of that village won't care." At this particular time, he had no destination in mind, so he thought that it might give him time to plan just what he was going to do.

"Fine and dandy," Teddy said. "We'll start back in the mornin'."

The trip to the Crow village took the five days that Teddy estimated. The northern foothills of the Absarokas were actually reached in four. Much of the fifth day was spent following a series of game trails that crossed deep canyons before climbing through dense pine forests that cloaked the steep slopes, broken occasionally by broad mountain meadows. It was easy for Slater to understand why his new friend had said it was an ideal place for someone who did not wish to be found.

In the afternoon of that last day, Teddy reined his horse to a stop and waited for Slater to come up beside him. "Hear that?" he asked.

"Yeah," Slater replied. "I've been hearin' it for a while, and it's gettin' louder. It sounds like the wind blowin'."

"It does, don't it?" Teddy said. "Sounds more like supper to me, though. Ride on up around that bend, and you'll see why."

Curious, Slater did as Teddy suggested. Rounding a steep granite formation that forced the trail to take a wide turn around it, he was amazed to find the source of the windlike sound. The spectacular beauty of a waterfall spilling over a rocky cliff would be a sight he would never forget, as it fell some two hundred feet to crash on the rocks that formed one bank of a crystal clear lake below. This was the paradise that Teddy had casually referred to.

A moment later, he was startled by a loud howl from Teddy, like that of a coyote, when he came up beside him. "Just lettin' Red Basket know I'm home for supper," Teddy said, grinning from ear to ear.

"Come on. It'll still take us fifteen minutes to follow this trail down there."

The trail took them to the lower end of the lake. They circled around the eastern bank to pass through a broad meadow where a pony herd grazed peacefully. A small group of people walked out to greet them as they approached the circle of seven tipis standing close up against the steep slope of the mountain. Leading them, a large-framed woman with coal black hair streaked with gray paused to wonder at the rider accompanying her husband. By the time the two dismounted, the rest of the people in the camp came out to meet them, curious to see who the stranger might be.

Slater stood beside his horse while Teddy strode forward to greet his wife. She pressed her face against his in a gentle gesture while still gazing at the obviously ill-at-ease boy. Speaking in the Crow tongue, she teased, "You went to hunt elk, and you came back with a white boy. Do you want me to cook him?" Her question caused those standing around her to laugh.

Answering her in her native tongue, he said, "No. I think he might be too tough and stringy." Then in English, he said, "This is Slater. He's my guest."

In the Crow tongue again, he told Red Basket that he would tell her the young boy's story later on. Then he again told the others gathered around that Slater was a guest. They responded cordially, smiling at Slater and nodding politely. A few offered words of welcome, which he didn't understand but could interpret as friendly. He nodded in return. It didn't strike him until later that the men he saw in the village were all older men. There were no young warriors and no children. He assumed that all the younger men were away from the village hunting.

"Welcome," Red Basket said to Slater, speaking in English now. Looking at her husband again, she said, "Come. You and your guest must be hungry. Maybe I should cook some of this elk you brought back," she said, still teasing Teddy. "Surely it must be the medicine elk you went looking for."

Teddy grinned sheepishly. "Nah, it's just regular ol' elk. I didn't have no luck finding the medicine elk."

It occurred to Slater that Red Basket was not as gullible as Teddy thought.

After the horses were unsaddled and turned out to graze with the Indian ponies in the meadow, Teddy took Slater to Red Basket's tipi, where he made room for him to spread his bedroll. While her guest was being settled, Red Basket and the other women prepared supper for them. Seeming more like a large family, the village was small enough for everyone to participate in the meal. The women baked bread made with wild turnips that had been dried and pounded into flour. As an extra treat, blue saskatoon berries were mixed in with the flour. This was served with fresh-roasted venison and hot coffee. It was a meal thoroughly enjoyed by young Slater, and the celebration of Teddy's return gave evidence of the village's regard for the burly white man.

"Where are all the young men?" Slater asked as he and Teddy sat by the fire after the celebration. "Off huntin' somewhere?"

"There ain't no young men in this village," Teddy said. "They're long gone—to the north, most of 'em. A good many are scoutin' for the army. You see, this used to be Crow territory, from here all the way to the Black Hills, till the Sioux and the Cheyenne crowded 'em out. There was just too many of 'em. These folks here in this little camp remember how it used to be, and ten lodges of us came back three years ago to finish out our time where the spirits of the Crow people still live. This is a special place for these folks. This mountain with the waterfall is Medicine Mountain. At least, that's what they call it, and they say that waterfall comes out of the mountain with water purified by the spirits. We're down to seven lodges now, and I reckon we'll be here till there ain't none of us left."

Slater didn't know how to respond to what he had just heard. His first impression was that he had landed in a camp of the living dead, all having given up the fight for life. He said as much to Teddy, but Teddy was quick to disagree.

"No such a thing," he replied. "The reservation's for the folks that give up the fight. We're determined to live free where we belong, and these mountains are our home. Every man here will fight for that right."

Slater began to understand, even though he still had questions. "But you don't look as old as most of these folks I saw tonight."

"I ain't," Teddy was quick to reply. "I followed Red Basket here. The old man settin' beside her tonight, Crooked Foot, that's her daddy." Slater remembered then that Red Basket had seemed to give special attention to the gray-haired old man. Teddy went on. "Crooked Foot is what the Crow people call a *maxpé* man, what white folks call a medicine man."

"Which one was her mother?" Slater asked, trying to remember the women that had been preparing the meal.

"Her mama's dead," Teddy replied. "Died last winter. The fever took her." He nodded toward the old man, who was just then returning from a visit to the aspen trees downstream. "Crooked Foot's been goin' downhill ever since she died. I think he's gettin' ready to join her pretty soon."

When it was time to turn in for the night, Slater remembered his manners and thanked Red Basket for her hospitality. "You are welcome," she said. "You must stay and visit with us."

"Oh no, ma'am," Slater said. "I reckon I'll be movin' on. I wouldn't wanna cause you folks any more trouble." He still had it in his mind that someone might be searching for him.

"What's your hurry?" Teddy asked. "Where are you thinkin' about headin'?"

"I don't know—just away from this part of the country, I reckon."

"What for?" Teddy pressed. "If you're worryin' about some lawman from Virginia City lookin' for you, he ain't likely to come into these mountains. And there ain't many Injuns know where this valley is—and no white man, except me—and now you. You'd be welcome, and I'd be obliged, if you stay a while and do some huntin' with me. In case you ain't figured it out yet, I'm the one who supplies most of the meat for these folks."

The invitation surprised Slater, but it made him think about the men sitting around the fire that night, and he could readily understand the problem. He hesitated for a few moments before accepting. Teddy was probably right about the difficulty anyone would have tracking him in these mountains. "I reckon I could help you do a little huntin'," he said. "But I don't have a whole lot of cartridges, and that's a fact."

"Then I reckon you'd best be a good shot," Teddy said with a laugh. "I'll take you down to Martin Greeley's place. He runs a tradin' post on the Yellowstone, and he'll trade with you for deer hides and most any kind of pelt—fox, raccoon, whatever you've got, long as they're prime."

"Fair enough," Slater said. "We'll hunt for a while, then."

Once the decision was made, he felt relaxed for the first time since he had left his mother and Henry Weed.

The days that followed turned into weeks as Slater and Teddy hunted the mountain slopes and valleys to supply the village with food. The mountains never failed to provide game in abundance, so there was plenty of deer, elk, and occasional moose prepared for the coming winter.

It was on these hunts that Teddy came to appreciate Slater's expertise with a Henry rifle. It seemed the boy never missed, and usually placed the kill shot behind the animal's front leg where it would puncture the lung. Teddy teased him, accusing him of being stingy with his cartridges, to which Slater would typically reply with a stoic grunt.

Before long, it occurred to Teddy that the young man never seemed to smile, and the stoic grunt was about as close to a laugh as he ever came. Word of his marksmanship soon spread among the others in the village, and they began to greet him with a Crow phrase each time he returned to the camp with fresh meat. Finally his curiosity got the better of him and he asked Teddy what the phrase meant.

"They're just callin' you by your name. That's your Crow name," Teddy said.

"What's it mean in American?" Slater asked.

"Shoots One Time," Teddy said with a grin. "How you like it?"

"Shoots One Time," Slater repeated, not particularly impressed. "What kinda name is that?"

"It's an Injun name," Teddy said, "and a good'un at that. It's better'n mine."

"What's yours?"

"*Hisshe Bishée*," he said. "Red Buffalo."

"Why'd they call you that?" Slater asked.

"My size, I reckon."

"Yeah, but red?" Slater wondered.

"When I first met Red Basket, my hair and whiskers were a little more reddish."

Slater considered that for a moment before commenting in his typical humorless fashion, "I reckon they could call you Gray Buffalo now."

"I reckon," Teddy said, shaking his head impatiently in response to Slater's total lack of humor. "You ever laugh?" he suddenly asked.

Puzzled by the question, Slater hesitated, then answered, "I reckon—if somethin's funny."

"Well, I'm mighty glad to know that," Teddy said. "'Cause I was beginnin' to think your sense of humor was broke. I reckon you just ain't run across anythin' that's funny."

At a loss as to why Teddy was going on with an obviously meaningless discussion, Slater paused to think about the comment. "I reckon not," he finally answered when he realized there was no incident he could recall.

Chapter 3

As the summer ran its course, Slater and Teddy provided plenty of meat for the women to prepare for the winter, as well as a good quantity of hides to trade for ammunition and supplies. Already it was past the season when the blue-and-purple flowers of the wild turnips dried up and broke off, making it difficult to find and dig up the plants.

On this late-summer morning, Slater paused to watch Red Basket as she prepared the last of the turnips the women had gathered. She could feel his intense gaze as she peeled the hard dark skin from the turnip and sliced the root so it could be dried and stored.

By now, she was accustomed to the strangely sorrowful young man's interest in everything that was necessary for survival in the high mountain country. She knew that he planned to leave them before the severe weather arrived. He had delayed his departure at Teddy's urging to accompany him on a hunt for mountain goats, the horns of which would be ground up for medicine that Crooked Foot used to treat certain ailments.

To find the goats, they planned to ride up into the Beartooth Mountains east of the Absarokas. With higher mountains, vast treeless plateaus that fell off steeply into the canyons that surrounded them, the rugged Beartooth Range lay in sharp contrast to the forested slopes of the Absarokas. Teddy wanted to go before the first heavy winter snows closed the high passes, making access to the peaks impossible. "Are you still planning to leave as soon as you get back from the Beartooths?" Red Basket suddenly asked.

"Yes, ma'am. I reckon so," Slater answered.

"It was good that you have stayed with us. Everyone in the village is happy that you came to help us." She stopped slicing the turnips for a moment to look directly at him. "It is a bad time of the year for you to start out on your own. It would be better to wait for the spring. That is what I think."

He couldn't argue with her reasoning. It would be a lot easier to wait the winter out there with the Crow people, but he had been threatening to leave for over a month by this time with something always causing him to postpone it. Unlike Teddy, he was not content to wither on the vine with the older members of the camp, even though he had come to be fond of them, especially Crooked Foot and Red Basket.

"What you say is true," he said, "but it is time I made my own home."

"You can make your home here at Medicine Mountain with us," she insisted. "In the spring, we will make your tipi. Teddy and I will help you make it."

"I've put you folks to an awful lot of trouble," he said. "You're already makin' me some clothes. I don't know how I'm gonna pay you for that."

She smiled. "You grow so fast, they might not fit when I'm through with them. I think you should stay with us till spring." He made no response to her suggestion, so she continued to stare at him. Finally she blurted, "Where is your family, boy?"

Her question took him by surprise. He shrugged, not wishing to go there. "No family," he said.

"Teddy say your father dead."

"That's a fact," he said.

"Where is your mother? Is she dead?"

"Same as," he replied.

She thought about that for a moment before repeating, "I think you should stay here till spring." Then she turned her attention fully back to her turnips, in effect dismissing him to contemplate it.

"Well, me and Teddy better get started if we're gonna find Crooked Foot a goat," Slater said. "I reckon we can talk about it when we get back."

The two hunters followed an old game trail down into the Boulder River Valley, crossed the river, and followed it upstream for a few miles before climbing up into the mountains on the other side. The farther they rode and the higher they climbed, the more the terrain changed as they left the heavily vegetated slopes of the Absarokas behind them.

To Slater, there was a feeling that no man had set foot on these treeless, glaciered peaks before. This was not the case, however, since Teddy had ridden the broad barren plateaus in search of goats and sheep before. By his admission, it was not often, simply because there was more game in the Absarokas that was far more easily hunted. That and the fact that he was not as young as he once was.

"I reckon this is about as far as we can take the

horses," Teddy said after they had scaled a steep slope to gain a flat grassy plateau with a small lake, bordered by pines, at the narrow end. "We'll have to leave them here and go the rest of the way on foot." Slater looked at the twin peaks high above the plateau and decided it was going to be a hell of a climb.

They made their camp by the lake, hobbled the horses, and began the climb up toward the Alpine-like meadows, already wearing shrouds of snow. It was close to dark when they were forced to abandon the hunt after no sighting of a suitable male goat, although several females had been spotted.

"Maybe we'll have better luck tomorrow," Teddy said as they descended to the lake below. "With all them nannies, there's gotta be a billy around somewhere."

It was not until two days later that the opportunity to complete their hunt presented itself when a handsome billy was spotted on a granite ledge on the far side of the mountain. Not eager to make the difficult climb, Teddy remained near the foot of a fissure in the granite wall while Slater continued to climb up to get within the Henry's effective range. As Teddy had hoped, Shoots One Time did just that and dropped the goat with one shot. The hard work was not finished, though, for Slater was obliged to make his way down into a narrow gorge to retrieve the body from the rocks where it had fallen. It was after dark when he made it back to the camp where Teddy was waiting.

"I swear," Teddy said, "I was startin' to think I was gonna have to go lookin' for you."

Slater dumped the carcass on the ground by the fire Teddy had built. "It was a long climb outta that canyon," he said in simple explanation.

"Well, I'm glad you found your way back," Teddy said, "'cause I was plannin' to have goat for supper."

"I thought we were gettin' this goat for Crooked Foot."

"He don't need nothin' but the head," Teddy said. "I plan to have me some fresh goat meat roasted over the fire. I like goat, and I don't get any very often, so let's get to skinnin'." He uttered a little groan when he got to his feet and complained. "I swear, I'm gettin' too old to climb all over these mountains. My legs is plumb wore out. I'm damn glad we found this billy today. You mighta had to go huntin' by yourself tomorrow."

In a short time, there were strips of goat meat sizzling over the flames while Teddy wrapped the goat's head in the hide to be delivered to Crooked Foot. "Maybe that won't get to stinkin' before we get back to the village," he said.

It was Slater's first experience eating goat meat. He decided it was not bad, but he preferred venison. After he had eaten his fill, he sat back against a huge boulder that seemed to be perched precariously at the edge of the lake, as if about to roll forward into the water. It had probably looked that way for a hundred years, he imagined, as he drank his coffee. He could feel the spirit of the stark granite peaks, standing even taller than the neighboring peaks of the Absarokas, and he knew that this was a good place, a safe place for him.

Lost in his thoughts for a long moment, he suddenly glanced up to find Teddy watching him intensely. He realized that Teddy had not spoken for several minutes, which was not a normal thing for his talkative friend.

"You thinkin' 'bout leavin'?" Teddy asked.

"No," Slater said, after a long pause. "I'm thinkin' 'bout stayin'."

"Good," Teddy said. "I'm damn glad to hear it. You're damn sure welcome, and that's a fact."

The news came as a great relief to Teddy. He and Red Basket had talked about how much easier things had been on him since Slater came. And he had promised her that he would do his best to convince Slater that this would be a good place for him. It had been a most worrisome matter as to how he could persuade the young stallion to stay. And now he found that he had worried for naught, because the mountains had done the job with no help required from him.

Although Slater's decision to stay with the tiny band of Crows had been made with the intent to merely wait out the winter, and possibly hunt with Teddy in the spring, four more years would pass to find him still vacillating between staying and leaving.

This was the fifth summer since Teddy Lightfoot had brought the serious young boy to the base of Medicine Mountain for what was planned to be a short visit. In that time, the boy had grown to be a powerful young man. A skillful hunter and tracker, he had become expert with either rifle or bow, and was held in highest regard in the tiny Crow camp. He was even more somber as a man than he had been as a boy, a fact that puzzled Teddy, causing him to remark to Red Basket, "I swear, in the time since I brought him here, I ain't knowed him to laugh out loud a single, solitary time, and that's a fact."

"It is Slater's way," Red Basket said. "That's all. What does it matter?"

"It just ain't natural for a man to go through life without findin' something to smile at," Teddy insisted. "He's likely to wind up bitter as bile before he's my age." He shook his head and frowned. "And he's got to ridin' off up in the mountains by hisself for two or three days at a time."

Red Basket smiled patiently. "I'm sure he would ask you to go with him if you were able to ride." Owing to a stiffness in his hips, it became extremely painful for him after a long time in the saddle, and Teddy no longer accompanied Slater on his extended hunting trips. The past couple of years seemed to have taken a toll on her husband, and she knew how much the effects of his advancing age bothered him. She was not immune to the effects of aging herself, although she was not nearly as old as Teddy. She was convinced that had it not been for Slater, however, the whole camp might already have crossed the river of life. "Besides," she said to Teddy, "he always brings plenty of meat back from his hunts."

"I reckon that's because I taught him how to use a bow and shoot a rifle," Teddy said.

"Maybe so," she said, still smiling as she thought of the Crow name he had been called ever since the first time he went hunting with Teddy—*Shoots One Time*. "He is fortunate to have you as his friend."

"I expect me and him need to ride down to the Yellowstone to Greeley's tradin' post and trade that big stack of hides Slater has got piled up in his tipi," Teddy said. "I know he oughta be gettin' low on cartridges, and we need some flour and coffee." He smoothed his mustache with his fingers unconsciously as another matter entered his mind. "We ain't been down to Greeley's for a spell. Maybe he's got some new word on ol' Red Cloud's war with the army."

The Sioux and Cheyenne had been attacking cavalry haying and woodcutting details all summer near the forts supposedly protecting the Bozeman Trail.

Teddy was anxious to find out if any Sioux war parties were roaming anywhere close to the Absarokas.
Even if they were, he doubted they would venture
deep enough in the mountains to discover the small
Crow camp. But it was something to cause him concern, since the little camp of old men and women
would be hard put to defend themselves against a
Sioux war party. If Slater would ever get back from
his latest hunting trip, the two of them could get the
latest word from Martin Greeley.

"Ain't no tellin' when he's liable to be back," he said.
The words had barely passed his lips when he heard
Crooked Foot call out a greeting to the returning
hunter. "Speak of the devil. . . ," Teddy muttered, and
got up to go out of the tipi.

Outside, Teddy joined the small collection of people who gathered around Slater's packhorse to examine the recently killed elk. "We'd better butcher it
right away," Red Basket said. "The weather is still too
warm to leave the meat uncooked."

"It ain't been dead very long," Slater said. "I run
up on it no more'n a couple of miles from here."

"That close?" Teddy asked, surprised. "Looks like
we mighta heard your shot."

"I got him with my bow," Slater explained. "Seemed
to me like he was just wantin' to get shot. He crossed
my path when I was comin' up the other side of the
mountain, and he just stopped and stared at me. It was
a good chance to save some cartridges, so I shot him
with my bow. Figured he was so close I couldn't miss."

"I figured you was gettin' low on cartridges," Teddy
said. "We need some other stuff, too. So why don't we
ride down to Martin Greeley's place in the mornin'
and do some tradin'?"

"All right with me," Slater said as he pulled the

elk's carcass off his packhorse. "We might as well have this one for supper. After we go to Greeley's, I'll go huntin' for more meat to store for winter."

Early the next morning, Slater loaded the hides he had accumulated on his packhorse, then threw his saddle on the paint gelding he'd ridden since trading his father's sorrel. The paint was an Indian pony, a stout horse that had harbored a strong dislike for his previous owner, Walking Stick, who was one of the oldest men in the village. Walking Stick had traded two mares for the paint with Martin Greeley, and soon found out why Greeley hadn't been difficult to bargain with.

"Whoever gelded him musta done a sorry job," Teddy had commented. "They didn't get all the stallion outta him."

After several attempts to negotiate a peace treaty with the spirited horse, Walking Stick was more than willing to trade horses with Slater. Fully expecting to meet with the same difficulty that had caused both Greeley and Walking Stick to get rid of the horse, Slater was surprised when it submitted to his authority willingly. Teddy could only surmise that the paint recognized a strength in Slater that it had not sensed in his previous owners.

"It's downright disgustin'," Teddy said to Red Basket, "the way that damn horse nuzzles around Slater like a pet puppy. And if you try to get on him, you're liable to get bit."

There was no real explanation for it, because Slater was certainly not likely to make a pet of the horse. He believed in taking care of the horse's needs before he took care of his own—and never applied the whip—but he was never one to coddle the animal.

After waiting by the waterfall for over fifteen min-

utes for Teddy to come out of his tipi, Slater led his
horses over beside the tipi flap and called out, "Come
on, old man, we're burnin' daylight."

In a minute, Red Basket came out and was about to
speak when Teddy yelled from inside, "I'm comin',
dad-burn it. Just give me a dad-blamed minute."

Red Basket looked at Slater and shook her head.
"He can't ride," she whispered. "He woke up with the
bad pain in his hips again."

"The hell I can't ride," Teddy blurted, overhearing
as he pushed the tipi flap aside and made an uncon-
vincing effort to walk normally. "It just took me a
while to get myself up and goin'. I'm all right now."

Slater was not convinced. He looked at Red Basket
and nodded. He was inclined to believe her. Back to
Teddy, he said, "You don't look ready to me. You'd best
stay here and look after the people. I'll go do the tradin'."

"The hell you say," Teddy protested. "Ol' Martin's
liable to skin you if I ain't there to do the tradin'." It
was obvious to Slater that his friend was in pain, even
as he stood there denying it. He suspected Teddy was
most concerned about missing an opportunity to buy
a jug of the poison Greeley called whiskey.

"Climb up on my saddle," Slater said.

"What for?" Teddy replied.

"I just wanna see if you can," Slater answered.

"Hell, that crazy horse of your'n will buck me off
if I try to ride him. And I don't see no sense in gettin'
on your horse anyway."

"He won't buck you," Slater said. "I'll hold his head
while you get on him."

"I don't wanna get on your horse. You're talkin'
nonsense. We've got to get started, if we're goin'."

Slater didn't say anything more, just stood watching Teddy while holding the paint's bridle. Teddy took

hold of the saddle horn but made no move to mount the horse. When he still made no motion after several minutes, Slater said, "That's what I thought. You can't even raise your leg to put your foot in the stirrup. Red Basket's right. You ain't ready to ride outta these mountains today. I'll take care of the tradin' this time."

Red Basket placed her hand on Teddy's arm. "Come, Red Buffalo, I'll feed you some more of that elk—make you strong—fix your hip."

"I can ride," Teddy protested weakly, but made no effort to pull away.

"I'll bring you a jug of Greeley's medicine," Slater whispered in his ear. "I'll be back tomorrow evenin'."

He climbed aboard the paint and set out for the trading post on the Yellowstone. As the hawk flies, it was no more than twenty miles, but because of the difficulty of the winding route he had to take, and the mountains he had to cross before reaching the Yellowstone Valley, he planned to make it an overnight visit.

"Somebody's comin'," Clyde Rainey said to Martin Greeley. He stood in the open door of the trading post, watching a rider following the trail down from the bluffs leading a packhorse.

"Who is it?" Greeley asked the old man who had been working for him for more than six years.

"Don't know yet," Clyde answered. "He ain't close enough for me to tell. He's leadin' a packhorse that's got a heavy load, though." He remained in the doorway, watching until the rider was close enough for Clyde to recognize him. After a few minutes more passed, he said, "I swear, it looks like that scary-lookin' feller that lives with them Crows back up in the mountains. But Teddy ain't with him. Wonder how come? I ain't never seed him ride in here 'cept when Teddy was with him."

Curious now, Greeley walked to the door to see for himself, since Clyde's eyesight was not always accurate. "That's him, all right," Greeley said. "Reckon this time he's gonna have to say something." On prior visits, the somber friend of Teddy Lightfoot never seemed to utter more than a single grunt or two while Teddy did all the talking.

When Slater pulled up to the hitching rail, Greeley and Clyde walked out to meet him. "Looks like you're wantin' to do some tradin'," Greeley said in greeting.

"That's a fact," Slater answered.

"Where's Teddy?" Greeley asked. "Don't usually see you if Teddy ain't with you."

"He's ailin' a little," Slater replied, "stove up in his hips, so I reckon you'll be dealin' with me today."

"Well, let's see what you've got."

Slater stepped down, and he and Clyde untied the buffalo hide that had served as a cover for the load of pelts. Greeley briefly considered testing Slater's knowledge of the worth of the hides, thinking that he might not be as hard to deal with as Teddy. On second thought, however, he decided to play it fair and square, although he would miss the haggling that usually went on between him and Teddy. There was just something about the stony countenance of Teddy's young friend that discouraged Greeley from thinking about cheating him. So he graded the hides one by one as he and Clyde pulled them off the horse. As was usually the case, most of them were prime. When he had tallied up the stack, he told Slater how much credit he would allow for the bundle, and Slater nodded his acceptance and started listing the things he needed.

After buying ammunition for both Teddy and himself, Slater bought coffee beans, flour, and dried beans. Once the essentials were taken care of, he asked, "Is there enough left for a jug of whiskey?"

"Maybe just enough," Greeley said. "I never saw you take a drink. I didn't know you used it."

"I don't," Slater replied. "It's for Teddy."

"Well, be sure and tell him I hope he gets back on his feet pretty soon," Greeley said as he stood watching Slater tie his purchases on the packhorse. "Tell him I'm hopin' we'll see a boat up the river this far in a week or two, with the water up as high as it's been since spring. So you boys better keep huntin', 'specially if you can get some more as prime as these you brought in today."

"I'll tell him," Slater said, and stepped up into the saddle. "He wanted me to ask you if you've heard anything about Sioux war parties over this way."

"Well, not over this far," Greeley said, "but east of here, I'm told they've been causin' the army a lot of trouble. A feller came through here last week and said there was a war party that attacked some soldiers workin' in a hayfield near Fort Smith, over on the Bighorn—had a big fight. But I ain't heard nothin' else."

Slater nodded thoughtfully. "Well, much obliged." He turned the paint's head away from the hitching post and gave him a nudge of his heels.

Greeley and Clyde watched him until he disappeared back up in the bluffs. "Well, he still don't say much," Clyde said. "But he can talk if he has to."

Slater guided the paint up an almost hidden game trail at the end of a box canyon that led up into slopes that were so dense with pine trees there was almost no penetrating sunlight. He thought about the first time he had entered these mysterious mountains, when he had followed Teddy Lightfoot to the tiny gathering of Crow tipis by the waterfall. He remembered how totally lost he had felt as Teddy led him up narrow ravines and across wooded slopes. That was a long time ago, and now he knew the mountains as if they were his backyard, both the Absarokas and the Beartooths. They *were* his backyard, and he had hunted and scouted every inch of them. In fact, in the past four-plus years, he had seldom ventured out of these mountains. The few times that he had were when he was in a mood to ride back to the mountains where he had first met Teddy, a range that Teddy said some called the Tobacco Root Mountains. He didn't know the origin of the name, but he remembered the boy who had fled to them to escape a posse. What Teddy had told him then, that he would never be found in the Absarokas, had turned out to be an accurate prediction.

He thought then about his present situation as he nudged the paint a couple of times with his heels when the horse hesitated before crossing a rocky stream. There were even fewer people left in the tiny camp now than there had been when he arrived. And the burial ground below the village had almost as many platforms as there were people left alive. He wondered how many years were left before all of the old people died. There could not be many. Then where would he, Teddy, and Red Basket go? Teddy was already so stove up in his joints that he couldn't ride as he used to, but Slater was sure he had many years left before he had to permanently sit by the fire. He decided it was a good thing that he had met Teddy Lightfoot, and he was content to remain there in the mountains and provide for the people who had become his family.

They will be glad to see me, and the supplies I'm bringing, he thought, *especially Teddy when he sees the jug.*

The thought almost brought a smile to the stony face where smiles seldom strayed. No more than a second later, a frown of concern settled upon his brow, followed by immediate alarm, for he detected the first hint of smoke coming to him on the gentle breeze from the east. There was still a mountain between him and the Crow village, so he couldn't determine the source of the smoke. But he knew he was too far away to be able to smell smoke from the cook fires in the village, even with a helping wind. He hurried the paint gelding along, although the horse was already maintaining a good pace up the steep climb.

When he reached the point where the trail took a wide turn around the giant granite column and the first view of the waterfall presented itself, he discovered the source of the smoke. It drifted up to him from the burning remains of the tipis by the lake far below him. The sight struck him like a solid blow to his chest, and he felt the blood in his veins go cold. It was the same feeling he had experienced when he first saw his father hanging from a pole beside the saloon in Virginia City. Anxious to get to the village, he hurried his horse down the winding trail, hoping desperately that he would find someone alive.

The cruel sight that met him when he finally made his way down into the canyon struck him with devastating force that made him feel sick to his very core. Scattered among the smoldering tipis, the bodies of his Crow friends told the story of the tragedy that had befallen them on this day. Only a couple of the bodies were found in the ruins of their tipis. The others were slain as they had attempted to run from their attackers, some between the tipis, some near the meadow where the pony herd had been, and some at the edge of the lake. The little village smelled of death. Slater hurried from body to body, identifying each one, frantically searching for Teddy and Red Basket, hoping they would not be among the scalped victims. He found Teddy, however, beneath the low bank of the lake, his body mutilated and scalped, the broken shaft of an arrow protruding from his neck. On the gravel beside the body, Slater saw five empty cartridge shells that told him Teddy had gotten off a few shots before they killed him. Still there was no sign of Red Basket.

Although a man of few emotions, Slater immediately felt the anger rising in his veins, and he vowed to find the people responsible for the massacre. That was the most important thing, to track them down and punish them. To mourn the dead and construct burial platforms for all of them would mean an important loss of time, so he immediately began scouting the scene of the attack. He would come back to take care of the dead, but only after the warriors had paid for their evil.

There was more than enough sign to give him an idea of the size of the war party that had surprised the peaceful Crow camp. He estimated ten or twelve, Sioux, by the look of the few arrows that had not been recovered. They had swept in from below the lake, probably with no idea the village was there until they stumbled upon it. He could only guess how much of a head start the war party now had, but judging by the still-burning tipis and the condition of the bodies, he estimated that it had been only a few hours. There was only one trail into the canyon from above the waterfall—the way he had come down. So the raiders must have left the village from the lower end of the canyon.

He had to be sure, however, so he scouted the trail at the lower end of the lake carefully, even though the many tracks leading away from the camp left little doubt. Not willing to waste any more time, he had started to step up into the saddle when he was startled by a splashing in the water behind him. He spun around with his rifle raised to fire, only to be startled a second time by the sight of Red Basket emerging from the lake, her long doeskin dress clinging to her body.

"Teddy said to hide till you come back," Red Basket gasped as she trudged up from the water. "I could not help him. I have no weapon, but he thought he could drive them away with his rifle. So I do like Teddy say." She turned and pointed to a bank of elderberry bushes at the water's edge. "I hide there and stay in the water after they kill Teddy." She seemed unusually calm considering the tragedy she had just witnessed, and the husband she had just lost. "I hide there again when I hear your horse," she said, explaining the reason for her wet clothes.

"I reckon you did the right thing," Slater said, "'cause there ain't nobody else left alive. I thought maybe they took you with 'em."

"Teddy fight hard," Red Basket said. "Killed two of them before they shot him."

"Who was it?" Slater asked, although he was pretty sure who the raiders were.

"Lakota war party," Red Basket confirmed. "They sneak up through trees at lower end of lake. They were on us before we knew they were there."

"How many?" he asked.

"I count twelve after Teddy killed two," she said as she stood dripping water from her hair and dress, still remarkably calm after the horror she had just witnessed.

"How long ago?" he asked.

"Not long," she replied. "I not stay in water long before you come."

"I've gotta go after 'em," he said, "while I've still got a chance to catch 'em before dark. Will you be all right here till I get back?" She nodded. "Here," he said, and handed her his pistol. "I don't think they'll be back here, but I'll leave this with you. I reckon you'll wanna do what you can for Teddy and your father. I'll help you with the others when I get back."

She nodded again, equally in need of vengeance against the Crow's bitter enemies. "I go with you," she said, now that she had a weapon.

He did not doubt her intent. "All the same, I'd rather go alone. I need you to take care of the packhorse with all our supplies. You keep that .44 just in case you need it." Moving quickly then, he loaded his cartridge belt with ammunition and climbed aboard the paint gelding. "I'll be back as soon as I can. If I don't come back by tomorrow evenin', go to the tradin' post. Martin Greeley's a good man. I think he'll help you."

"I stay here," she said. "You be careful."

"Suit yourself," he said as he gave his horse a nudge of his heels. He knew she was a strong woman and could most likely take care of herself whether he returned or not.

It was not difficult to follow a trail left by more than two dozen horses, so he wasted no time going after them. He could tell the general direction the Sioux were intent upon driving the horses they had captured. And if he was correct in his assumption, they were heading down to the valley to strike the Boulder River.

Since the afternoon was already well along toward sundown, they probably were aiming to camp by the river where there was water and grass for their horses. Obviously not as familiar with the mountains as he was, the warriors tried to drive the horses along trails that seemed to follow the ridges down toward the valley. Slater knew that they were heading for a box canyon and would be forced to turn back to find another route to the river. He, on the other hand, rode down through obscure gulches and gullies that led him on a more direct line, enabling him to reach the valley in far less time than his prey had taken.

By design, he struck the river about half a mile upstream from where he estimated they would come down from the hills. He tied his horse in a small grassy pocket near the water with a length of rope sufficiently long to permit the animal to get to the water to drink. Then he sat down to wait for darkness to close in on the narrow river valley, no longer in a hurry since he now had a pretty good idea where the Sioux camp would be.

When he felt that the warriors had had time to fill their bellies with the stores of meat he had personally provided for his Crow village, he started out along the bank of the river on foot. He carried both rifle and bow, planning to use both weapons in his attack. With only the soft light of a three-quarter moon to guide his moccasins over the rocky shore, he made his way downstream until he saw the glow of a campfire lighting the pine trees that bordered the river. It was time to be

more cautious. He slowed his pace, walking more carefully, to make sure he didn't announce his presence.

When he had approached close enough to see the
cook fire flickering through the trees and the warriors
as they sat around it, he paused to study the camp. As
he had expected, the horses were downstream from
the camp and he could not see them clearly from
where he now stood. If things went according to his
plan, it would be best to approach from the horse herd,
so he went deeper into the trees and circled around
the camp until he could see the horses. They were neither tied nor hobbled, but left to graze on the grass
and small shoots near the riverbank. It was obvious
that the Sioux warriors were not concerned about their
safety. There were no guards watching the horses.
Slater could imagine that the war party's objective was
to raid any white prospectors they happened upon
along the river. They could not have expected to find
the tiny village of Crows back up in the mountains.
That had been an unexpected gift of a dozen ponies,
and the satisfaction of acquiring a few scalps.

When he was certain there was no one watching
the horses, Slater walked in among them, gently herd-
ing them with a tap of his bow on a croup, or a pat of
his hand on a neck, until he got them moving quietly
away from the camp. Making a soft clicking sound
with his tongue, he kept behind the hindmost until
most of the herd shuffled quietly downstream. When
they were some distance from the circle of warriors
still taking their leisure around the fires, he gave one
of the horses a sharp rap with the butt of his rifle. The
horse reacted with a squeal and bumped another horse
that promptly answered with one of its own. Hoping
that would have the desired effect, Slater positioned
himself behind a fallen tree. He propped his rifle beside

him, drew an arrow from the quiver on his back, and
notched it. Then he waited.

"Something's bothering the horses," Wounded Hawk
said, and got to his feet to listen. "Maybe a coyote or
a wolf." He peered out into the darkness. "I can't see
them now. I think I had better go look."

"It could be a wolf," Two Bears said. "I'll go with you."
The other warriors were not concerned enough to accompany them, and elected to remain seated around
the fire, their bellies filled with the meat they had found
in the Crow camp.

Walking into the darkness of the trees, the two warriors found that the herd of horses had wandered farther downstream. Ahead of his companion by several
steps, Wounded Hawk said, "Something has caused
them to move." Then he heard the solid thump of an
arrow when it impacted Two Bears' back, and the grunt
of pain emitted by the stricken warrior.

Startled, he turned to discover Two Bears on his
knees. Then he looked up to see a dark shadow no
more than twenty feet from him, his bowstring fully
drawn. There was no time to react before the arrow
struck him in the chest, knocking the wind from his
lungs and sending him staggering drunkenly to fall
against a tree. He had time to call out once before his
throat was sliced.

With the same absence of emotion shown when
putting a deer out of its misery, Slater moved up
behind Two Bears and finished him with his knife as
well, but not before the wounded warrior yelled out
in pain. Unhurried, Slater wiped his knife blade
clean on Two Bears' shirt and positioned himself to
await the response of the rest of the war party.

The reaction in the Sioux camp was what Slater had

hoped for, because he fully intended to kill all twelve of the Lakota warriors. And it would be impossible for him to do so if they all came at him at once. The leader of the war party, Plenty Scalps, got up from his seat by the fire and looked out toward the pony herd.

"What were they shouting about?" He looked around him at the others, but no one had understood the two calls. "They must need some help," Plenty Scalps said. "The ponies must have wandered too far." Sighing impatiently, he said, "Someone come with me, and we'll help them."

Slater watched as the war chief and three others walked out of the circle of firelight and entered the shadows. When they had moved into the trees, he remained where he waited until they had passed him. Then he circled around behind them, until he was between them and the camp. Again, he laid his rifle down and notched an arrow on his bowstring, knowing that as soon as he fired his rifle the element of surprise would be gone. And he did not think his odds would be very good if the remaining six warriors in the camp were able to escape into the cover of the trees. If that happened, they would all be stalking him. So he waited, knowing that the four warriors going to help their friends would not go far before finding the bodies.

"Wah!" Plenty Scalps suddenly blurted when he almost stumbled over Wounded Hawk's body. A second later, he cried out in pain when Slater's arrow penetrated his back. Startled, the warrior to his right turned to help him, but was stopped by an arrow in his side. He screamed out in pain, and Slater knew his element of surprise was gone. He dropped his bow and grabbed his rifle. Two rapid shots found their marks and the other two warriors went down. With no time to lose, Slater turned at once toward the camp where the remaining six warriors were scrambling up from their places by the fire. Making every shot count, he laid down a continuous series of fire as fast as he could pull the trigger and crank a new cartridge into the chamber. Selecting his targets carefully, he picked the first warriors to get to their feet, then targeted those who were slower.

The chaotic confusion caused by the sudden attack on their camp enabled the determined avenger to reduce the remaining warriors by half, while three were able to scramble out of the firelight to plunge into the berry bushes on the riverbank. Slater had fired so rapidly that the remaining three Sioux were convinced there was more than one shooter, so there was no thought of trying to fight.

Pushing frantically through the bushes, they fled into the rapidly flowing water of the river. Slater, grim and unyielding, made his way along the bank until he spotted two dark forms bobbing up and down as the swift current swept them downstream. He dropped to one knee and tried to take steady aim at the unsteady targets before they were out of sight. He could only be sure of one more kill, but not certain of the second shot. It had been his sincere intent to kill every member of the war party. He felt that the merciless massacre of the peaceful Crow village called for nothing less than the same punishment for their murderers. But at least he had accounted for one execution for each one of the old folks slaughtered.

He got to his feet and walked down along the bank, searching for any sign of the survivors. As he walked, he reloaded the magazine of his rifle, using his bandanna to protect his hand from the heated barrel of the Henry. Convinced that he was in no danger of an immediate counterattack, he returned to search for the wounded. There was still danger from that source, more so from those shot with his bow than the victims of his Henry rifle. As he expected, there was still killing to be done before his vengeful mission was completed. One of the warriors, with an arrow in his back, had crawled almost all the way back to the camp for his weapon.

Finally he felt that he had done all he could to avenge Teddy Lightfoot and his Crow friends. It did not occur to him how unlikely it was that a single man with a rifle could destroy a Sioux war party of this size. He had never known deep emotions of any kind, no matter what the source, so he felt no feelings of triumph or passion in the taking of lives. He saw only a balancing of the scales. The Sioux warriors had been wrong in slaughtering a village; therefore it was necessary that they pay for what they did.

Half a mile down the river, Striped Otter crawled out of the water and paused to listen for sounds of pursuit. When he was certain there were none, he pulled himself up on a rock while he thought about what he had seen. This was his first war party at fourteen, and he had to admit that he had been afraid when they were attacked. Fights With Lance and Black Arrow yelled for him to run for the river. They were sure they had been attacked by the soldiers because the bullets were so many and so close around them. They made it to the river, but Fights With Lance and Black Arrow were both hit as they swam. If Striped Otter had not hidden behind a rock at the water's edge, he might have been hit as well.

Watching from behind the rock, he saw the man with the rifle walking along the bank, looking for them. The man did not look like a soldier. He was dressed in animal skins. Where were the soldiers? Striped Otter had wondered, but no one else ever came to join the one man. He must have special powers to turn his rifle into many rifles. Convinced he had been witness to some form of magic, Striped Otter decided he should get back to his village as quickly as possible to warn his people about this strange man.

Chapter 4

Slater decided to wait until morning before returning to the Crow village to help Red Basket with the
dead. As a precaution, he thought it best to lie in
ambush for the Sioux warriors he could not account
for, in case they came back looking for him. He felt
confident in Red Basket's ability to take care of herself, so he went back upstream to the small grassy
pocket where he had tied his horse and settled in for
the night.

With the first rays of the sun, he was up. He climbed
aboard the paint gelding and slow-walked the horse
down toward the Sioux camp, scanning the river-
banks carefully for any sign of activity. He pulled up
for a few moments at the edge of the clearing to look
the camp over before proceeding to ride in. Everything was the same as it had been the night before,
with three bodies lying close-by the remains of the
campfire.

Off to one side, he saw a saddle that he recognized
as Teddy's, his rifle still in the sling. There were various

blankets and animal hides arranged around the ashes of the fire, some with bows close-by, the surprised owners never having had the chance to use them. He was suddenly startled by a movement in the choke-cherry bushes, and instantly whipped his rifle up to fire, only to find it was one of the horses that had wandered back to the clearing. Looking out beyond the bushes then, he saw several other horses. He felt sure he would find the rest of them not far away, but since he was not inclined to take care of a sizable herd of horses, he intended to take only the few that he could handle easily. Many of the ponies taken from the Crow village were not in prime condition anyway.

Before going in search of the other horses, he checked the camp for anything that might be useful to him or Red Basket. He found very little of any value except a few firearms and a quantity of arrows. He tested the bows he found, but decided he preferred his own, although he did replace the arrows he had broken or lost with some from a Lakota's quiver. Of the firearms he found, a Springfield single-shot rifle and a cavalry Spencer carbine were the only ones worth keeping. He set them aside while he went after the horses.

They were not hard to find, as they had not wandered far from the camp. He found them peacefully grazing next to the river's edge and spotted Teddy's dun gelding nibbling on some tender shoots among the rocks along the shore. The bridle was still on, so it was no trouble to lead the horse back to be saddled. Slater felt sure that Red Basket would want to have Teddy's horse for her own. He also spotted Crooked Foot's sorrel, but he decided there were several other horses in the bunch that were in better condition.

Thinking ahead, he worked through the herd and

culled out the older, worn-out ponies, which resulted in leaving almost all of the horses that had been taken from the Crow camp, and a few from the Sioux war party.

Ready to return to the village, he left the site of the one-man massacre, leading a string of eight ponies and leaving nine bodies to feed the buzzards. It was his hope that he could sell the extra horses at Martin Greeley's trading post.

Because of the narrow trails, he had to cut the horses loose again when he started back up into the steep mountains to return to the Crow village. But they followed along after him and Teddy's dun, which was the only one he kept on a lead rope. He speculated that the only reason the others followed was that the narrow trail left them less inclined to wander.

When finally he approached the lower end of the lake, he saw no sign of Red Basket until he rode up to the still-smoking ruins of the camp. She stepped out from behind a tree, with his .44 in her hand.

"I not sure it was you when I hear the horses," she explained.

He did not comment when he noticed that she had cut her hair short, and saw the fresh gashes on her arms, both a sign of her mourning for Teddy and Crooked Foot. The gashes were purposely cut deep enough to ensure that they would leave permanent scars. Slater figured that she had exhausted her tears of grief while he was dealing with the Sioux war party.

The rest of that day and most of the one following was spent caring for the dead. Red Basket insisted on constructing the burial scaffolds for Teddy and her father herself, using poles from the tipis that were not burned too badly. Slater erected the frames for most of the other bodies.

When all the dead were taken care of, Red Basket and Slater sat down by the campfire to eat and talk about what to do now that there were only the two of them. Slater was not sure what he should do. The only thing that he was certain of was that he would not abandon her.

On the other hand, Red Basket could not expect him to stay with her. Slater had known that the day would come when the village would die. He and Teddy had talked about it before, and he knew that Teddy had been concerned about it. He had planned to return to the family farm in Arkansas where he and Red Basket would spend their final years. What worried him the most was the fact that Red Basket, although not a young woman, was much younger than he, and would likely outlive him by quite a few years. His younger brother had taken over the farm when Teddy's father died, while Teddy chose to follow his natural call to see the far side of the mountains. He figured his family would have no choice but to accept his Crow wife as long as he was alive, but it might be a different matter when he died. Now, with Teddy gone, Red Basket could not expect to be welcomed by the brother and his family.

"Where are the rest of your people?" Slater asked. "Have you got any kin somewhere else?"

"Do not worry about me," Red Basket said. "I am strong. I will take Teddy's pony and his rifle, and I can take care of myself. You are still very young. You must go where your heart calls you. I will go to find my father's people, the Apsáalooke. That is where Teddy found me, in Chief Lame Elk's village in the

Musselshell country. My brother, Broken Ax, is with
Lame Elk, and Teddy said they were still on the Musselshell River. I will go there."

Slater considered that for a moment. Teddy had told
him that the Fort Laramie Treaty of 1851 had specified
that the northern boundary of Crow territory was the
Musselshell River. But he had no earthly idea where
on the Musselshell her people might be. There was a
later treaty in 1868 that further reduced the land area
designated as Crow territory. Teddy had said that the
Crows had agreed to live on the reservation and learn
to farm and live as the white man did.

But there were still many small villages that had
not moved onto it. It was not a normal way of life for
the Crow. They were hunters. They knew nothing
about farming, and as long as there were buffalo on
the plains, there was no need to move close to the
agency on Mission Creek. Lame Elk's band was one
of those that vowed to live as they had always lived.

"We'll stay together and go find the rest of your
people," Slater said. "Then I'll decide what I'm gonna
do." She nodded, pleased that he was concerned for
her safety. Slater continued. "First thing, we'll go to
Greeley's tradin' post and see if we can sell some
horses and a couple of these rifles."

He decided to keep one of the eight horses he had
brought back as a packhorse for Red Basket. She would
ride Teddy's dun, and that would leave him with six
horses to sell. He wasn't sure whether Martin Greeley
bought and sold horses. If not, maybe he would extend
him a line of credit for the horses.

After pushing his small herd of horses down out of
the mountains, he and Red Basket drove them along

the river toward Greeley's trading post. Watching the Indian woman as she helped drive the horses, Slater was impressed with her control of Teddy's powerful dun gelding. Sitting comfortably in her late husband's saddle, his .44 strapped around her waist, she obviously intended to take Teddy's place as a working partner. Slater was not surprised.

He reined the paint back for a moment when they started down through the bluffs above the trading post and discovered the horses of a cavalry patrol tied out front. It was a natural reaction for him, even after all the years that had passed since Virginia City.

Red Basket guessed at once why he hesitated. She pulled up beside him and said, "Too much time. They not looking for that boy anymore."

"I reckon you're right," Slater said, and gave the paint a gentle kick.

They followed the extra horses, which had already loped down toward the water's edge. When they rode up to the store, there was no room left at the hitching rail, so they looped their reins in some bushes on the side of the building. Behind the store, close to the water, a group of a dozen soldiers were taking their leisure, eating hardtack and drinking coffee. Slater, with Red Basket close behind him, walked in the front door.

"Here's somebody who might be able to tell you a little more," Martin Greeley said when he saw Slater walk in, surprised to see him back so soon. The lieutenant he had been talking to turned to look at the rangy young man dressed in animal skins, with the Indian woman following. "Slater here knows these mountains better'n anybody," Greeley explained. "If there's any Injuns holed up back in those hills, besides that little village of Crows he lives with, he'd most likely know it." Turning to Slater then, he said, "This here is Lieutenant Russell. He's leadin' a patrol of cavalry outta Fort Ellis, lookin' for some Sioux warriors that have been raidin' some of the settlers' farms." He paused to look beyond Slater at Red Basket. "That's Teddy Lightfoot's woman, ain't it?" he asked, still addressing Slater as he stared at the obvious slashes on Red Basket's arms, and the absence of much of her hair.

"Mr. Slater," Lieutenant Russell said before Slater had time to reply. He stepped forward and offered his hand. Slater accepted, and nodded in reply to the lieutenant's greeting. Russell continued. "Like Mr. Greeley said, we've had reports that a Sioux raiding party has struck a couple of families east of here on the Yellowstone. Anything you might have seen that could help us?"

Slater was distracted for a moment when Clyde Rainey walked over to join them, after selling three soldiers some tobacco. "Howdy, Slater, Red Basket," he said, also staring at the Indian woman. "Where's Teddy?"

"Teddy dead," Red Basket replied.

"What?" Greeley exclaimed. "When? What happened?"

Slater glanced at Red Basket, but the somber woman did not flinch, leaving him to explain. "Mighta been that Sioux party you're lookin' for," he said to the lieutenant. "They struck Crooked Foot's camp the same day I was last here. That's when they got Teddy."

"My Lord," Greeley exclaimed. "That's terrible news." He looked at Red Basket. "I'm mighty sorry to hear that, ma'am." He turned back to Slater. "Anybody else killed?"

"Everybody but her," Slater answered, nodding toward Red Basket.

"My Lord in heaven," Greeley started again, but was interrupted by the lieutenant.

"Do you have any idea where they might be now?" Russell asked.

"Pretty much," Slater replied stoically. "They're over on the Boulder River. I ain't sure where they all are, but there's nine or ten of 'em over by the Boulder."

Impatient with Slater's lack of urgency, Lieutenant Russell pressed. "Where on the Boulder River? Can you take us there? That is, if they're still there. They're likely moving pretty fast."

"I doubt they're still there now," Greeley speculated as well. "They'll be long gone."

"They're still there," Slater said, "least what the buzzards left of 'em."

Russell was not quite sure what Slater was telling him. "Are you saying they're dead?" Slater nodded. "Who killed them?" Russell asked.

"I did," Slater answered.

Russell was not yet ready to believe what he was hearing. "And you say there are nine or ten dead Sioux warriors over on the Boulder. Are you telling me you killed all of them? Who helped you?"

When Slater didn't answer, Russell looked at Greeley as if asking for confirmation. Greeley nodded solemnly, never doubting that Slater did what he claimed.

Figuring the topic of conversation was done with, Slater turned to Greeley again. "I'm wonderin' if you're interested in buyin' some horses. I've got six good, stout horses I just brought in, and I'm lookin to sell 'em."

"Well," Greeley responded, "I ain't usually in the business of buyin' and sellin' horses. I reckon it wouldn't hurt to take a look at 'em."

Lieutenant Russell spoke up right away. "The army

is always in need of good horses," he said. "If Mr. Greeley isn't interested, I might be."

Slater looked to Greeley for his reaction. Greeley hesitated for a moment. He had no interest in horse trading as a rule, but he was clearly disgruntled by Russell's remark. Being a natural-born trader, he had immediately seen the possibility of gaining Slater's horses at a pittance, then selling them to the army at a profit. But Russell had destroyed that possibility by effectively eliminating the middle man.

"I reckon you might as well sell 'em to the army," Greeley said. He glanced at Red Basket in time to see the knowing smile on the silent Crow woman's face. She seemed to have read his mind.

"Fine," Russell said. He called to one of the three men who had just purchased tobacco from Clyde. "Sergeant Bell, go with Mr. Slater and take a look at those horses." He looked back at Slater. "Sergeant Bell is a pretty good judge of horseflesh. If they are in good shape, the army will pay you the current price we're buying stock for in this territory. This year, the quartermaster has been paying an average price of around a hundred and forty dollars for top-quality Virginia- or Kentucky-raised horses. But you can expect a good bit less than that for the typical Indian pony." He paused, waiting for Slater's reaction.

"Whatever the army thinks they're worth," Slater said. He had no idea what the horses were worth to the military, and he was willing to take just about any price offered.

"Very well, then," Russell said. "Sergeant Bell will go with you to look them over."

"He warn't lyin' when he said they was in good shape," Sergeant Bell reported back to the lieutenant.

"But they's Injun ponies, unshod, and most likely ain't up to that Morgan you're ridin', sir. Most likely, the quartermaster would give about seventy dollars apiece for 'em."

Russell turned to Slater. "Whaddaya say, Mr. Slater? Will you sell them for that?"

"I will," Slater replied immediately.

"All right," Russell said, "but you'll have to deliver them to the stables at Fort Ellis, and that's where you'll get your money." Slater nodded and the lieutenant continued. "But before you do that, I'd appreciate it if you could tell me where this Sioux war party is. I need to investigate the site for my report to my superiors." He still found it hard to believe that the young man had killed a war party of Lakota warriors of that size with no help from anyone else.

"Like I said," Slater replied, "over on the Boulder River."

"But where on the Boulder, man?" Russell asked, losing a bit of his patience with the stoic young man. "That's a helluva long river."

"I reckon," Slater said, "it's pretty nigh straight east from where we're standin'." He nodded toward the mountains. "About twenty miles or so as the crow flies, on the other side of those mountains. It's a good bit farther if you have to follow the Yellowstone around the mountains till you strike the Boulder and then head south."

"It would save us a great deal of time if you could lead us through those mountains so we wouldn't have to take the long way around," Russell said.

"I don't know. . . ." Slater hesitated. "I've got those horses to take care of, and I've got Red Basket to think about."

"I'll see that you get a day's pay for every day it takes

to lead us there and get back to Fort Ellis," Russell said. He considered taking Slater's word that he had killed the entire war party with no help from anyone, and returning to Fort Ellis at once. But he found it hard to accept it as fact. He wanted to see the site himself.

"You can leave your horses here in my corral if you want to," Greeley offered.

Slater glanced at Red Basket to see her reaction to the lieutenant's request. He wasn't quite sure how she would feel about riding with a cavalry patrol. She met his gaze with a solemn nod. Turning back to Russell, he said, "All right, I'll take you through the mountains."

"Good," Russell said. "About twenty miles, you say?"

"Yes, sir," Slater replied. "As the crow flies, but you'd best figure it closer to twenty-five or more of slow goin', 'cause we'll be doin' some hard ridin' for those army mounts. But it'll still be quicker than goin' the long way around."

Since there was a good bit of daylight left, the cavalry patrol set out as soon as the lieutenant got his troopers in the saddle. Slater decided to take only one of the packhorses with what he and Red Basket would make camp with, as he didn't expect to be gone but a couple of days.

The patrol rode up out of the bluffs, following their somber scout up into the formidable mountains, the solemn Indian woman riding close behind him. By the time sunlight began to hurry from the deep gulches and tree-covered ravines, the horses were ready for rest. Slater led the patrol to a small glen with a lusty stream rushing down from the peak above, a place where he had once killed an elk. This was where the soldiers made their camp.

Red Basket collected enough wood for her cook fire,

which she made at the upper end of the meadow, about twenty yards from the soldiers' campfires. In a few minutes, she had coffee boiling and strips of jerky roasting over the fire for Slater and herself. After taking care of their horses, Slater came to sit by the fire to eat.

Lieutenant Russell poured a cup of coffee for himself and walked up to the edge of the meadow to talk to Slater. When he was out of earshot, Trooper Trask sat down next to Sergeant Bell.

"Hey, Sarge, what's the story on the Injun woman? Is she that scout's squaw? She looks damn near old enough to be his mama."

"What the hell do you care, Trask?" Bell answered him. "She ain't none of your business."

"Hell, I was just askin'," Trask said. "She ain't no young girl, but she don't look bad atall. I was just thinkin' if she ain't that feller's squaw, maybe she might wanna make a dollar or two."

Sergeant Bell got to his feet, disgusted with Trask's attitude. "That poor woman just lost her husband," he said, "and her father, too. I don't expect she'd have anything to do with you, even if she was in the market." He walked away to find better supper companions.

"Well, ain't he on his high horse?" Trask snarled to Corporal Jarvis, seated on the other side of the fire. "When did he get so uppity? I was just makin' conversation."

"I swear, Trask," Jarvis said. "You ain't got a lick of sense. You say anything to that woman and she'll like as not slit your throat, and if she don't, that feller with her will."

The next morning Slater led the cavalry patrol down from the steep mountainside, following an old game trail into the narrow valley of the Boulder River. After taking a moment to be sure he recognized this point on the rugged river, he told Lieutenant Russell that the site of his battle with the Lakota was about a mile downstream.

"If we're that close," Russell said, "we might as well keep going and rest the horses when we get there."

It was not an easy ride along the rocky riverbank. There was no trail through the thick stand of spruce and fir trees and the thick mountain juniper that grew right down to the water's edge. They continued along the river for a hundred yards until they came to an easy place to cross over to the eastern side. Cautioning the weary troopers to follow carefully, lest their mounts stumble on the gourd-sized boulders that covered the river bottom, Slater led them across. After riding a couple of hundred yards farther, they passed the spot where he had left his horse before launching his attack on the unsuspecting Sioux camp.

"About half a mile farther," he told the lieutenant when Russell asked. After weaving their way through a thick growth of pines along the boulder-strewn banks of the river, Slater pointed to a clearing ahead. "That's where they were camped," he said.

Expecting to find the bodies of at least nine Lakota warriors, they rode into the camp finding none. The ashes of two fires were evident, proof that someone had camped there, but that was all at first glance. Russell already harbored a suspicion that Slater's claims of single-handedly killing a Sioux war party might be nothing more than a tall tale that a typical mountain man was noted for. His first thought, upon finding no bodies, was that his suspicion was confirmed. He pulled up beside the puzzled scout to hear his explanation.

"Where are the bodies of those you say you killed?" he asked. "You didn't bury them, did you?"

As surprised as he was to find the bodies missing, Slater was still stoic in his answer. "I reckon somebody musta moved 'em."

"Somebody moved them?" Russell echoed. "Who the hell could have moved them?"

Emotionless in his response, Slater answered, "How the hell would I know? Some more Lakota, most likely. Most Indians will pick up their dead if they can."

With no particular regard for the lieutenant's opinion of him, but a need to see for himself, Slater stepped down to satisfy his curiosity.

"I'd be interested to hear more details about your attack on the war party you say was here," Russell said, not entirely successful in masking his skepticism. Slater gave him a brief account of the assault, starting with his drawing half of the party out to tend to their horses, then his rapid fire on those still by the fire.

"Interesting," Russell commented, remaining in the saddle for a few moments, watching Slater as he proceeded to scout the camp. Stepping down then, he ordered Sergeant Bell to take care of the horses. Every bit as interested in Slater's account of the fight, but with no thought of disbelief, Red Basket slid off her horse and went with him to scout the campsite.

When Russell and Sergeant Bell walked over to join the white scout and the Crow woman, the lieutenant informed them that they would rest the horses and let his men eat. Then he intended to start back to Fort Ellis, since the war party had obviously moved on.

"Like I told you before," Slater said, "you ain't gotta worry about the war party that camped here. What you've gotta worry about now is the war party that picked up the dead." When Russell appeared to be skeptical still, Slater continued. "If you look down at your feet, that dark spot you're almost standin' on is a bloodstain. He was one of the first ones that jumped up when they heard the gunshots." Slater pointed to another stain several feet away. "There's another one, and there's the third one," he said, pointing to a third stain.

While the lieutenant and his sergeant stared at the ground dumbfounded, Red Basket walked across the small meadow where Slater had said the Lakota's ponies had been grazing, leaving him to continue his report.

"The thing that oughta concern you the most," he said to Russell, "is all these pony tracks around this camp." He indicated a wide area around the burned-out remains of the fires. "Hard to say how many, but that was a good-sized party that came in here and picked up their dead. And these tracks are fresh, not more'n a few hours old, I'd say." He was about to say more, but was interrupted by a shout from Red Basket from the trees beyond the meadow.

"Here is where you killed the other four," she called out, and started walking back to join them. "They are all gone." She held a broken arrow shaft in her hand, which she handed to Slater. "Here is one of your arrows," she said, and pointed to the Crow as well as Slater's personal markings on the shaft.

"Damn. . . ," Russell muttered softly. "I've got to admit, I had my doubts, but there's no question about it now. That means there's at least one other war party raiding up and down the Yellowstone, and you think it might be bigger than this one." He turned to gaze up at the steep mountains on either side of the river. "But what are they doing back here on the Boulder?" he wondered aloud. "There sure as hell aren't any settlers along this river—maybe a prospector or two, but nobody else."

"I expect they're holin' up in these mountains between raids," Slater said, "knowin' they'd be mighty hard to find." He looked at Red Basket then. "I reckon they wouldn'ta stumbled across our village if they hadn't been lookin' for a place to hole up where the army wasn't likely to find 'em." She nodded solemnly in agreement.

Russell was thinking hard now. He had a decision to make. Without knowing the true strength of the second war party, should he pursue them, or return to the fort to reinforce his fifteen-man patrol? If he did, that might give the Indians time to strike another farm and be gone before he could take to the field again. He decided that he should at least try to find out where they were heading. Turning to Slater again, he asked, "Can you tell where they headed from here?"

"I reckon," Slater replied. "I expect they're gonna take their dead somewhere where they can make up some kinda platforms for 'em in the trees. They ain't likely to do much raidin' if they're carryin' bodies behind 'em on their ponies. And I doubt they brought extra horses with 'em to tote the bodies."

"So maybe they aren't that far ahead of us. Is that what you're saying?" Russell asked. Slater nodded. Russell continued. "Maybe you could track them and get close enough to see how many we have to deal with. I don't want them to discover this patrol if we're too greatly outnumbered. I want to know what I'm getting into before I commit my men to attack."

"I reckon I can do that," Slater replied. "This is as good a place as any to hold your men till I get back. After I rest my horse a little, I'll go on up ahead and see if I can find 'em. All right?"

"Good man," Russell replied. "I know you're taking a helluva chance and I appreciate it."

"I'll find 'em for you, as long as I know you'll see that Red Basket gets to Fort Ellis safely if I do wind up with a Lakota arrow in my behind."

"You have my word," the lieutenant said.

"And she'll get my pay for scoutin' for you," Slater said, "and she'll get the money from the army for those horses."

Russell could not help smiling. "That's right. She'll get all the money owed to you."

"I go with you," Red Basket interrupted then, "help you scout."

"I druther you didn't," Slater said to her. "I've done lost Teddy. I don't want anything to happen to you. Teddy'll come back and haunt me if I don't get you back to your people. You stay with the soldiers." He went to check on the condition of his horse then while the soldiers took advantage of the rest period. In a few moments, Red Basket followed him.

He turned when he heard her come up behind him. Stroking the paint gelding on its neck, he said, "He's ready to go now, but I'm gonna make him wait a little while." The Indian pony stood in sharp contrast to the weary cavalry mounts. A strong mountain horse, the paint was at home on the difficult steep trails that wound through the Absarokas.

Looking at the army horses, Slater couldn't help thinking, *I hope to hell they don't have to make a run for it.*

"You must be careful," Red Basket said. "The Lakota are skillful fighters."

"Don't worry," he said. "They ain't even gonna see me."

Chapter 5

"Maybe you could not see the others," Iron Pony said. "Maybe the soldiers were hiding in the bushes around the camp."

"No. There were no others. There were no soldiers," Striped Otter said. "It was just one man, but his gun spoke like many guns. It was a medicine gun that did not miss. Black Arrow and Fights With Lance told me to run to the river, so I ran. But when I saw them sink under the water, I hid behind a rock and stayed there until he was gone."

Iron Pony was not sure that Striped Otter had not panicked. He was a young boy and this had been his first time, so it would not have been unusual for him to be confused. But he insisted that one man had killed all of the war party but him. It was difficult for the Lakota war chief to keep from venting his sorrow and anger upon the boy, for Black Arrow, Iron Pony's brother, was one of the warriors killed by this white Crow warrior.

"I will kill this white devil with the medicine gun," Iron Pony swore. "My brother will be avenged. I will not rest until he is dead and his entrails are hanging in the trees for the buzzards to feed upon."

Iron Pony's heart was heavy with the grief he felt for his younger brother's death. It was going to be a difficult thing to take this sorrowful news back to his mother and father when the war party returned to their village on the Tongue River. He was determined to avenge Black Arrow before he returned to tell his father that his son was dead.

The burial beds made from limbs crisscrossed and tied together were nearly completed. The bodies were wrapped in blankets with hides protecting them from the weather and supported by the limbs of a grove of aspens where they would be safe from predators. To add to Iron Pony's grief, there were two empty beds. Black Arrow and Fights With Lance had been swept down the river, and Striped Otter said that he had not been able to find their bodies. Iron Pony told his warriors to construct the supports for the two missing men.

"When we have finished here," Iron Pony said, "we will search the river where it comes out of the mountains. I will not leave their bodies to rot and feed the buzzards."

Iron Pony returned his attention to Striped Otter then, remembering how guilty the young warrior had felt for not staying to face the white Crow. "You did the right thing," Iron Pony said. "If this white devil has the medicine gun that kills without reloading, it was best to come to look for us."

He was familiar with the repeating rifles that some of the soldiers carried, weapons that he and several of the war party carried as well. But Striped Otter was convinced that the demon that attacked their camp used a medicine gun that fired by itself, never ran out of bullets, and never missed. Iron Pony started to give Striped Otter additional encouragement but was interrupted with the arrival of Two Wounds.

"It is finished," Two Wounds said. "We are ready to ride on your signal."

He spoke for the twenty-seven warriors left of the forty who had followed Iron Pony on this war party. The burial was complete and the grove of quaking aspens was now hallowed ground. There had been some in the war party who spoke in favor of taking the bodies of their brothers back to their village on the Tongue River. But Iron Pony persuaded them to leave them in this narrow ravine, halfway up the side of this rugged mountain, where they would not be disturbed.

"We will ride back down to the valley and search the river for our missing brothers," Iron Pony told the warriors gathered around him and Two Wounds. "We must not waste any more time, and try to find their bodies before they are found by wolves or buzzards. Then we will find this white Crow that killed them."

"Maybe we should split up," Medicine Hat suggested. "Half of us could look for Fights With Lance and Black Arrow. The rest of us could go back to that place where we found our dead and search for the white Crow."

His suggestion was met with grunts and utterances of agreement. The raiding party had been away from their village for several weeks, and many of the warriors were ready to return home. This was especially so since the army had begun patrolling the Yellowstone Valley with more troops. Medicine Hat, like the others, was gratified with the success of their raids. Four white homesteads had been massacred, cattle slaughtered, a small Crow village destroyed, and ranches burned with just two losses until this disastrous defeat of Black Arrow and the others. That was a very bad sign, and surely a warning that they should now return home, and maybe a sign that Iron Pony's medicine was no longer strong. Some of the others felt the same as he but, like him, were reluctant to challenge the war chief's leadership.

Iron Pony considered Medicine Hat's suggestion for a few moments before responding, "What you say is wise. It would be quicker. But if what Striped Otter says about White Crow is true, it might be better not to split up. If Black Arrow and the others had not left to look for a better place for us to make our camp while we raided in the valley, they would not have been rubbed out after they killed the Crows. Striped Otter has told us what happened. They were taken by surprise by this white Crow. He will not take us by surprise. I think maybe his medicine gun will not be strong enough to protect him if he is surrounded by twenty-seven Lakota warriors."

No one spoke in opposition to Iron Pony. He had been a powerful war chief for a long time, so there was no one strong enough to challenge his leadership. There were some, however, like Medicine Hat, who were not confident in the possibility of finding this phantom rifleman. So when all were ready to go, they followed him down the winding game trail that traced the narrow stream through the aspens and into the band of firs that skirted the base of the mountain.

When they reached the valley floor, they followed

the river north, riding carefully along the rocky bank, searching for the two bodies.

It was difficult to hide the tracks of a large party of mounted warriors, so Slater had no trouble following the trail left by Iron Pony's warriors. For long stretches along the wild river it was impossible to ride close to the water because of the rocky walls that formed much of its banks. For this reason, a man on horse was forced to follow an old game trail that paralleled the river's course, weaving in and out of heavy stands of fir and spruce trees on the slopes above it.

At first, he thought that maybe the war party was intent upon leaving the mountains, possibly following the river toward its confluence with the Yellowstone, some thirty-five miles away.

He wondered if he should continue tracking the Indians. It appeared that they were heading back to the Yellowstone Valley, but Lieutenant Russell wanted to know how many they were, so he continued on.

It was well past noon when he came to a section of the river that he remembered quite vividly, for he had found it to be a fascinating place when he first found it. The river had been low then, as it was at that moment, and he was fascinated to discover that the whole river disappeared through a mass of rocks to go underground, only to reappear one hundred feet later to gush through the porous limestone rock under a natural bridge.

Slater had also seen this special place when the river was high, and the section of dry bed, where the river was now underground, was raging with surging current. At that time of year, the river formed twin falls, the upper one flowing over a ledge some one hundred feet over a pool below.

It was a place that left man in awe of the untamed marvels of nature, the Sioux not excluded, for he could plainly see where the braves had ridden down on the dry riverbed to examine it. It was Slater's guess that they had been so struck by the mystical falls that they decided their burial ground should be close-by. They had left the river and followed a narrow stream up a ravine into the mountains. Maybe, he thought, they had made a camp higher up on this mountain. If that was the case, then he might conclude that the war party planned to remain in these mountains to continue to harass the settlers along the Yellowstone. Lieutenant Russell would like to know that, so he supposed it would be wise to confirm it.

There was a very narrow path leading up the ravine, and one that might be hard to approach without being seen. He paused to think about it before proceeding. There was still a possibility that they were just looking for a place to leave the dead they carried. There were tracks coming down the trail beside the stream as well as those going up, which tended to agree with his thinking. He couldn't be sure, but it appeared to him that none of the tracks either way were very old. After a moment's speculation, he decided that the whole war party had ridden up the trail, then came back down together. He felt sure he had guessed right, and if he followed the tracks up the ravine, he would probably find a burial site and no camp. He told himself there was no use following this trail up the mountain.

But his curiosity got the better of him, however, so he decided to confirm his thinking. It wouldn't hurt to make sure they didn't have a camp up there, so he turned the paint's head toward the ravine.

He didn't think it a very good idea to ride on the one narrow trail leading up the steep ravine. If the warriors were still up there, he'd be in a mighty tight spot if he happened to meet some of them coming down. He decided it much safer to leave his horse and go up the other side of the ravine on foot, where there was no trail.

He led the paint deep into the trees above the waterfall and tied him. Then he drew his rifle and started making his way up through the rocks and trees on the back side of the ravine. It was a slow climb because of the massive boulders that lay on the mountainside. But after approximately half an hour, he reached a point where he could see the upper end of the ravine and made his way carefully over to the top of the ridge to a point where he was close enough to look down into it.

It was what he had expected. The top of the ravine was empty of living souls. He knelt on one knee and looked at the bundles lying in the limbs of the trees, like large cocoons awaiting rebirth. He could not resist moving down the side of the ravine to get a closer look. There were eagle feathers tied to the branches at the four corners of the trees that held the bodies, in effect marking the boundaries of the burial ground. This was meant to warn people that this burial site was sacred and not to be violated.

As the sun dropped closer to the mountains on the far side of the river, a brisk breeze swept across the top of the ravine. In ghostly response, the aspens began to quake and gently stir the cocoons, as if the souls of the dead warriors were at that moment leaving their bodies. He could not deny the eerie feeling that crept over him, even though he felt sure these souls had long since departed to seek the Sioux god, Wakan Tanka. He abruptly decided that he had best get back on the trail

of the living warriors while there was still a little daylight left.

He had never ridden scout for the army before, so he
had no idea how far, or how long, Lieutenant Russell
expected him to continue tracking the Sioux war party.
But he was beginning to think they had left the valley
and he might never catch up with them, considering
the fact that they had a good head start on him already.
He had not ridden far from the natural bridge falls
when the sun dropped down behind the highest peak
to the west, and it was as if God had blown out the lantern, casting the narrow river valley into darkness. It
helped him make a decision.

"Well, boy," he confided to the paint, "looks like
we'd best find a place to make camp. We'll go back in
the mornin' and give the lieutenant the word that the
war party has left the valley."

Walking carefully, lest he misstep on the slippery
boulders in the shallow water next to the bank, Slater
led his horse to a small clearing on a tiny island near
the eastern side. He pulled the saddle off the paint
and let him go free, knowing he wouldn't stray off
the island. The paint had spent many a night in the
mountain wilderness, so he was content to nibble on
the grass and shoots near the edge of the river.

Once his horse was cared for, Slater went about the
business of making a fire. He gathered a pile of small
branches to use for kindling, then got his flint and
steel from his saddlebag and bent low over his kindling to strike a spark in a double handful of dead
grass he had stuffed under his kindling. Working
patiently, he finally got a spark to take hold in the
grass, and a tiny flame was born. With his hands

cupped around the flame to protect it from the breeze, he started to lay it carefully under his kindling when suddenly the wind changed.

Caught off guard, he hastened to protect his fragile flame as the wind reversed and now came from downriver. Moments later, he was startled by the faint sound of voices carried on the breeze. He immediately smothered his tiny fire and stood rigidly still, listening. He had been certain that the party of Lakota warriors was far ahead of him, but it could be no one but them.

Without being aware of it, he had caught up with the war party and was making his camp within hearing distance of them. He had not anticipated that the warriors would stop to camp, having assumed they were on their way to the Yellowstone. He did not know that they had established a camp on the river while they searched the rocky rapids before the river reached the flatter plain and the Yellowstone, in hopes of finding the two bodies of their missing dead.

"Well, if that ain't something," he remarked to the paint. "Reckon I'd better not start this fire just yet." He was more than a little perplexed to think that he had almost blundered into the war party. *Helluva scout,* he thought in silent criticism. "Maybe I coulda just rode on into their camp and took a head count," he said sarcastically. With no further delay, he set about finishing the job the lieutenant sent him to do.

Satisfied that his horse was fine right where he was, Slater pulled his rifle from the saddle and started downriver on foot. The Sioux camp could not be far, as he had heard voices over the sound of the water flowing around the rocks. So he was not surprised to see the glow of campfires in the trees ahead after only a short walk. From that point, he moved cautiously toward what appeared to be an open meadow surrounded by tall trees. It was obvious that he was going to have to cross the river to be able to see into the meadow without risk of being discovered.

After reaching the other side, by carefully moving from boulder to boulder, he climbed a high bluff that afforded him an unobstructed view of the Sioux camp. The meadow, he discovered then, was quite large, and the Indians had made their camp there to take advantage of the grass for their horses.

Close to the water, Slater saw several different fires with warriors gathered around each one. It was as he had expected; they were a sizable war party. He counted twenty-four that he could see near the fires, including two individuals coming from the trees below the camp. He realized that there were more than likely other warriors that he could not see for one reason or another.

At any rate, he felt his job was completed. He had found the Lakota war party and had a fair assessment of their size and strength. He considered the prospect of remaining there until the war party was on the move again, but decided that he could conceivably find himself following them halfway up the Yellowstone. Better to get back to the cavalry patrol, he concluded, and tell Lieutenant Russell what he had found. Then if the lieutenant decided to go after the war party, it was up to him. He and Red Basket could go about their business and the army could go about theirs. That settled, he came down from the bluff and retraced his path across the river.

When he got back to the little island where he had left his horse, he decided to saddle him and put a little more distance between himself and the two dozen armed warriors he had seen. He moved slowly back up the river, until a three-quarter moon rose above the mountains to help light his way. With better light, he rode for what he figured to be a couple of miles before he picked a spot to make his second camp of the night.

It was early the next morning when Slater made it back to the site of his execution of the Indians who had slaughtered his Crow friends. A silvery mist still lay quietly on the river valley as he rode into the upper end of the meadow where Red Basket had made her fire. The somber Indian woman rose to her feet and came to meet him. "I make coffee," she said.

"I could sure use some," he replied, and stepped down from his horse.

"You find Lakota?"

"I did," he said.

"I will roast some deer meat," she said. "You hungry?"

"Yes, ma'am, I am, but first I'd best go tell the lieutenant about his Lakota war party. Pour me a cup of that coffee, though. I'll take it with me." He didn't comment on it, but he thought it a little careless of the soldiers when he had been able to ride right into their camp without being noticed. He took the coffee cup Red Basket offered and walked toward the lower end of the meadow, where he saw Lieutenant Russell, Sergeant Bell, and a couple of other soldiers gathered around one of the campfires. "I'll be back in a minute to take care of my horse," he said to Red Basket as he walked away.

"Mr. Slater," Russell called out in surprise when he glanced over to see Slater approaching. "When did you get back? I didn't see you come in."

"Didn't look like anybody saw me come in," Slater replied. "I reckon it's a good thing it was just me and not some of those Lakota warriors comin' in to say good mornin'."

"I suppose that's true," Russell said, blind to the criticism casually implied. "Did you find them?"

"I found 'em," Slater said. "They ain't but half a day's ride from here. They rode up in the mountains a ways to take care of their dead. Then they came back down and headed down the river again. But they stopped for some reason and made camp, and from the looks of it, they're gonna stay there awhile."

"So we could catch up with them if we march right away?" Russell responded. "How many are we talking about? Did you get a count?"

"I did," Slater answered. "I counted twenty-four in the camp, but I reckon there could be a few more that I couldn't see. As near as I could tell, a good many of 'em are armed with rifles."

"Two dozen, huh?" Russell mused aloud, comparing that number to his fifteen troopers, all but one or two untested in actual combat with the Indians. He had not anticipated a war party quite that big, and the fact that most of them were armed with rifles had to figure in his decision. Frankly he felt their number called for a troop-sized detachment, but he also had to consider the need to attack the war party before they had the opportunity to raid again.

While Russell labored over his decision, Slater nodded to Sergeant Bell and said, "'Preciate you fellers lookin' after Red Basket while I was gone."

"Ha!" Bell blurted. "More like she was takin' care of us. You didn't have to worry about that woman. Ol' Trask found that out. He went over to her fire to see if she'd be interested in spreadin' her legs for a little money. Jarvis went with him." Bell hesitated then when he saw Slater's eyes narrow in instant anger. "Don't get riled. That woman can take care of herself. Jarvis said she pulled out a skinnin' knife and started to come at him like she was fixin' to peel him like an onion." Seeing the anger clearly in the buckskin-clad scout's eyes, Bell immediately regretted telling the story. "Don't be too hard on Trask," he said. "He didn't think he was doin' no harm, just askin'—her bein' an Injun woman and all. And she wasn't nobody's wife, or nothin' like that." With each word, the sergeant dug himself into a deeper hole.

"She used to be somebody's wife," Slater said, his voice deadly calm. "She was the wife of my best friend, Teddy Lightfoot. He was killed by that Lakota raidin' party, and that's why I killed those warriors. If that trooper had harmed Red Basket, I would have killed him." It was a simple statement, but there was no doubt in the sincerity of it.

Reacting to an awkward situation that threatened to become dangerous, Lieutenant Russell quickly interceded. "Rest assured, Mr. Slater, neither Sergeant Bell nor I would permit any behavior of that nature to go unpunished. Trooper Trask will be dealt with when we return to the fort." He cocked his eyes in Bell's direction. "Isn't that right, Sergeant Bell?"

"Yes, sir," Bell responded. "I've already give Trask the word on that," he lied.

Slater calmed down after a moment. Perhaps he had gone a little too far in threatening to kill the soldier, but it was not an idle threat. Red Basket was the only family he had, and he would have avenged any harm that came to her. Teddy would count on him to take care of her.

With the sullen scout seemingly peaceful now, Russell made up his mind. "Back to the business we're here for," he said. "We're going to move against that Sioux war party. It may be the only chance to stop them before they disappear off somewhere down the Yellowstone." His decision was influenced by a mental picture of himself, reporting to Colonel Brackett, his commanding officer, explaining why he had decided not to fight. He turned to Slater again. "I'm of course counting on you to lead us to that Sioux camp you found."

Had it not been for the fact that Red Basket was with him, the decision would have been easier for Slater. He hesitated before responding to Russell. "I have Red Basket to be concerned with," he started. "I don't want to put her in any danger." He shrugged indifferently and explained, "Their camp is on this river. All you have to do is follow it until you get there."

"I know," Russell countered. "But you know exactly how far it is, so we could move faster with you leading us, and you know when we need to be more cautious."

"It's just a short ride beyond a waterfall where the river goes under the ground," Slater tried to assure him. "You'll know that place when you come to it."

"I'm gonna need you, man," Russell insisted. "Otherwise we might blunder into their camp before we have a chance to plan an effective attack." When Slater still hesitated, he said, "You help me get my men in position, and you and Red Basket can withdraw from the actual battle. Whaddaya say? Can you help us out?"

"Hell," Slater snorted, exasperated. "I reckon. I'll go talk to Red Basket."

"Good man," Russell said. He turned to Sergeant Bell at once. "Sergeant, get the men ready to ride as soon as breakfast is over, and that'll be in twenty minutes from now."

"My horse could use a little rest," Slater said. "How 'bout givin' me a little more time before we start out?"

"Hold on, Sergeant," Russell said, then turned back to Slater. "What if I make it an hour? Will that do?"

"That'll do," Slater replied. The paint had really not been ridden that hard, but he wanted a little rest for him, since he was not sure what the horse would be called upon to do when they encountered the Lakota.

He returned to Red Basket's fire and pulled the saddle off his horse before accepting the roasted strips of venison she had prepared for him. "You not eat enough," she said as she refilled his coffee cup. "Teddy say you don't ever eat enough."

Her comment caused just the hint of a smile on his always serious face, as he thought about the tendency Teddy had had to mother him. *It appears now that Red Basket is going to take over that job,* he thought. "I eat when I'm hungry," he said. "I ain't gotta feed a body as big as Red Buffalo's," he added, referring to Teddy by his Crow name. While he ate his breakfast, he told her what he had agreed to do for Lieutenant Russell. "I ain't comfortable with you gettin' anywhere near the fightin', so all I told him I'd do is find that war party for him, and you and I'll head back to Greeley's to get our horses. The soldiers can take care of the fightin'."

Her eyes locked on his, a deep frown furrowing her brow, as she insisted, "I fight."

He could not say that he was surprised by her response, knowing the depth of her devotion to the gentle giant who was his friend. He realized that she was as determined to seek her vengeance against those who had killed Teddy as he was. And even though he had killed almost every one of the war party that had descended upon the Crow village, it had not given her the satisfaction of striking the killing blows herself. A big woman, she was likely the only one suited to mate with a man of Teddy's size, and she was like no other woman Slater had ever met.

Still, he felt obliged to tell her, "I can't take a chance on you gettin' too close to any fightin' the soldiers run into. Teddy wouldn't appreciate that."

He immediately saw the disappointment in her eyes, and it occurred to him that she had been anxiously awaiting the chance to take her revenge ever since they joined the cavalry patrol. Still, he could not feel justified in putting her in danger.

"I fight," she said again, but voiced no further protest.

"We'll see how it comes out when we get past the falls," he conceded, still planning to do no more than what he had committed to do for the lieutenant. "We'll pull outta here in about an hour, so you've got plenty of time to pack up."

He settled back then and ate the meat she had cooked for him.

Chapter 6

The cavalry patrol moved out, led by the rangy buck-skin-clad scout with the sullen Crow woman leading the packhorse close behind him. Making their way along the narrow river valley, they rode until noon when the lieutenant called for a break to rest the horses and eat the noontime meal.

Back in the saddle after a brief respite, they pushed on until coming to the double falls and natural bridge, where Slater pulled up and waited for Russell to catch up to him and Red Basket.

"Are we close?" Russell asked.

"Not yet," Slater said. "I'd say we're five miles or so, but I thought I'd give you an idea of how far you've got to go, in case you wanted to rest your soldiers and horses. I expect after we ride a couple of miles farther, you might wanna tell your men to quiet down as much as they can, in case somebody might be listenin'. 'Cause somebody might."

"Right," Russell said. "I don't think it's necessary to stop, but I'll give the order to quiet down now." He started to turn back to relay the order to Sergeant Bell, but hesitated to ask, "Would you like me to take Red Basket back to the rear of the column now?"

"I reckon not," Slater said. "I'd rather she stay with me." He wanted to have Red Basket where he could protect her, but there was another reason. He figured that if they might blunder into an ambush, the Indians would most likely let the whole column pass before they closed the trap behind them. If Red Basket was riding at the tail end of the column, she might be the first to get hit. The front of the column would be under fire, too, but he felt their chances to fight were better at the head.

They pushed on past the point where the river seemed to sink into the ground. When within a mile or so of the Sioux camp, Slater rode on about a hundred and fifty yards ahead of the column. Alert for any sign of Lakota hunters or scouts, he proceeded cautiously as he neared the site of the camp.

When he had found it the night before, he crossed the river to get a better look so he could count the warriors. It was unnecessary to do so now, for he knew how the camp lay. He left the trail by the river and made his way up through the trees on the ridge above the meadow until reaching a point high enough to see down into it.

The meadow was empty. The Indians were gone.

Although he did not voice it, Lieutenant Russell was not overly disappointed to hear that the Indians were no longer encamped, still thinking about the size of the war party.

"Well, I guess we're just a little too late. They've evidently moved on back to the Yellowstone Valley. I could push on, but we've already been out longer than we had planned, so we'll head on back to Fort Ellis before what little supplies we've got left are exhausted."

"I reckon we'll ride out to the Yellowstone with you," Slater said. "Then Red Basket and I will ride on down to Greeley's to pick up our horses, and we'll go to Fort Ellis from there."

Russell dismounted and called to Sergeant Bell, who was looking over the abandoned Sioux camp. "Sergeant, we'll rest the horses here before we start back to the fort. The men can build fires if they want to make some coffee—if they've still got any. But I don't plan to stay any longer than it takes to rest the horses."

The bodies of Black Arrow and Fights With Lance had been found no more than thirty yards apart. Both had been lodged against boulders on opposite sides of the river just before the valley began to widen.

Thinking it important to lay the bodies to rest with those of their brothers who had been killed by White Crow, Iron Pony and his warriors returned to the burial ground high on the mountainside. The two platforms that had been constructed for his brother and Fights With Lance were now no longer empty, and he returned his mind to concentrate on the vengeance he so passionately needed. His thoughts were interrupted when Medicine Hat came to stand beside him.

"It is done," Medicine Hat said. "Black Arrow and Fights With Lance are at rest with their brothers. Maybe we should return to our village now. We have been away for a long time."

Iron Pony scowled in response, making no attempt to hide his irritation with Medicine Hat's dogged attempts to dissuade his determination to find the one they called

White Crow. Iron Pony knew that some of the other warriors were of the same mind as Medicine Hat, even to the point of questioning Iron Pony's power as their war chief. "Would you counsel me to leave our dead without revenge?"

"Some of us think it is a bad sign that we have lost thirteen of our warriors since we came to these mountains," Medicine Hat said. "Maybe we should have continued our raids in the valley where our medicine was strong. Maybe our medicine is not strong in these mountains because the time is not right. So maybe it would be good to return to our village to make our medicine strong again. That is all I want to say."

Iron Pony was about to respond in anger when the discussion was interrupted by the arrival of Angry Bear pressing his pony hard up the steep trail below them. "Soldiers!" Angry Bear called out excitedly as he slid off his laboring horse. His alarm brought all the warriors to surround him.

"Where?" Iron Pony demanded.

"On the path below, following the river," Angry Bear replied. "They are almost at the place where we camped last night."

"How many soldiers?" Medicine Hat asked.

"I counted fifteen and a war chief, but there were two more with them." Angry Bear paused then, anticipating Iron Pony's reaction to his next statement. "There was a white scout and an Indian woman leading them."

"White Crow!" Iron Pony gasped. "It is the white Crow!" His mind was racing, already assuming it could be no other than White Crow. "With only fifteen soldiers," he said, relishing the two-to-one odds his warriors would have. "Our medicine is strong. We are called to avenge our brothers we leave here, to find this demon, White Crow, and Wakan Tanka has brought him to us." The reaction from his warriors told him that they believed in him again.

The always cautious Medicine Hat asked a question, however. "How can we know if the scout with the soldiers is White Crow?"

"I would know," young Striped Otter spoke up.

"Yes!" Iron Pony exclaimed. "Striped Otter will know. But even if it is not the white demon, it is still a chance to kill the soldiers while they are outnumbered. It will be a great chance to get more weapons and ammunition. We must plan our attack so they will not know we are about to strike. First, we must be sure where they are going so we can set up an ambush. Angry Bear and Little Paw, go and see if they are still where we camped." Then, remembering, he said, "Striped Otter, go with them so you can tell us if it is White Crow with them."

Acting immediately, the three scouts set out down the steep trail by the creek, hurrying to overtake the unsuspecting cavalry patrol. The rest of the war party ran to their horses as well, preparing to follow close behind the scouts.

Slater could understand Lieutenant Russell's assumption that the Lakota war party had had no plans to remain in the Boulder River Valley. There were no farms on that wild river through the Absaroka and Beartooth mountains, and no land suitable for farming until leaving the mountains about sixteen miles south of the river's confluence with the Yellowstone. So there were no settlers in that section to serve as targets for the Sioux raiders. While a couple of the soldiers tended to two fires they had built to boil their coffee, he walked downriver to the lower end of the meadow to confirm the lieutenant's assumption, as well as his own. There would be tracks showing where the Indians had left the meadow.

A close inspection of the gravel and soil beyond the meadow failed to expose tracks of a large party of horses leaving the area, however. Puzzled, he intensified his search, walking along the edge of the meadow to see if they had ridden up through the trees instead of following the river trail. He could find no tracks anywhere to indicate they had actually ridden north.

Concerned now, he hurried over to the upriver side of the meadow, where the trail entered it. Here he found what he had hoped not to find, plenty of fresh tracks leading back the way they had come. He chastised himself for failing to notice them when the patrol rode in, then turned to look at the campsite behind him. Half of the detail was down at the edge of the river, watering the horses. He turned again to look at Lieutenant Russell, who was already drinking a cup of coffee and talking to Sergeant Bell. It struck him then. *It was a trap!*

"Get back to the river!" he shouted. "Get out of this open space!"

Instead of reacting immediately, Russell turned to stare at the scout, sprinting toward him and Bell as they talked. Both men were openly astonished by his sudden yelling. A moment later they were startled by the first shot fired from the wooded slope above them, the slug catching Bell in the shoulder. That shot was followed almost immediately by a barrage of rifle fire from the trees, sending the leisurely campsite into near pandemonium as the troopers caught in the open meadow ran for the cover of the trees and bushes along the riverbank.

"Get to the river!" Slater yelled out again. One who had not been slow to react to Slater's first warning,

Red Basket had immediately grabbed the reins of her and Slater's horses and led them quickly to meet him.

With only one foot in the stirrup, they each hung on the side of their horses as they galloped toward the river. Reaching the bluffs, they dropped down behind the bank, pulling their rifles as they did. Behind them lay the bodies of three troopers not lucky enough to have escaped the fire from the trees above them. The rest of the patrol followed Slater's lead and hunkered down behind the low bank of the river, scrambling over the rocky shore searching for cover of any kind. Sergeant Bell lay on his back behind a large fir tree, cursing angrily, while Corporal Jarvis stuffed a makeshift bandage on his shoulder.

Still confused by what had just happened, Lieutenant Russell crawled over closer to Slater. "Where the hell did they come from?" he gasped. "How did they get behind us?"

"I ain't sure," Slater replied, "but I'm guessin' they musta gone back up that mountain behind us where they made their burial ground. They musta found one of the bodies that were missin'. Maybe one floated down the river."

"Damn," Russell swore. "I've got three men lying out there." He said it as if he held Slater responsible.

"You'da had more'n that if we hadn't run when we did," Slater said. "I expect they were waitin' for the rest of your men to come up from the river."

With his hand, he raked out a trench in the gravel big enough to rest his rifle in. He glanced over when Red Basket crawled up a few feet away and did the same. Then she laid Teddy's Winchester '66 in the trench and prepared to return fire. Knowing it a waste of time to tell her to crouch down beneath the bank and let the men do the fighting, he offered advice instead.

"Save your cartridges until you see a target. Watch that tree line up there and see if you can catch a muzzle flash. That'll give you something to shoot at. Even if you don't hit anything, it'll be close enough to give 'em something to think about."

She didn't say anything, but after a couple of minutes, he heard her fire.

Overhearing Slater's instructions to Red Basket, Russell ordered his men to do the same. "Watch for a muzzle flash," he called out. "Don't waste ammunition just shooting at the damn woods."

The barrage of shots that had erupted from the riverbank before tapered off then to random shots up and down the line of troopers. After about twenty minutes of stray bullets stinging the air over their heads and spitting up plumes of sand from the bank, Russell pressed Slater for more answers. "They've got us pinned down here. They could keep us pinned down all day."

"I expect that's so," Slater replied. "But they can't come outta those trees and cross that open meadow without gettin' shot, either." He pulled his rifle back to reload. "And we've got water and our horses behind us. So when it gets dark enough, me and Red Basket are gonna slip away from this bank and get the hell outta here. I'd advise you to do the same."

"We're going with you," Russell replied at once, without taking the time to try to think of an alternative plan. His concern now was to escape without taking any more casualties, and something told him he'd be wise to hang on to the stoic scout.

"You're certain?" Iron Pony asked again.

"It's him," Striped Otter insisted. "I got a good look at him. It's White Crow. I'm certain he's the man who killed Black Arrow and the others."

Iron Pony's forearms began to ache, as a result of the force with which he had clenched his fists upon seeing the tall white warrior, dressed in animal skins, decorated in the fashion of the hated Crow. It had taken all of Iron Pony's strength to control the desire to kill him when he began to walk up the meadow toward the trees where the Lakota warriors lay in ambush.

Close by his side, Medicine Hat had continued to caution him not to fire unless White Crow came into the trees and saw them. "We want to kill this devil," Medicine Hat reminded him, "but if we shoot him now, the soldiers will get away."

Iron Pony had managed to rein his passion back while White Crow searched the edge of the meadow for tracks. He studied his enemy intensely, trying to memorize every line on his face, clean-shaven, without the facial hair that so many white men wore. His hair, though not coal black, was long, reaching his shoulders in the style of the Crow men. After a few moments more, White Crow had looked toward the river, then walked away toward the lower end of the meadow.

When he had left, Iron Pony signaled his warriors to leave their hiding places and move down to the edge of the trees. The soldiers would have been easy targets when they all came up into the open meadow. But then White Crow called out the warning and those soldiers in the meadow fled to safety. Angry Bear was the first to fire his weapon. Seeing the soldiers suddenly break for the riverbank, he didn't wait for Iron Pony's command, aimed at the lieutenant, but missed and hit the sergeant. Furious, Iron Pony shot at White Crow, but he also missed his target.

Instead of running in a panic to the river as the

soldiers had done, White Crow and the Indian woman had clung to the sides of their ponies, using the horses as shields, as an Indian would have. He had not fired the medicine gun that Striped Otter had described. But he might possess big medicine, for it was he who commanded the soldiers to run to the river to take cover, spoiling the planned ambush. How could he have sensed Iron Pony's presence unless his medicine told him he was in danger?

Angry and frustrated, Iron Pony cautioned his warriors against wasting ammunition shooting with no clear targets, just as the lieutenant had cautioned his soldiers. "They have no place to go," he said to them. "We will move across the grass when night comes and kill them all. Then we will see why White Crow did not use the medicine gun, if he truly has such a weapon."

"Keep your damn head down, Trask," Corporal Jarvis blurted.

"I gotta fill my canteen," Trask said. "I've gone plumb dry settin' here up under this bank. Besides, I think that hole in the bank between us is a yellow jacket nest. I just saw one come outta there."

"You're gonna get stung with somethin' stronger than a yellow jacket if you show your head over the top of that bank," Jarvis said. "Long as you're gonna fill your canteen, though, you might as well fill mine."

"Yeah, we wanna make sure you don't stick your neck out," Trask replied sarcastically. He waited a moment for Jarvis to toss the canteen over to him.

"Be careful," Jarvis said, "but if you get your ass shot, toss my canteen back up here."

"Right, I'll throw it up in the air and see if those Injuns can hit it."

Listening to the senseless conversation between the two soldiers, Slater wondered if any of the others were as casual about their predicament as they were. Even with the coming of darkness, he was thinking it was not going to be easy to slip across the river without the Sioux knowing it. He figured they would be moving down across the clearing as soon as it got dark. But if they were smart, they would send half of their warriors down the back side of that wooded hill to cross the river farther downstream and circle around behind the soldiers. He decided that he didn't want to sit there and wait for the Indians to think of that. He had hunted this far down this river before, and he was almost certain he remembered following a wounded deer up a narrow ravine on the other side of the same hill. He glanced over at Red Basket to find the imperturbable woman studying him.

"What are you thinking?" she asked, sensing that he was about to do something about their situation.

It no longer surprised him when Red Basket seemed to know when he was contemplating taking action of some kind. "I'm thinkin' I don't particularly like our chances of outlastin' that bunch of Sioux, if we just sit here. So before it gets dark, I'm gonna make my way along the river far enough to get down below the foot of that ridge they're perched on. There's some pretty heavy brush between here and there, so I might be able to sneak down there without being seen. I think I can get up to the top of that ridge they're settin' on, maybe get up behind 'em. And if I get there at the right time, I might be able to keep 'em from splittin' up and tryin' to get around behind us."

She nodded thoughtfully. "It is a good plan. I will go with you."

He shook his head. "You need to stay here and help the soldiers," he said.

"Teddy say you shoot fast and you don't miss," she said. "That's good, but two guns better than one gun. I go with you."

Even though her aggressive confidence no longer amazed him, this was a little too much to expect of the woman. "I need to have you stay here and keep an eye on our horses," he said. "I'm gonna have to go on foot. I'd never slip out of here with a horse. They'd damn sure see a horse sneakin' down the river before dark. Besides, with me gone, the soldiers will need your rifle when those warriors come down offa that hill."

"I stay," she conceded reluctantly. "You be careful."

"I will," he replied. "You make sure you keep your head down, and we'll get outta this mess if we're lucky."

With his rifle and a full cartridge belt, he crawled over to tell Lieutenant Russell what he planned to do. "If I can get up there behind 'em while there's still enough light to see, I might be able to keep 'em from sendin' somebody to get behind you."

"Very well," Russell said, unable to think of any suggestion of his own to offer, "if you want to take the risk."

"If I don't," Slater said, "I'm afraid all of your soldiers ain't gonna make it across the river."

Russell turned his head to look at the expanse of open space on the other side of the river between the water and the first growth of fir trees at the base of a hill. It was a long sprint to run, even in the dark. The prospects of losing more of his men were high.

"I appreciate your willingness to go," he said. "Do you want me to ask for volunteers to go with you?"

"No, I work better alone," Slater replied, thinking

that if he figured he needed help, he probably would rather have had Red Basket with him.

Not waiting for any further discussion, he turned at once and was away, running in a crouch behind the taller bushes along the bank. When he came to the end of one patch of taller growth, he dropped down on his hands and knees until reaching taller cover again. He moved along the riverbank in this fashion for almost one hundred yards before he reached a small stream that emptied into the river at the foot of the hill. He paused to peer back toward the forest over the meadow. If his movements had been seen from the trees, he was not likely to know it until he was met on the back side of the hill by a delegation of Sioux warriors coming to intercept him.

Only one way to find out, he thought, checked his rifle to make sure it was ready to fire, and set off up the stream.

The stream emerged from the mouth of a narrow ravine that led up through the heavy growth of spruce trees that covered the side of the hill. When he started climbing, he was sure it was the ravine he remembered. He was almost certain he recognized the spot where he had found the deer as it lay dying. He couldn't help thinking that on this hunt his prey was a bit more dangerous, and he was still undecided as to who was the hunter and who was the hunted.

The ravine led him to the top of the long ridge, and he started making his way back toward the Sioux war party, feeling lucky that he hadn't met anyone coming toward him so far. It was not easy to estimate how far back the Indians were. The trees were thick, and he could not see any of the meadow below, so he proceeded very cautiously. At this point, at least, he concluded that he had evidently not been seen leaving the cover of the riverbank.

Knowing that he had to be close to a point over the war party's ambush, he moved slowly from tree to tree, straining to see down through the dense forest. It occurred to him that he might have gone too far and had missed them. But if that was the case, why had he not found their horses? He had counted on finding their horses corralled somewhere up the hill behind the warriors' positions. Right on cue, he heard a horse whinny, and he froze, uncertain if he had been discovered. After a few seconds, he heard another whinny, this one with a little grunt at the end, like that typical of a stallion, or a gelding, different from that of a mare. It was enough to tell him that he had found their horses, and they were scattered among the trees, their owners having found no clearing to corral them.

His task now was to work his way down far enough to see the warriors' positions, but first there was the matter of spotting the one watching the horses, if there was one. He looked straight up at the sky, trying to guess how much time was left before the sun went down. The light was already getting dim there in the dense growth of trees, but the sky told him that he still had ample time to find the horse guard.

Relying on his instincts and the ability to move almost silently from tree to tree, stopping each time to listen and observe the actions of the horses he passed, he soon concluded that there was no one watching them. And since there was not a convenient place to corral the horses together, it appeared that each warrior had simply tied his pony to a bush or tree limb. In some places, Slater found two or three horses tied to the same tree. The warriors had apparently had no concerns that they might be attacked from the rear.

A few yards farther down the ridge brought him to a spot where he got his first sighting of the waiting warriors. Spread in a line no more than five or ten yards above the edge of the open meadow, the Lakota crouched, awaiting the order to attack. Slater glanced up at the sky again.

It ain't gonna be much longer, he thought.

The problem facing him now was the dense growth of the forest, making it much more difficult for him to get off a volley of quick shots. He had hoped to find several of the Indians exposed to his surprise assault, giving him more than one target for his rapid fire before they could dive for cover. By firing and moving quickly from spot to spot, he could still kill one or two, but he needed to do more damage than that to be effective. Then an idea occurred to him that might help to give him more targets.

Withdrawing a few yards back up the slope, he moved quietly through the trees, untying each Indian pony as he came to it. In a short time, he had untied almost all of them. At first, they stood close to the place where they had been tied, so he crept back among them, gently encouraging them to move down the slope.

For a few long moments, it looked as though his plan was not going to work, until one, then another moved, and the rest of the horses followed, their natural desire for water and the grass that the meadow provided drawing them. Below him, near the edge of the trees, he heard a surprised exclamation from one of the warriors when one of the ponies emerged from the forest and walked slowly out into the grassy meadow. Soon a second horse appeared in the meadow, and in a matter of minutes Slater could hear the excited cries of the warriors as they saw all their horses filing out, heading for grass and water. It was enough to cause the confusion Slater had hoped for, and he moved quickly to get in position to take advantage of the Indians' befuddlement.

Surprised by the sudden appearance of their ponies in the meadow, the warriors tried to move quickly to stop them. They were forced to leave the cover that had made them difficult targets, and Slater was quick to take advantage of that opportunity. The Henry rifle spoke in rapid succession and two of the warriors dropped at the edge of the meadow.

While the rest of the warriors reacted in panic-stricken confusion, uncertain where the shots had come from, Slater moved to another position and fired at two more who had left their cover at the edge of the woods, killing one and wounding the other. Aware then that the shots were coming from somewhere in the trees, the Indians backed down into the fringe of the meadow, searching frantically for the source of the barrage. At that point, with visible targets suddenly appearing, shots rang out from the soldiers lying along the riverbank below.

Slater was certain the first one fired had the distinct sound of Teddy Lightfoot's Winchester '66. It did not surprise him when one of the vulnerable warriors cried out in pain and fell to the ground. Another shot from the river felled a warrior running to try to catch his horse, and the Lakota realized they were caught in a deadly cross fire. Their natural instinct was to seek the safety of the trees, but Slater made it costly for them when he hustled to a new position above them and cranked out five more rounds, two of which found their marks.

The meadow had become a killing field now with

the constant barrage of fire from the troopers firing as fast as they could. The Lakota war party had no choice except to run from the ambush that had been turned upside down and was taking a deadly toll. Those who could caught their ponies and fled the meadow, leaving behind a field strewn with the bodies of warriors and horses.

Seeing the Indians running, the troopers came up out of their defensive positions, firing at the retreating warriors for as long as they could see them. Slater remained in the cover of the trees until the last shot was fired and all the soldiers were up from the river to walk among the dead. He was not willing to risk being shot by a soldier in the excitement of the battle.

"Lieutenant!" he finally yelled. "I'm comin' outta the woods! Tell your men to hold their fire." When Russell yelled back to acknowledge, Slater walked down into the meadow to meet him.

"By God!" Russell exclaimed. "That was one helluva brilliant tactic! It negated their advantage of numbers." He looked around him to survey the Sioux bodies as an occasional rifle fired to finish off a mortally wounded warrior here and there. "They lost a good portion of their war party as well as several wounded that got away." He was filled with the excitement of victory for his patrol, already thinking about the boost this fight might give him in his career.

"I expect it'd be a good idea to get your men mounted up and get away from here while you've got a head start," Slater said, his tone absent the excitement evidenced by the lieutenant and his men. "We were lucky to get away with this. It'll take a while for those warriors to get together and decide what they're gonna do. There's still more of them than there are of us, so it just depends on what they decide to do about it. If you're smart, you won't wait around to see. We might not be so lucky next time."

"You're right, of course," Russell said. "We'll recover our dead and get under way." He was about to call for Corporal Jarvis when he heard a disgusted grunt from Private Trask, standing behind him. They turned to see Red Basket in the process of taking the scalp from one of the dead Lakota. In workmanlike manner, she placed her foot on the dead warrior's neck, twisted his hair around her hand, pulling it up while she sliced a circle around the crown of his head until the scalp came away, bloody and ragged.

"Damn," Trask swore in open revulsion. "What does she wanna go and do that for?"

Slater answered, "'Cause that was what they did to her husband, I reckon."

"Barbaric," Russell declared quietly, making no further comment on the matter.

"Damn," Trask muttered again weakly, all lecherous thoughts he had entertained regarding the somber Indian woman having left his imagination for good.

"Corporal Jarvis," Russell called out, "detail some men to pick up our dead, and help Sergeant Bell to get mounted. On the double, Jarvis, while we still have enough light to put some distance behind us."

In a short time, the patrol was mounted, with the bodies of the three men who had been shot in the meadow secured across their saddles. With Slater leading, they splashed across the Boulder River, heading northwest toward the Yellowstone, some twenty miles away.

As she had done from the beginning, Red Basket rode behind him. When she reached the middle of the river, she dropped her bloody trophy into the water and watched the current sweep it downstream. If they had not hurried away from the killing field, she would have lifted every scalp from the dead Lakota, so that none of them would find their way to hunt with the spirits.

Slater estimated that they had ridden close to seven miles by the time darkness threatened to stop them for the night. They pushed on a little farther until coming to a shallow stream that offered water for the horses.

Setting up their camp, they established a sentry detail to spell each other throughout the night. Russell was still aware of the possibility of a retaliatory attack by the Sioux.

The night, however, passed without incident and the patrol was in the saddle again in the morning.

They struck the Yellowstone River before noon, and Lieutenant Russell ordered a halt to rest the horses and cook what food they had left for themselves. "Well, I reckon this is where Red Basket and I will leave you," Slater said to Russell. "We'll go back to Greeley's and pick up our horses and the rest of our supplies we left there. You ain't forgot what you said about helpin' me sell my horses to the quartermaster, have you?"

"No, indeed, I have not," Russell replied enthusiastically. "After what you did back there on the Boulder, I'll be happy to help you any way I can. And that includes seeing that you get paid for every day's service since you joined us." Russell was very aware of the potential for the loss of many more lives had Slater not gone alone to create the confusion that brought the Sioux out in the open.

"I'm obliged," Slater said. "I expect I'll see you in a day or two."

He stepped up into the saddle, nodded to Red Basket, who was already on her horse. The ever-somber

Crow woman nodded once in return and turned her horse to follow him.

"It was White Crow," Medicine Hat said.

"It is hard to say who it was," Iron Pony replied. "I think it was more than one man. Not one of us saw this White Crow, so how can you be sure it was him? I heard no medicine gun like Striped Otter said he had before when the others were killed. Somehow some of the soldiers slipped up the hill behind us. We should have had someone watching the ponies."

"I think it would have been very hard for some of the soldiers to get behind us without being seen," Medicine Hat insisted. "This White Crow has big medicine, I think, and maybe it is best to leave him alone."

Iron Pony was still not convinced that White Crow had special powers, and he was becoming more and more impatient with those warriors who agreed with Medicine Hat.

"The shots fired from the ridge above us came from many different places," Iron Pony said. "Do you think White Crow can fly from bush to bush like a bird?"

"I think there was the same number of soldiers that charged up from the river as were there before," Medicine Hat countered.

Iron Pony exhaled loudly, expressing his frustration. "I was too busy to stop and count the soldiers that came up from the river. I say the best way to be sure is to track these soldiers and find out if White Crow is still with them." He looked around him then at the warriors who sat listening to the discussion. "I am not afraid of this White Crow, and I will test his big medicine." To his disappointment, there was no enthusiastic response to his boast. "The soldiers are running to get back to their fort. If we hurry, we can catch up with them." He looked around the circle of warriors who had fled to this ledge above the river, where they waited for their brothers to find their way there also. "We must not let them escape us again." No one rose to accept the challenge.

Angry Bear got to his feet to speak. "I know that Iron Pony is a mighty war chief," he started. "But I think that Medicine Hat is right. We have already lost many of our warriors since we crossed paths with White Crow. I think it is time to return to our village to fast and cleanse ourselves in the sweat lodge so that our medicine can be strong again. I think our spirits are telling us that it is time to go home. I think if we don't listen to them we are going to have to make the burial ground bigger."

Grunts and nods of agreement from the other warriors told Iron Pony that they agreed with Angry Bear and Medicine Hat, so he finally conceded. "If that is what you want to do," he said in defeat, "then I'll not argue further. But I will find this White Crow and I will tie his scalp to my lance so that everyone will know that my brother, Black Arrow, has been avenged."

Chapter 7

Martin Greeley and Clyde Rainey were more than a little interested to hear about the results of the cavalry patrol's search for the Sioux war party. So they greeted Slater and Red Basket anxiously upon their return to the trading post.

"Well, I reckon you came to get your horses," Greeley said. "They're down at the river with my horses right now."

"Much obliged," Slater said. "Do I owe you anything for keepin' 'em?"

"Nope. I didn't feed 'em no grain or nothin', just like you said, so there ain't nothin' I can charge you for," Greeley said.

Slater nodded. He had been specific about not feeding his horses grain. They were Indian ponies, raised on nothing but grass, and he didn't want them to develop a taste for oats or some other grain.

"I reckon I'll take 'em off your hands and drive 'em on up to Fort Ellis. Red Basket might need a couple of things from your store."

He looked at the stoic woman, who had waited for his nod before going inside. While she went with Clyde to make her purchases, Slater remained outside to answer Greeley's questions.

"What did you find over there on the Boulder?" Greeley asked. "Any sign of any more Sioux war parties?" Although there were no farms close to his store to tempt a Sioux raiding party on this stretch of the river, he was still concerned about being hit. If the Indians happened upon an isolated village like the Crow camp deep in the mountains, they could more easily stumble on his store right on the river.

Slater told him what they had found when he took the soldiers back to the site of his fight with the Lakota war party on the Boulder River. Greeley was concerned when told of the larger raiding party and the fight that followed.

"I doubt you got much to worry about from that bunch," Slater said. "They lost quite a few of their warriors, and I expect they headed for home after that fight. Course, I got no way of knowin' that for sure. I'm just guessin'."

"Well, I hope you're right," Greeley said. "You and Red Basket ought not to hurry off. You could camp here and rest up a little after all the fightin' you been in." His motivation for the invitation was not entirely selfless. He was also thinking it would be good to have Slater and his Henry rifle around for a while, and give the Sioux raiders a little more time to clear out of the area. It also came to mind that the formidable Crow woman would provide one more gun.

"I expect we'll be movin' right along as soon as Red Basket buys what she needs. I'm anxious to get rid of our extra horses, and I told Lieutenant Russell we'd be at Fort Ellis tomorrow. I'm thinkin' it's too late to start out today, so we'll camp here tonight and leave early in the mornin'."

Slater and Red Basket rode out early the next morning, each leading a packhorse. Before them, they drove the six extra Indian ponies north, back toward the point where they had left the cavalry patrol the day before. Upon Greeley's advice, they took a roundabout path to Fort Ellis, skirting the high mountains to the west, avoiding the difficulty they would have encountered had they attempted to drive their horses through them.

They reached the army fort early in the afternoon. With no idea where to go, they herded the horses to an empty field in the center of the fort and halted them there.

Dismounting, they both looked around them at the various buildings, and Slater realized that he had no idea how to find Lieutenant Russell. It was his first time on any army post, but he figured they were probably on what was most likely a parade ground. And he reasoned that, if that was the case, someone would probably soon come to tell him to move. There were many soldiers moving among the buildings, and so far, none seemed interested in Red Basket and him.

"Maybe we got spirit ponies," Red Basket deadpanned. "Soldiers can't see."

"Maybe so," Slater said. "We'll wait awhile longer. Somebody's bound to tell us to get the hell outta here." His assumption was confirmed a few minutes later.

Colonel A. G. Brackett, commanding officer, was distracted as he walked by a window in the headquarters building. He stopped and took a step backward to take another look. "What the hell?" he muttered, and stood gazing at the visitors for a few seconds before issuing an order to the sergeant major. "Sergeant Millward, go out there and see what those two Indians are doing in the middle of our parade ground."

Millward had not noticed the visitors up to that point. He got up from his desk and looked out the door. "Ha!" he exclaimed after a moment, then, "Yes, sir." He reached for his hat, stepped outside, and marched toward the man and woman waiting by their horses. "You need to move those horses off this parade ground," he called out as he neared them. "You speak English?"

"I reckon," Slater replied.

Millward jerked his head back in surprise when he realized Slater was a white man. "Damn," he said. "I thought you were an Injun till I got close enough to see your face." He squinted as he took a harder look at Red Basket. "She's an Injun, though." Getting back to his purpose for questioning them, he said, "Colonel Brackett sent me out here to find out what you're doin'." He shrugged and motioned toward the horses standing quietly behind them. "What *are* you doin'?"

"I'm lookin' to find Lieutenant Russell," Slater said.

It triggered a spark in the sergeant's mind. His face broke out in a grin as it occurred to him. "You're Statler, ain't you?"

"Slater," he corrected him, surprised that the sergeant knew who he was.

"Slater, that's right," Millward went on. "Lieutenant Russell's scout." He grinned at Red Basket. "And you're the Crow woman." He affected a polite nod in her direction before turning back to Slater. "Lieutenant Russell said you'd be showin' up with some horses you wanted to sell." He paused to look toward the buildings on the far side of the parade ground, as if trying to decide. "Tell you what. Why don't you move your horses over to the Second Cavalry stable and put 'em in the corral there?" He pointed out the stable. "Then you can come back to headquarters"—he turned and pointed—"right there, and I'll send somebody to fetch Lieutenant Russell. All right?"

"All right," Slater replied, puzzled by the gruff-looking sergeant's manner, as if he were trying to communicate with a backward savage. He would have understood had he known the fierce, untamed warrior's image that had been described by Lieutenant Russell.

"Just let 'em out in the corral," Millward repeated, "and come back to the office there." He pointed to the headquarters building again.

"Right," Slater responded, and turned to step up into the saddle. "They need waterin' first. I'll take 'em to that creek yonder. Then I'll be back." He and Red Basket herded the six extra ponies toward the creek.

Millward stood watching them for a few moments before turning about and heading back to the office. Colonel Brackett looked up from the Morning Report he had been reading when the sergeant stepped inside his office door.

"That was Lieutenant Russell's scout," he reported, "and damned if he don't look as wild as the lieutenant said he was." Before Brackett could ask, Millward answered his question. "He's gonna put his horses in the Second's stable, and then he'll be back here." He snuffled a little chuckle and added, "But first, he's gonna water 'em."

Brackett nodded. "Send somebody to find Lieutenant Russell."

"Yes, sir," Millward responded.

* * *

Upon hearing Sergeant Millward greet Slater when the scout walked in the outer office, Colonel Brackett got up from his desk and came out to meet him. His first look at the tall, broad-shouldered warrior did not disappoint him. He looked younger than he had expected, but every bit the figure that Russell had described, clad head to toe in animal skins, his shoulder-length hair framing a rugged, clean-shaven face, and his rifle held casually in one hand. Brackett had had doubts about his young lieutenant's accounting of his scout's accomplishments against overwhelming odds, especially his supposed annihilation of almost an entire Sioux war party. Upon seeing the white savage, however, he wavered a bit in his reservations. "Slater, is it?" Brackett asked and extended his hand.

Slater shifted his rifle over to his left hand and shook the colonel's hand. "Right," he answered.

"Is it Mr. Slater, or Slater something else?" Brackett asked, merely out of curiosity.

"It's just Slater," he said, impatient to get his business there completed. "Are you the man that buys the horses?"

"No, that'll be the quartermaster," Brackett replied. "He'll look them over and see if they're sound and up to cavalry standards."

Wary of being cheated, Slater said, "Lieutenant Russell and Sergeant Bell already looked 'em over."

Russell walked in at that moment. "Yes, sir, we did," he confirmed. "And I'm sure the quartermaster will agree that they are sound horses." He turned to Slater then. "I see you got your horses here all right. Where's Red Basket?" Slater's somber expression did not change to match that of the smiling lieutenant, nor did Russell expect otherwise.

"She took the packhorses up that creek a ways to make camp," Slater answered.

"We could probably have found some accommodations for you here at the fort," Russell said, "if you'd rather."

"Thanks just the same," Slater said. He suspected that they might find him a bed somewhere, but he wasn't sure what they would do for an Indian woman. He didn't want to take the chance that Red Basket would be treated poorly. "I'd like to get my horses sold so me and Red Basket can get on our way. I've got to find her people up in the Musselshell country."

"I'll go with you to the quartermaster," Russell said, "and see if I can hurry him along to get your money. It might take a day or two, but we'll see." The expression never changed on the stony face, but a slight shifting of his eyes told Russell that Slater was disappointed. "Sorry," Russell said, "but that's the way things are done in the army as far as paperwork is concerned. But if I can help, I will. In the meantime, why don't you take a little time to rest before you and Red Basket start out again? She might need it, even if you don't."

Slater almost smiled at the thought, picturing the somber woman astride Teddy's big dun gelding, her gun belt strapped around her waist, but her two long braids no longer floating on the wind. "I expect Red Basket might ride these soldiers into the ground. She don't need no rest. She's anxious to go."

"You're probably right," Russell conceded, having ridden with the determined woman. Then he got straight to the point. "I'd like to talk to you about signing on as a scout for the regiment. I've already mentioned it to Colonel Brackett. I told him there was nobody who knew this territory any better than you, especially the Absaroka and the Beartooth ranges. He'd like to talk to you about it. Whaddaya say?"

The proposal caught Slater by surprise. The possibility had never seriously entered his mind. There was always the thought in his head that if the authorities, civilian or military, ever found out his full name was John Slater Engels Jr. he might be arrested for the murder of Arlen Tucker in Virginia City. "I don't know anything about scoutin' for the army," he said. "I ain't ever done anything like that."

"The hell you haven't!" Russell fairly exclaimed. "You scouted for me and did a helluva job. What you did for my patrol was all you'd be required to do for any detachment you were sent out with. The army would be paying you for your knowledge of the territory, and from what I've seen, you've got plenty of that." Watching the young man's reaction, Russell could see that he was turning it over in his mind. "Come on, we'll go see about selling your horses while you think about it."

The sale of the horses took less time than either Slater or Russell had expected, primarily because of Slater's lack of his old friend Teddy Lightfoot's tenacity at trading. In spite of Russell's efforts to praise the quality of the six Indian ponies, the quartermaster's men would not offer more than half the price of a typical cavalry horse. Slater appreciated the lieutenant's attempt to gain a bigger price for him, but as far as he was concerned, almost any amount would give him more than he now had.

When the deal was done, he was told that he would not receive the money until all the paperwork procedure was completed. Then the money would be taken to the commanding officer's desk to be approved. The cash would be released to Slater the next day at the earliest. He did not understand the delay, but Russell assured him that he would have money in hand tomorrow. He also reminded Slater that the colonel wanted to talk to him, so they left the stable and returned to the headquarters building.

"Come on in, Lieutenant," Colonel Brackett called out when he saw Russell and Slater enter the outer office. "Did you get your horses sold?" Brackett asked Slater. When Slater allowed that he thought he had, although he hadn't seen any money so far, the colonel assured him that he would shortly, and then he proceeded to get on with the purpose for the conversation.

"We lost three good men in that encounter with the Sioux, and we don't take that lightly. But Lieutenant Russell reported that our losses would probably have been much greater had it not been for the steps you took to ensure the outnumbered patrol the chance to escape an ambush. So, first of all, I'd like to commend you for your actions. You have our thanks, especially since you put your life in danger when you routed the savages out of their hiding places all by yourself." He paused to witness Slater's obvious discomfort to his praise. "At any rate," he continued, "we'd like to have a man like that to serve as a scout." He paused again to hear Slater's response.

Realizing he had just been offered a permanent job, Slater had to take a moment to think about it. He was sorely tempted to accept, since he had never had a paying job before, but he knew he could not. His responsibility for Red Basket prohibited him from accepting. When he had made no reply after a few seconds, Brackett sought to persuade him.

"You'd be paid the same as a U.S. cavalry soldier," he said. "Plus, the army would supply your ammunition and food. Think you might be interested?"

"I would be," Slater replied, "but I promised Red Basket I'd take her to find her people. So I reckon I'll have to say no, but I surely do thank you for the offer."

Brackett nodded in silent understanding. Then he said, "Well, I certainly appreciate your position. You made a promise to the woman, and I respect your decision to make good on it." He paused to think for a moment before continuing. "Where is this Crow village?"

"She says it's Chief Lame Elk's village," Slater said. "I don't know exactly where it is right now, just somewhere on the Musselshell."

"Well, my offer still stands," Brackett said. "After you find Lame Elk and get the woman settled, come on back and take the job." He was thinking about the reason Fort Ellis was built, to protect the farmers and the miners who were moving into the Yellowstone Valley. He sorely needed a scout who knew not only the valley, but the daunting Absarokas and Beartooths as well. He had a complement of scouts, but none who knew these mountains as well as the young man standing in his office today. "Whaddaya say? You wanna scout for the army?"

Slater nodded solemnly, thinking hard. "I reckon I would," he finally decided, since it appeared that he would never be asked his full name.

"Good," Brackett said. "Have a safe journey and we'll see you back here sometime soon, I hope."

"Yes, sir," Slater said, "but I ain't got my money yet."

"Come by here tomorrow morning," Brackett said. "I'll see that your money is here, all right?"

"Yes, sir," Slater said, and turned to leave. Lieutenant Russell walked out with him.

"I'll see you tomorrow," Russell said when they were outside. "You've still got several days' pay coming that I promised you. You won't get that until the regular troops' payday at the end of the month, when everybody gets paid. So don't worry—you'll get your money."

"Much obliged," Slater said as he stepped up into the saddle. He turned the paint's head toward the creek and loped off to find Red Basket, feeling like a very wealthy young man. When he got his money for the horses, he would give Red Basket half of it, and she would then have enough money to set herself up with her brother's family and enough left over to last her for a good while. If he saw her safely to her brother's family, then Teddy's spirit should be satisfied.

A short ride along the bank of the creek led him to a line of cottonwoods, broken by a small grassy clearing. He found Red Basket and the horses in the clearing. A fire was already maturing, with her old coffeepot sitting in the coals.

"Coffee ready," she said in greeting when he rode into the clearing. "You like Teddy, all time want coffee."

"I reckon that's so," Slater said, and stepped down.

She immediately took out her knife and sliced some salt pork from the side meat they had bought at Greeley's trading post. "We need fresh meat," she said, and laid the strips in her frying pan. "Maybe you need to go hunting soon."

"Maybe," he replied as he pulled his saddle off the paint. "We might find something to hunt after we get a ways from this fort tomorrow." After he turned his horse loose to graze with the other three, he told her about the offer he had from the colonel.

She listened with interest and with mixed emotions. She had already become too dependent on him, and had hoped he would find his place in Lame Elk's village, just as he had done in White Pony's. Maybe, she had thought, he might find a young girl there, as Teddy had done, and be content to live with the *Apsáalooke*. Her brother, Broken Ax, had a daughter who should have been about the right age for Slater, if she had not already been spoken for. She stopped herself from further speculation then, telling herself that the fearsome warrior who had come to live with the Crows when still a boy would not be content to live on the reservation. He was older than his years— a result of having killed a man when he was still a boy, and being a fugitive from such an early age. And although he'd been forced to become a man before his time, he still felt the call of the mountains and the wilderness beyond, just as Teddy had when he was a young man. Finally deciding what was best for him, she said, "I think it is a good thing for you to scout for the soldiers."

He put a lot of trust in Red Basket's advice, so he decided. "Maybe that's what I'll do. If I've gotta give 'em a first and last name, I'll just make one up," he said, still concerned about the shooting in Virginia City. "But the first thing I'm gonna do is find that Crow village and make sure you're gonna be all right before I leave you."

Early the next morning, Slater and Red Basket broke camp, packed up their belongings, and rode back to the headquarters building, just as the bugler sounded reveille. They found no one in the commanding officer's post but a sleepy-eyed corporal, who told them that they were far too early to see the colonel.

"Hell, feller," the corporal told Slater, "Colonel Brackett ain't likely to be here till after breakfast."

"When's that?" Slater asked.

"Well, mess call won't be for another hour yet," the corporal said, glancing at the clock on the wall. "Then it depends on how long the colonel takes to eat his breakfast. You can wait and talk to Lieutenant Morse when he gets back if you want to. He's the officer of the day. He went down to the Officers' Mess to get a cup of coffee."

"Colonel Brackett is supposed to have some money for me," Slater said naïvely. "I sold the army some horses. He didn't by any chance leave it here for me, did he?"

"No, there ain't no money here," the corporal replied, "and I wouldn't be authorized to give it to you if there was."

Slater looked at Red Basket, perplexed. Looking back at the corporal, he said, "I reckon I ain't got no choice. I'll wait for the colonel." He was eager to get started toward the Musselshell, but he didn't want to leave without the money for Red Basket. This was his first experience with the army in garrison, and he wondered how they ever got anything done, if they couldn't move until a bugle told them to.

Thinking it a better idea to take the horses back up the creek a little way, rather than have them stand in front of the headquarters building, Slater went with Red Basket to find a suitable spot. Then he came back to wait for the colonel.

By the time he finally got his payment for the horses, it was early afternoon, and he was thinking seriously about changing his mind about scouting for the army. However, the delay actually saved them some time in the long run, because a detachment of cavalry returned

to the fort that morning that had been ten days in the
Musselshell country. The officer in command of the
patrol reported that Lame Elk's village was on the river
just northeast of the northern slopes of the Crazy Mountains.

When Lieutenant Russell heard about it, he immediately went in search of Slater to relay the information. Consequently, when he and Red Basket left Fort
Ellis, it was with a much better idea where they might
find her brother's village.

Chapter 8

With less than half a day of daylight left, they departed Fort Ellis on a course to skirt the eastern side of the Crazy Mountains. Sunset found them still short of the southernmost slopes of the mountain range. With darkness approaching, they were fortunate to find a small stream that saved them from having to make a dry camp for the night.

Early the following morning, they skirted the southern end of the mountains, heading in a more northerly direction, with the mountain range to the west of them. That evening, they made their camp on the bank of Sweet Grass Creek in the shadows of the lofty peaks of the Crazy Mountains. It was a range that Slater had never explored, and looking west toward the setting sun, he could almost feel the mountains calling to him. He recognized the feeling. He had experienced it many times before.

Gazing at him as he looked toward that lofty wilderness, Red Basket recognized the faraway gleam in his eye. She had seen it many times before in the eyes of Teddy Lightfoot. She knew then that Slater would not be settling down in Lame Elk's village. It would be much like teaching a hawk not to fly.

The third night's camp was beside the Musselshell River. "We'll follow the river east in the mornin'," Slater said. "If what Lieutenant Russell said is true, we'll run up on your village sometime tomorrow."

"I will be glad to see my brother and his wife again," Red Basket said. "I am sorry that I bring him sad news about our father."

Her comment caused him to think about his father, and it occurred to him that he had very seldom thought about the man he was named after. Whenever thoughts of his mother strayed into his conscious mind, they were quickly blurred by an image of Henry Weed. And he immediately endeavored to erase the picture from his mind. Still, it was difficult to keep from wondering if she was getting along all right with the small-time outlaw. His thoughts were quickly returned to the present when Red Basket held a cup out to him.

"Thanks," he said. "I expect we'll find that village before noon tomorrow, if it's still where that soldier said it was." She smiled and nodded.

As Slater had predicted, they sighted the village in the middle of the morning. There looked to be about sixty-five tipis in a half circle facing the river. Beyond the tipis, a large pony herd grazed near the riverbank. Several small children played at the edge of the water, not far from some young women who were filling water sacks. The image struck Slater right away. It was in sharp contrast to the village of Red Basket's father, Crooked Foot, where there had been no children and no young women. He glanced at Red Basket. The usually stoic woman was sitting up straight in the saddle, straining to see the village, eagerly awaiting a reunion with her people.

They were suddenly spotted by one of the children playing near the water, and he called to his mother, who looked up to see what had caught his attention. Seeing the two riders and their packhorses approaching, she stood and watched, shading her eyes against the sun with her hand.

When the visitors were close enough to see that they were a man and a woman, the young mother alerted the other women filling water containers at the river. Curious, they walked up to stand beside her and waited to greet the strangers.

"Welcome," the young woman said when they rode up to them.

"Is this the village of Chief Lame Elk?" Red Basket asked, speaking in the Crow tongue.

"Yes," the woman answered. "This is Lame Elk's village." By then, the visitors had been noticed by others in the village, and several more came to join the women.

"I am Red Basket, sister of Broken Ax, daughter of Crooked Foot. I have come to find my people again. This is Shoots One Time, a good friend to the Crow."

"I remember you, Red Basket," the young woman said. "I was a young girl when you left our village with a white man. Welcome back to our village." She turned to one of the small boys and said, "Run and find Broken Ax. Tell him his sister has come home." She turned back to Red Basket then. "You must be tired after your journey. Come and we will fix you something to eat."

A crowd of people had gathered by then, and all made the visitors feel welcome. Slater dismounted and stood by his horse while Red Basket explained the circumstances that brought her back to the village of her youth. He nodded politely, exchanging greetings with those who offered them, otherwise having little to say.

Although they welcomed him warmly, he wasn't really comfortable, for no reason he could explain. He just had a feeling that he would not be long in this village. Already he was thinking about leaving, but he told himself that Red Basket might be disappointed if he did not stay until she was settled. His immediate concern was where he could unload the packhorses. He looked toward the village then when he heard a welcoming shout for joy from a tall, well-built Crow man as he trotted along after the boy who had been sent to find him. Slater remained by his horse, silently watching the affectionate reunion between brother and sister. He was satisfied that Red Basket would be fine here.

Red Basket introduced him to her brother and told Broken Ax of the attack on their village by a Lakota war party that resulted in the death of their father and her husband, Teddy Lightfoot. She then told Broken Ax of the vengeance taken by Slater upon the war party, killing almost all of them single-handedly, which brought nods of respect from everyone.

Broken Ax turned to face Slater, placed his hand on Slater's shoulder, and said, "Thank you, my friend. This is grievous news you and Red Basket bring. It gives me more peace in my heart to know that they who killed my father have paid with their own lives. Thank you for bringing my sister home to us." Looking back at Red Basket, he said, "Summer Rain will be glad to see you again. Come, we must not make you stand out here, after you have ridden all this way. You must take your things to our tipi."

They started toward the circle of lodges, but Slater hesitated. "I reckon I'll just make my camp down by the river," he said, switching over to English.

"There is room for you in my tipi," Broken Ax assured him, answering in English as well, even though he knew it would be crowded.

"I thank you for your hospitality," Slater said. He had a pretty good picture of the lack of space for him and Red Basket, especially since Red Basket had mentioned that Broken Ax and Summer Rain had a young daughter still living with them. "But I like to camp in the open."

"As you wish," Broken Ax said. "But you must come and eat with us."

"I'd be glad to do that," Slater said. "I need to take care of my horses first, though."

He and Red Basket followed her brother and his wife to their tipi, leading the horses. When they got to Summer Rain's tipi, Slater pulled the saddle off Red Basket's dun gelding and helped her carry it and the supplies from her packhorse inside the tipi. When she was all moved in, with help from Summer Rain's daughter, Little Wren, Slater left to make his own camp before turning the horses out to graze.

He picked a spot under a large cottonwood to park his saddle and arrange his possibles and supplies from the packhorse. Then instead of turning his horses out with the herd of Indian ponies, as he had done with Red Basket's two horses, he hobbled them close-by his camp. He figured his stay in Lame Elk's camp would be a short one, so he might as well have his horses close.

He felt comfortable with the warm welcome Summer Rain had extended to Red Basket, and he was satisfied that she would be all right there while she acquired the buffalo hides and poles to build her own tipi. He had left her with sufficient funds to buy what she needed to make her home.

With his camp set up, he walked down the riverbank a short distance, picking up dead limbs to use as firewood later on. When he had gathered a sizable armload, he returned to his camp to find Little Wren waiting for him. He had to take a second look to realize she was Summer Rain's daughter. He had not really noticed the young girl when he had been unloading Red Basket's possessions because Little Wren had been working hastily inside the tipi, making room for her aunt.

"Little Wren?" he asked to make sure.

"Yes," she answered. "My mother sent me to tell you there is food prepared for you to eat." Looking quizzically at the armload of firewood he carried, she asked, "Are you going to cook your food?"

Suddenly finding himself dumbfounded, he realized after a moment that he was openly staring at the lithesome young girl, who returned his gaze with a puzzled frown. Moving closer, her steps as graceful as a fawn, she was about to repeat her question when he recovered and answered, "No, I just picked up this wood for a fire later, maybe not till mornin'."

"Come, then," she said, smiling, "and we will eat."

He followed her back to the tipi, still mystified by the strange disruption the girl had generated in his emotions, causing him to be speechless for several long moments. He had never been around anyone before who caused him to lose control of his voice. In truth, he had never really been around anyone as young as she, male or female. The more he thought about the effect she had on him, the more he was convinced he should get her out of his head.

He found a place beside Red Basket and sat down

by the large fire built outside the tipi. Many of the other people of the village were there to welcome Broken Ax's sister home as well. They ate freshly killed antelope that some of the young men had shot that morning, and Summer Rain baked bread using the flour Red Basket had brought. There was coffee, too. Red Basket laughed as she teased Slater.

"He is like Teddy Lightfoot," she said. "He has to have coffee to drink or he will turn to stone."

All during the feast, she watched Slater's reactions around Little Wren. He seemed to display discomfort whenever she came near him. To Red Basket, that was a good sign. Maybe the lissome young girl would melt the steel-like somberness in his heart.

It would please Teddy if this were so, she thought.

As the evening progressed, more and more of the people of the village came to welcome Red Basket and to hear about the Lakota war party that had slaughtered the tiny camp of old people in the Absarokas. Red Basket related the tragic attack again, repeating the story of the devastating vengeance taken upon the Lakota by Slater.

In spite of the grunts of approval from those around the campfire, it once again made Slater uncomfortable. The evening was still young when he thanked Summer Rain and Broken Ax for their hospitality and got up to leave.

"Sleep well," Red Basket said to him as he walked by her. He nodded in response.

"Your friend seems very sad," Broken Ax said to Red Basket. "Is he mourning the loss of those who were killed in Crooked Foot's village?"

"No," she replied. "Shoots One Time has always been like that. Teddy had hoped that he would learn to laugh, but he has always been sad. Teddy used to say that he had broken his funny bone." She smiled, thinking about the huge man.

"From what you have told us, he is a mighty warrior," Broken Ax said. "Yet he does not seem to be proud." He watched the departing man until he could no longer see him in the darkness. "Is he a cruel man?"

Red Basket shook her head. "Only to those who would harm his friends," she said.

"I think it would be good if Little Wren were married to such a fierce warrior, even if he is a white man." Remembering then that Red Basket had married Teddy, he added, "Some white men are honorable men, like Red Buffalo."

"She would be a good wife for him," Red Basket quickly agreed. "She is certainly of age. I'm surprised that she has not married yet."

"She has no interest in marriage," Broken Ax complained. "Lame Elk's youngest son, Running Fox, was willing to offer ten ponies for her hand. The disrespectful girl said she would cut her hand off and give it to him before she would let him enter her tipi. And Running Fox is the best hunter in our village." Broken Ax shook his head in frustration.

"The soldiers at Fort Ellis want him to come and scout for them," Red Basket said. "I don't know if he wants to do that or not, but I think that's what he will do."

Slater walked down to the edge of the river where his horses were drinking. Although the sun had set, hard darkness had not yet settled over the valley. Looking back downstream, he could see the many glows of campfires, since everyone cooked outside as long as the weather permitted. He could still hear the faint sound of voices from the people who had gathered around Summer Rain's tipi to welcome Red Basket home. He was glad that she was well received, and he no longer felt any necessity to stay.

He stroked the paint's neck when the horse came up to greet him, nudging his chest with its nose affectionately. Slater could not help remembering the trouble that old Walking Stick and Martin Greeley had had with the spirited horse.

"How you doin', boy?" Slater asked as he gently scrubbed the paint's neck. "You gonna be ready to ride outta here in the mornin'?"

"When you talk to the horse, does he ever answer?"

Startled, Slater spun quickly around to discover Little Wren standing behind him, holding something wrapped in a cloth. "Not all the time," he blurted in answer.

She laughed softly, enjoying his embarrassment for not having heard her approaching. "You mean sometimes he does?"

Recovering slightly, he replied, "Most times he does, just not by talkin'." He gave the paint a dismissive pat and walked up from the water's edge, still feeling discomfort at having been surprised. "I reckon I woulda heard you comin' if the wind hadn't been blowin' back toward you," he said in his defense.

"Maybe," she allowed. Then, holding her bundle up for him to see, she said, "Red Basket was going to bring this bread to you, so you would have it to eat with your coffee in the morning. She said you would most likely make coffee as soon as you woke up." She pulled the cloth back so he could see the end of the bread loaf. "I told her I would bring you the bread. She was still greeting old friends."

She extended her arms and he took the bread from her. "Much obliged," he mumbled. "This'll go good in the mornin'."

To his surprise, she walked right up to the paint then, gently pulled its head against her breast, and started scratching behind its ears. "Red Basket said your horse was an angry horse and was hard to train," she said as she stroked the paint's neck.

Astonished by the horse's affectionate reaction to the girl, Slater said, "That's a fact. He ain't a mean horse. He just don't like nobody to touch him but me." He hesitated before adding, "And you, I reckon."

Seeing then that it was missing out on the petting, the red sorrel packhorse plodded over to beg for a portion of Little Wren's affection, nudging her in the back with its nose.

Slater couldn't help blurting out, "Damn, my horses ain't gonna be fit to ride if you don't quit pettin' 'em." He experienced that uncomfortable feeling again that he had felt before when he first met the girl, still unable to explain a reason for it. He gave the sorrel a smack on its croup and chased it away. "Thank you very much for bringin' the bread," he said, and walked back to his campsite.

Pleased with the obvious effect she had on the fierce warrior, she followed.

When he got to the rudimentary camp he had set up, he thanked her again and said, "Well, I reckon it's about time to turn in. You need me to walk you back?"

"No," she said, smiling warmly. "It's only a little way. Sleep well."

"Yeah, I will," he said, and watched her stepping gracefully along the riverbank until he could see her no more. "I will," he repeated, but he found that he

couldn't when he pulled his blanket over himself and
tried to sleep.

He turned on his left side, which was usually the
side he slept on, but he felt uncomfortable. So he
turned on his right. It was no better, so he alternated
sides for what seemed hours with no chance of sleep.
His mind was too full of troublesome thoughts and
questions that he had no answer for.

Why did the young girl bother him so?

He realized that he had never before thought about
girls in general. Whenever he had given any thought
about taking a wife, he had figured that it would be
when he was much older, like Teddy when he took
Red Basket to wed. Hopefully he would find one who
was a good cook and had a sensible disposition.
Those feelings he was experiencing mostly frightened
him, for he didn't know what to do about them.

Having never had the advice some boys had gotten
from a wise father, he didn't realize that he was going
through a phase that other boys experienced at a
much younger age. He troubled over it until weariness eventually came to claim his troubled mind, and
he fell mercifully to sleep.

Red Basket woke early the next morning, surprised to
do so, since she had been up so late talking to the people who came to sit at their fire. Seeing that the others
in the tipi were still sleeping soundly, she got out of
her blanket as quietly as she could so as not to wake
them. It was obvious that she was one of the few early
risers in the camp as she left the circle of lodges and
walked downstream beyond the pony herd to answer
nature's morning call.

When she got back to the tipi, she took some small

sticks and rekindled the fire that was still fighting for life, thinking Slater would be up soon, since he had gone to bed early. She smiled as she thought, *And he will want coffee.*

When the fire was showing signs of recovery, she walked upstream to Slater's camp. He was not there. She looked around her. There was nothing there. His two horses were gone—the packs of supplies, his saddle and blankets—all gone. She exhaled a long, weary sigh.

Well, that's that, she thought, disappointed that he didn't stay long enough to feel as though he belonged.

When she returned to Summer Rain's tipi, the two women were up. "Did you sleep well?" Summer Rain asked. "We will cook some breakfast when the lazy men leave their blankets."

"We will only need to cook for one lazy man," Red Basket said. "Shoots One Time is gone."

"You could not find him?" Summer Rain asked. "Maybe he went to the bushes."

"He is gone," Red Basket repeated. "His horses, his saddle, his packs, everything is gone."

Summer Rain looked surprised, then shrugged, accustomed to the changing nature of a man's mind. The concerned look of disappointment on Little Wren's face did not escape Red Basket's notice.

It only lasted for a few moments, however, before being replaced by one of smug confidence. "He will be back," Little Wren said, trusting what she had read in the young man's eyes.

At the time the three women were discussing his unannounced departure, Slater was more than fifteen miles south of their village on the Musselshell. He had decided sometime during the near-sleepless night that the best thing for him was to report back to Colonel Brackett and sign on as a scout.

Approaching the majestic peaks of the Crazy Mountains, he was once again in awe of their mysterious splendor, and he was aware of the beguiling call of their slopes and canyons. Unfamiliar mountains always beckoned to him, and the urge to know their secrets was pulling hard on his mind.

When he came to a shallow creek, he decided to stop and rest his horses. He found enough wood on the creek bank to build a small fire. When it was going well, he got his coffeepot from the packs, found a couple of flat rocks to grind his coffee beans, and before long had coffee boiling.

When it was ready, he got out the bread Little Wren had brought him the night before and sat down to eat his breakfast. He picked a large rock for his seat and faced the east so he could gaze at the early-morning sun shining upon the tree-covered lower slopes of the mountains.

By the time he had finished the generous portion of loaf that Red Basket had sent him, he was fighting an overpowering desire to follow that creek up to see where it was born. The more he thought about it, the less important it seemed to report to Fort Ellis right away.

What the hell? he thought. *Wouldn't hurt to go see what's up in those hills.* His mind made up, he packed up again and headed up into the mountains, following the creek.

The climb up the lower slopes was not especially hard on his horses, so he continued to follow the creek until he came to a clearing and he found himself facing a steep cliff. There was a small pond at the base of the cliff, formed by a waterfall that spilled over the edge some eighty feet above.

"Looks like we'd best find another way up this mountain," he said to the paint, and looked around the pond for sign of game, figuring it an ideal place to find it. There was no lack of tracks—deer, antelope, and elk.

I'll damn sure be back here to hunt, he thought, but at the moment he was more interested in exploring the slopes above him. Noticing a game trail that crossed the creek below the pond and led around the mountain, he decided to follow it.

The trail began a gradual climb as it circled the mountain, so he figured it might eventually take him up to what now appeared to be a grassy summit at the top, devoid of the trees that cloaked the lower slopes. He was certain that when he reached that meadow, he would get a better look at the higher peaks, but the trail descended after crossing a long ridge, leading him down to the base of the mountain again. He looked around him to see if there was another easy way up to the meadow. There seemed to be none, so he continued on the game trail.

After a few hundred yards, it curved in the direction of a narrow gulch between two steep mountains. He was about to abandon the trail when he was suddenly startled by a mule loping out of the gulch and coming straight at him.

His first thought was that the mule must have escaped from its owner. It was wearing a bridle, but no saddle, and no collar or hames, so his natural reaction was to stop the mule. Since the trail was narrow, with rocks and brush close in on each side, it was not difficult to corral the runaway. Slater could not help feeling disappointed to find that there were people here already—prospectors, he supposed.

Once it had calmed down, the mule obediently

allowed Slater to tie it on behind the sorrel packhorse. In the saddle again, Slater proceeded to follow
the trail down into the gulch, expecting to meet the
mule's owner frantically giving chase.

Riding deep into the chasm, he came to a wide, busy
stream that took up most of the width between the two
rocky walls. There was still no sign of anyone chasing
the mule. Even more curious now, Slater continued up
the stream. Upon rounding a sharp curve where the
water flowed between two giant boulders, he discovered a mining claim. Unaware of his presence, two
men were hunched over a sluice box, oblivious of
everything else around them. Slater pulled up short to
look the situation over.

On one side of the stream, a tent was rigged between
two pine trees that appeared to grow right up beside
two boulders. Beyond the tent, there was a small clearing where four horses grazed on the little bit of grass
they could find. Thinking the men must have no idea
that their mule had escaped, Slater started to announce
his presence.

But before he could call out, a woman suddenly
popped out of the tent. She froze when she spotted
the stranger, dressed in animal skins, astride a paint
Indian pony.

"Injuns!" she screamed, and ducked back in the
tent, causing both men at the sluice box to scramble
for their weapons.

His reactions natural, and lightning fast, Slater
quickly leveled his rifle ready to fire. "Hold on!" he
yelled. "I ain't an Injun. I'm just bringin' your mule
back."

With no chance to reach their weapons before being
cut down by the stranger, the two had no choice but to
freeze in their tracks.

Not at all surprised by their reactions, since he had not had a chance to announce his presence beforehand, Slater went on to explain, "Sorry. I didn't mean to surprise you. I just wanted to bring your mule back."

The two men looked at each other as if astonished to still be standing. For a long moment there was a frozen standoff until the woman appeared at the tent flap again, this time brandishing a rifle.

"Hold it, Lola!" one of the men yelled. "He's just bringin' our mule back. He'da done shot us, if he was of a mind to." When the woman eased the rifle down, the man turned back toward Slater. "Come on in, mister. You kinda surprised us there. My wife thought you was an Injun." He forced a chuckle. "Can't blame her none, can you? And the best rule when you see an Injun is shoot him first, then decide if he's friendly or not, right?"

Slater was undecided; their reaction seemed strange. They had obviously not been concerned about their mule escaping, based on what he had seen when he first rode up. He wondered if they had even been aware that the mule was loose. "I'll just leave you your mule, and I'll be on my way," he said, and dismounted to untie the mule.

"Why, we wouldn't be very neighborly if we didn't show a little appreciation for you goin' to the trouble of catchin' that mule." He took the reins from Slater and handed them to his partner, a gaunt-looking man with an oversized head and narrow shoulders. "Here, Slim, lead this critter over there with the horses." Back to Slater, he said, "My name's Tom Leach. He's Slim Posey. . . . Oh, and that's my wife, Lola." The woman, a large buxom woman with long red hair, and still standing by the tent flap, responded with a bored nod. Leach continued. "Where's the rest of your party?"

"I reckon I'm the whole party," Slater answered.

Leach affected a huge laugh. "He says he's the whole party, Slim." Their laugh seemed out of proportion to the comment. "Well, Mr. . . . I didn't catch your name."

"Slater," he said.

"Well, Slater," Leach went on, "my wife was just fixin' to cook us up somethin' to eat." He shot a quick glance in her direction. "Weren't you, honey?" With a wide smile on his heavily whiskered face, he turned back to Slater. "Least we can do is have you share some supper with us."

"If I can find somethin' to cook," Lola complained.

"There's side meat in a sack up there," Leach shot back. "Look for it."

"I'll not put you to the trouble," Slater said. He had no desire to spend any more time in their camp. "I'd best be headin' on back toward Fort Ellis."

"It's a long way from here to Fort Ellis," Posey offered, having just come back from hobbling the mule. "You might as well take supper with us and camp here tonight—get you a fresh start in the mornin'."

"Slim's right," Leach said. "Too late to get very far tonight before you'll have to stop anyway, and we don't get many chances at havin' visitors. Ain't that right, Lola?"

Lola took a moment to look the tall, broad-shouldered young man up and down before replying, "Yeah, we don't get much company up here in these miserable mountains. I'll get some side meat cookin', if I can find the fryin' pan."

"It's over there by the fire," Slim said.

Slater was already wishing that he had taken some other trail into the mountains. These folks seemed genuinely interested in being hospitable, but they were an odd bunch. To begin with, how could they not know their mule was gone when it most likely walked right by the two men at the sluice box? And the woman, Lola, was just about as scatterbrained. She couldn't seem to remember where anything was. He wondered if they had found any gold, and if they would even know it when they saw it. Maybe, he thought, they had spent too many lonely days in the mountains without having contact with other folks.

Well, he thought, *I reckon it wouldn't hurt to eat with them, since they seem to want some company.*

"Well, if you're sure it won't be too much bother," he said.

"No trouble atall," Lola spoke up then. "It'll be nice to have somebody to talk to besides these two."

While Lola was cooking what would turn out to be a basic meal of beans, bacon, and coffee, Leach and Posey were busy questioning Slater about any possible Indian threats he might have heard about in this part of the territory.

After that, their questions were mostly about whether or not he had been working a claim. When he said that he was not a miner, they seemed to lose much of their interest in him. They found that he was not much fun as far as drinking and gambling were concerned.

In fact, they soon realized what Teddy Lightfoot had found about his young friend—he had never developed the capacity to have fun. It was still an early hour when Slater thanked them for the meal, said good night, and left to make his bed a short way back down the stream.

He lay back and pulled his blanket over him, thinking what an odd trio of people he had encountered. He realized that he had no experience in dealing with everyday white people. Not since he was a boy in his

father's home had he even talked to anyone other than
Teddy, Greeley, or lately, a soldier. He decided he was
not good at it. He also decided that he would leave early
in the morning, as he had done when he left Lame Elk's
village. It was his way—when he was uncomfortable
with a situation, he removed himself from it.

His thoughts were interrupted then by the sound of
something pushing through the chokecherry bushes
that shielded his camp.

Instantly alert, he rested his hand on the Henry
rifle by his side. In a moment, he heard her voice.
"Slater, you awake?" He answered yes, and she said,
"It's just me, Lola. I just came to see if you're all settled
for the night."

"Yes," he said. "I'm all right. Is there something
wrong?"

"No, no," she said, "nothin' wrong. It's just that I ain't
sleepy, and Tom and Slim are already snorin' away. And
a woman like me, I don't get to talk to anybody new
very often, so I thought if you were awake, too, you might
wanna talk."

He was dumbfounded, for he had no idea what the
woman wanted to talk about. It was time for sleep
now. "I'm afraid I ain't much for talkin'," he said.

She recognized at once how naïve the young man
was. "You know, all the talkin' that went on at supper
was just Tom's and Slim's mouths flappin'. You hardly
said nothin' at all. I'd like to know about you."

Totally confused now, he answered simply, "There
ain't nothin' to know about me."

"Come on, now," she teased. "A big, strong, handsome man like you, I'll bet you've got a little bit of
money, too. Am I right?"

"Well, I've got a little bit," he answered foolishly,
"enough to get by on, I reckon."

She knelt down beside him. "What would you like to spend some of it on, if you could? You know, I'm married, but Tom Leach don't own me, and I like to have a good time once in a while."

At last it registered in his innocent brain what she had in mind, and he was immediately disgusted with the idea. He felt the blood in his veins turn to ice.

"You're barkin' up the wrong tree, lady," he blurted. "You'd best go on back to your husband now. And don't expect to see me here when you get up in the mornin'."

Inflamed, she got to her feet. "You dumb jackass!" she bellowed. "You ain't got sense enough to know what you just missed." She spun on her heel and added, "And you probably ain't man enough to handle it, anyway!" Then she pushed her way violently through the branches of the chokecherries and was gone. The boy and young man who had been sorely deficient in the education that most boys gained in the towns and saloons at a much earlier age was now a much wiser man—although he felt like the dumbest man on the earth.

There were other things to think about, now that he had belatedly realized the larcenous intentions of the woman. She had been more interested in whether or not he had any money than actually seeking to share his bed. More than likely she was intended to be the distraction while Leach and Posey went through his packs. He figured they were just thieves, but there was also the possibility that they were more than that. So he decided it was in his best interest to saddle up and be on his way.

Working quickly, in case he would have more visitors when the woman went back to report her failure, he threw his saddle on the paint. After he made sure his rifle was in the saddle sling and his bow securely tied on, he started to load his packs on the sorrel. He didn't get very far before he heard the voice behind him.

"You fixin' to go somewhere, partner?"

He turned to face a Winchester '66 leveled at him.

"I swear, Tom," Slim Posey said as he stepped out of the bushes on the other side of the paint, "I believe ol' Slater here was gonna run right off without so much as a fare-thee-well."

"Yeah," Leach drawled, "and after we showed him so much hospitality."

Stepping out from behind her husband, a revolver in her hand, Lola commanded impatiently, "Quit your japin' and cut him down so we can see that little bit of money he's carryin'."

"I'd like to see what he's totin' in those packs, too," Posey said. Still somewhat reluctant to end the enjoyment of watching a man squirm when he was about to die, both men waited, hoping he would make a move in desperation.

Caught by surprise, Slater found he had few options. He stood silently waiting while the two miscreants amused themselves at his expense. It did no good at all to chide himself for not finding cover to defend himself, instead of trying to run.

In the few moments he had to act before one of the three pulled a trigger, he saw no way he could get out of his predicament without getting shot by one or more of the three. He saw his odds improve, however, when Posey stepped up to the paint gelding.

"I've been admirin' that horse of your'n ever since you rode up. I'll most likely keep my saddle, though."

"Don't go puttin' your brand on that horse just yet," Leach said. "I been admirin' that paint myself."

"Kill the son of a bitch," Lola demanded, tired of

hearing the bickering between the two men, and still smoldering from Slater's rejection.

"We will, darlin'," Leach said, and started to raise the Winchester, then hesitated when the thought struck him. "You wanna shoot him?"

"Yeah," she said. "Let me do it, since it don't look like you're gonna get it done."

Posey laughed at her response. Still more interested in the paint gelding, he reached for the horse's bridle. It was Slater's signal to act, and the only one he was likely to get.

Faithful to its reputation, the cantankerous horse took a bite out of Posey's hand, causing him to yell out in pain, dropping his .44 as he jumped back, jolting Lola in the process. The result of the collision between the two resulted in Lola squeezing the trigger and firing a bullet into the ground.

Like a great cat, Slater sprang for his horse. With one foot in the stirrup, he flailed the horse for speed, and the paint did not fail him. Lola was unfortunate to be directly in the horse's way and was consequently knocked to the ground as horse and rider galloped away down the stream.

In all the chaos of the moment, one remained clear of the confusion. Leach raised his rifle to draw a bead on the fleeing man. Knowing he was not safe yet, Slater threw his leg over the saddle and dropped down to cling to the paint's other side in an effort to present a smaller target and put the horse between him and Leach. He felt the impact of the bullet behind his shoulder as he switched over, and he grabbed the saddle horn to keep from falling. There were two more shots fired after him, both misses. They told him that Leach and one of the others had shot at him, either Lola or Posey; his money was on Lola.

As soon as he felt it was safe, he pulled himself up to sit in the saddle, and reined the paint back to a lope. After a short distance, he reined the horse back further to a fast walk. He wasn't sure how bad he was hurt. The pain was intense, but not debilitating. He felt that he would be all right once he stopped the bleeding. He had been right when he figured that there were long odds on getting away without being shot.

Damn lucky it was my shoulder, he thought.

But he had left his packhorse and all of his supplies behind, and that would be the next order of business. He had no intention of losing them.

Chapter 9

"Boy, he lit outta here like a rabbit with a bobcat on his tail," Slim Posey crowed. "We ain't gonna see that jasper again. He left damn near all his possibles and a right fine horse to boot. I'd say it was a pretty good night's work."

Tom Leach continued to stare in the direction of Slater's departure. "Maybe he'll keep on runnin' and maybe he won't. I ain't willin' to take a chance on him sneakin' back here."

"Hell, you shot him," Slim said. "I saw him when the bullet hit him. He liked to fell outta the saddle then."

"I know I hit him," Leach insisted, "but I'd still like to know he's hurt too bad to cause us any trouble."

"He might already be dead," Slim said. "But I reckon you're right, we oughta see if we can find out. Why don't we walk on down this stream a ways and see if he's fell off his horse? Hell, he was just hangin' on when he rode outta here."

"That sounds like a good idea to me," Leach said. "I know I'd feel a lot easier if we was to find his body deader'n hell." He looked at Lola then, who was busy pulling Slater's packs apart, looking for anything of value. "You stay here. Me and Slim are gonna walk down this stream a ways till we find him, or know pretty sure he's gone from these mountains."

"If you find him, just make sure he's dead. I don't want him sneakin' around here. He looks like a damn Injun, anyway. He's liable to try to steal his things back if he ain't dead." She returned to her search of Slater's packs.

As the two outlaws made their way carefully down the stream, a full moon rose over the mountain to shine its light on the steep gulch, making it much easier to see what lay ahead of them. It caused them to proceed with even more caution, for they were aware that they would be more easily seen as well.

"Keep your eyes sharp," Leach whispered as they approached a bend in the stream where it worked around a stone column protruding from the spruce trees that lined the bank. Not willing to take a chance on being ambushed, Leach flattened his back against the stone column and eased his body around the bend. "Well, lookee yonder," he exclaimed. "I got him, all right."

Posey eased himself around behind Leach to see what he had seen. There, about thirty yards down the stream, the paint gelding stood close to the bank, its reins hanging down in the water, the saddle empty.

"Ha," Slim barked triumphantly. "I reckon you did." They hurried then to find the body, splashing through the cold mountain water. The paint moved its hindquarters around nervously as they ran up to it, looking right and left.

"He couldn'ta got far," Leach said, straining to look downstream. He heard a solid sound like the thump of an ax on a stump, and turned back to discover that Posey had dropped to his knees in the water.

"Slim, what the hell—" he started, but was stopped by the gleam of the moonlight on the smooth shaft of the arrow protruding from Posey's chest. "Wah!" Leach wailed fearfully, and turned to run, only to be stopped by the solid blow of an arrow when it struck his stomach.

Staggering backward, he gawked in disbelief at the cruel shaft buried almost to the feathers in his stomach. A fearful whine issued from his lips as he struggled to turn away, grunting painfully when a second arrow, this one in his back, dropped him into the water.

Slater climbed down from the columnlike stone outcropping where he had waited for the pursuers he had felt sure would follow him. With no feelings of compassion for the two would-be murderers, he waded out into the stream to confirm their deaths.

Reaching Posey first, he saw that he was not dead yet, although he was losing his battle with the devil. Slater put his foot on Posey's back and pinned him under the water until no more bubbles came to the surface. Then he tried to pull his arrow out but broke it off in the process. It had buried itself too deep, a result of the close range of the shot.

He then checked Leach but found him already dead. He pinned him underwater for a while anyway, just to be sure. He had similar results with those two arrows to what he had had with Posey. He had decided it best to use his bow when the two men came without the woman. Rifle shots would have given her warning, and he still had to deal with her.

He rearranged the bandanna he had stuffed in his shirt to slow the bleeding from his shoulder before rescuing the weapons now lying on the bottom of the stream. Then he pulled the bodies out of the water and left them on the bank to make it easier for the buzzards to feed on them. It would also improve the quality of the drinking water.

He took the cartridge belts from each body, then started back toward the camp.

When within about fifty yards below the little clearing where he had made his camp before, he tied the paint to a bush on the side of the stream. Then he went the rest of the way on foot, holding close to the shadows near the bank. When he reached the spot where he had left his packhorse, he found the sorrel still there. His packs were strewn about, evidence of the woman's frantic search for money, but she was not there. Figuring she had gone back to her camp to wait for the men to return, he decided it best to circle around the tent and approach the camp from above it.

Placing each step carefully on the rocky sides of the gulch, his wet moccasins leaving tracks in the moonlight, he dropped down into a narrow gully to keep from casting a shadow near the tent. The bottom of the gully was dark, making it difficult to see where to place his feet, and as he moved past the tent, he tripped over a mound of what he guessed was dirt, causing him to drop to his knees.

Feeling around in the darkness of the gully bottom, he tried to determine how wide the mound was. Suddenly he groped something that felt like a hand, but it was cold and rigid. Confused, he pulled on it and discovered it was still attached to an arm, and he realized at once that he had stumbled upon the original owner of the mining claim.

The discovery immediately brought to mind the unconcern over the runaway mule, and the woman's inability to remember where anything in the camp was. They had murdered the poor bastard. He wondered how many more bodies of unfortunate miners had been dumped in ravines and gullies in these mountains.

He returned his thoughts to the woman sitting on a rough stool by the fire in front of the tent and tried to make up his mind what to do about her. It would be a quick and easy solution to the problem to simply shoot her with his rifle. He hesitated to choose that option, however, because she was a woman, and consequently should not be treated as harshly as a man, even considering what she had been a part of.

And yet he had never encountered a more evil being than Lola Leach.

I'm wasting time, he told himself, and climbed up out of the gully.

Feeling very pleased with herself for having thought to check the straps of the packsaddle rig on the sorrel, Lola sat counting the money she had found under one of them. Wrapped in an oilskin sack to protect it, it had been carefully folded and tied to the main cross strap where it would not be easily seen. It had held the money Slater had received for the sale of the extra horses to the army quartermaster. It had been a pleasant surprise, for it was a tidy sum, one she would not have expected to be in the possession of a simple drifter who seemed half Indian and was as naïve as a young boy.

She smiled to herself as she thought, *Ain't no sense*

in telling Tom and Slim about this money. I'll just keep it to myself.

In the next instant, she jumped, startled by a voice behind her.

"I reckon I'll just have my money back now."

She knocked the stool over in her effort to get to her feet quickly, only to trip over it in her panic and land on her backside, just barely missing the fire. Staring wide-eyed at the .44 leveled at her, she scrambled to her feet, still clutching the oilskin sack of money.

"Wait! Wait!" she begged. "I didn't have no part in this! It was Tom and Slim. I wanted to let you go, but they told me to keep outta the way. I swear that's the truth. They're the ones you gotta worry about."

"Not anymore," Slater stated dryly.

"You got 'em?" she asked excitedly. "Oh, that's good. That's a good thing! Now I'm free of that evil pair. I'm so glad you came along. I've been prayin' for someone like you to come along and set me free of that man. There ain't no reason me and you can't be together now. I knew I was the woman to take care of you the first time I saw you, and I know how to give a man what he wants." Reading the obvious contempt in his eyes, she hastened to say, "There's gold, too! I know where it's hid. The old man they killed had found some in this stream. You and me, we can have that, too."

He let her rattle on for a few moments, still trying to decide what to do with her, amazed by her attempt to sway him after her earlier efforts to kill him. In spite of everything, though, he was still reluctant to simply execute her, only because she was a woman.

"You might as well save your breath," he finally said. "I'd sooner pair up with the devil himself."

"Damn you," she spat when it was apparent that he was not gullible to the extent she had hoped. "Tom shoulda shot you as soon as you rode up." She glared at him with all the hatred a pair of eyes could hold. "Whaddaya gonna do, just shoot me down?"

"I ain't decided yet," he replied.

"You don't look so good yourself," she said, nodding toward his bloody sleeve. "You're gonna have to do somethin' about that pretty soon. I bet you're already feelin' the loss of that blood, ain't you? Won't be long now before you'll wish you'd partnered up with me." She was beginning to realize his reluctance to shoot her, and it encouraged her to try to tempt him again. "Hell, I'm willin' to say to hell with what happened up to now and make a clean break of it. The way I see it, you got Tom outta the way, and you deserve to win the woman. Whaddaya say?"

"Just hand me my money," he said. "I'm tired of hearin' your lies." She glanced at the gun belt and pistol, lying several feet away near the tent flap, and took a casual step in that direction. He had noticed it as well, so he said, "Ain't no use to even think about it. You'd never make it. So just hand me the money."

"You want your money?" she taunted. "Here it is. Go get it!" She tossed it past him into the rapidly moving stream. Counting on his reaction to lunge after it before it was swept downstream, she sprang toward the pistol.

Without hesitation, he took one step in her direction and landed a right-hand punch that caught her flush on the side of her jaw, rattling her brain and knocking her senseless to land flat on her back.

Confident that she would be helpless for a few seconds, he quickly hopped into the water and retrieved the sack of money from the rock it had conveniently gotten hung on. She had still not recovered her senses when he stepped back to confront her again.

Spotting a coil of rope hanging on one of the tent poles, he took advantage of her helpless state and tied her hands behind her back, her feet together, and then tied her hands and feet together.

"That oughta keep you outta mischief till I get finished here," he said.

It had been a long sleepless night, but when the first rays of the morning sun shone in the trees high above the narrow gulch, he was prepared to leave. From the constant pain in his shoulder, throbbing with every beat of his heart, he was not certain he could last much longer before he was forced to lie down to rest. His head seemed a little unsteady, and he figured it was because of the blood loss he could not seem to stop completely. He was afraid that if he gave in to the urge to sleep, he might not be able to do what needed to be done before he could leave. So he managed to put his packsaddle on the sorrel and load the horse with his packs and all the weapons he could find in the mining camp—all this to the near-constant whining of the woman in an effort to play upon his sympathy.

Whether or not her moaning had anything to do with it, he couldn't say, but when he was ready to ride, he found that he could not kill her, in spite of her wickedness. He stood over her to state his decision. "I'm leavin' here now and I suspect I oughta kill you, but I ain't gonna."

"You can't leave me here like this," she cried. "That's the same as killin' me."

"I'll tell you what I'm gonna do. I'm gonna give you a chance, which is more than you were gonna do for me." He took a long skinning knife that had been in one of the gun belts of her companions. Then he reached down and cut the rope that held her hands tied to her ankles. "That oughta free you up a little."

"Is that all you're gonna do?" she protested. "You gonna leave me tied up like this?"

"If you set your mind to it, you can cut yourself loose," he said. "I'm gonna leave this knife stuck in the ground over by the tent, and I left the mule tied to a tree back there on the grass. I reckon that's all you'll need if you're really wantin' to get outta here. I wouldn't take too long if I was you. I've seen some bear tracks down the stream a ways," he couldn't resist saying.

"You low-down bastard," she spat.

"I reckon so," he allowed. As he stepped up into the saddle, making an effort not to show the strain it caused on his shoulder, he said, "I cut the other horses loose and they wandered off downstream. I'll let them decide if they wanna go with me. If you've really got some gold dust hid somewhere like you said, you can buy yourself another horse when you get to wherever you're goin'." He paused again to say one last thing. "Wherever you end up, I'd advise you to get into another line of business." He rode off down the stream to the sound of her cursing.

Following the trail he had ridden up the day before, he made his way back down through the foothills to the spot where the stream became the creek that had fanned his desire to explore the mountains. He found the three missing horses grazing nearby. Had it not been for the weakened condition caused by his wound, he might have taken the trouble to drive the horses, but at the moment, he didn't feel well enough to care.

He needed help. There was no way he could tend the wound behind his shoulder. It was impossible for him to even see it clearly, much less to remove the rifle slug.

There was only one place for him to go, so he started back the way he had come, back to Red Basket and the Crow village.

Chapter 10

Little Wren rose to her feet when she heard some of the young boys yelling that someone was coming. She was curious, because people came and went most of the day, so the boys would not shout to alert the village unless it was a stranger or there was something unusual about the approaching party.

She took a few steps up the riverbank to a place where she could see the prairie more clearly. The pony herd had been moved south of the village where the grass was not grazed down, and she could see what had caught the children's eyes. A rider leading a packhorse was approaching the herd of ponies, and there were four riderless horses that looked to be following him—three of them with saddles.

Little Wren squinted in an effort to see if it was someone who had been to the village before, but she could not see clearly because the rider was slumped forward on the horse's neck. He was apparently injured, and the empty saddles on the horses behind him led her to believe that the rider had just escaped

an ambush. And then she realized that it was a paint
pony he was riding, and her heart began to race.

It was Slater—she knew it was!

And he was not sitting tall in the saddle as Slater
usually rode. Forgetting the pot of beans she had just
filled with water, she ran back to the tipi, yelling for
Red Basket.

Kneeling by the fire, preparing to roast some of the
antelope Broken Ax had killed that morning, Red
Basket looked to see why Little Wren was shouting.
When she saw the young girl running toward her, she
got to her feet and looked around to find the cause of
her excitement. It was then she saw the wounded man
on the paint pony pushing through the herd of horses.

Like Little Wren, she knew immediately that it was
Slater. She left the meat by the fire and ran to meet
him. The two women arrived at the edge of the herd at
almost the same time. Red Basket took the reins from
Slater's hands and led the horse toward the lodges.

Having ridden the last five miles on determination
alone, Slater was content to surrender his weakened
body to Red Basket's care. He slumped heavily on the
paint's neck, saying nothing as she led him to Summer Rain's tipi. Little Wren walked beside the horse,
her face a mask of anxious concern.

By the time they reached the tipi, a dozen more
curious people had crowded around them, with many
willing hands ready to help get the wounded man off
his horse. He uttered a soft grunt of pain as he was
lowered to stand on the ground on unsteady legs.

"Gotta take care of my horses," he insisted weakly,
although he was standing only because Red Basket
and Summer Rain were supporting him.

"Don't worry about them," Red Basket said. "Broken Ax will do that."

Broken Ax was already pulling the packs from the sorrel. He nodded in reply to Red Basket's remark and said, "I will turn them out with the other horses, but first, we must take you inside the tipi."

"I'll be all right back where I was by the river," Slater said, thinking that he would be crowding the tipi, since they had already taken Red Basket in.

"Not until I fix your wound," Red Basket said emphatically. She had not had the chance to look at the wound closely, but it was obvious that it was pretty bad, judging by his weakness. "Who did this thing? Lakota?"

"No, white men," Slater said. "I'll tell you later."

Little Wren was already inside the tipi, making a bed for him, so the two women were able to get him settled right away. Red Basket immediately got him out of his shirt and turned him to lie on his side while she examined the ugly wound behind his shoulder. Summer Rain took the blood-soaked shirt from Red Basket and held it up to look at it. It was obvious that he had lost a great deal of blood.

"He needs to build his blood back up," she said. "I must go get Looks Ahead."

"No, I fix," Red Basket said. She was sure the medicine man was a true *maxpé* man, but she felt more confidence in her ability to treat gunshot wounds. And she wanted to be sure that Slater was taken care of properly. She started to work immediately. "First, I need to clean the wound," she said, and sent Little Wren to get some water to heat.

While the girl ran back to the river's edge, Red Basket went to the saddle packs on the ground to fetch the small jug of whiskey that Slater had bought for Teddy at Greeley's trading post. It was still full, since Slater had no interest in drinking it, and it could be used to sterilize the wound. Little Wren was back with the fresh water to boil, as well as the pot of beans she had forgotten all about in her excitement.

When the wound was cleaned enough to see better, Red Basket puzzled over it for a few moments. "What kind of gun were you shot with?" she asked.

"A rifle," Slater muttered painfully, "like the soldiers use. It's with the others I had on my packhorse. The bullet's still in there. I can feel it—like a big rock in my shoulder."

Surprised that a rifle slug had not gone straight through, as it was too low to have come into contact with the bone, she took another look at the front of his shoulder. Noticing then a distinct blue bulge in the skin close to his armpit, she saw that the bullet had almost gone all the way through, but had not gotten far enough to exit. "Does that hurt?" she asked, and touched it lightly with her fingertip.

He recoiled and responded, "Hell yes."

She nodded thoughtfully. "It's gonna hurt a lot more," she said. "I'm gonna have to cut it. The bullet almost went all the way through, but it'll be easier to get it out from this side."

He didn't like the sound of that, but he understood her logic. "Do whatever you gotta do, just dig it outta me."

"Maybe you better drink some out of that jug," Red Basket said as she sharpened her skinning knife. "This gonna hurt like hell."

"I don't need to hurt and be sick in my belly, too," he said. "Let's just get on with it."

She poured some of the whiskey over the knife blade while he got himself set for the operation. Without warning, she made the first incision, quick and firm, a deep slash north and south. He uttered a deep grunt, but made no other sound as his back stiffened with the pain. Before he had time to think about the next slash, she cut him again, east and west, making a cross that filled with a bloody mass.

It was enough to force him to exclaim, "Damn!" Watching from behind Red Basket, Little Wren couldn't help making a face while Broken Ax and Summer Rain watched with interest.

With the incisions made, Red Basket cleaned the wound again before going in after the slug embedded in the muscle surrounding his chest. As she had predicted, she did not have to probe very far before reaching it, although it took some additional probing before freeing it.

"I got it," she finally proclaimed, just as Looks Ahead arrived, having learned of the wounded man only minutes before.

He gave his approval of her treatment, and left a healing potion for Slater to drink, supposedly to hasten his healing. Then he watched as Red Basket bandaged Slater's shoulder with a large piece of cloth wrapped under his arm and over his shoulder to hold them in place.

As a sign of respect, she thanked Looks Ahead for coming to help. Then she shooed the spectators out of the tipi so her patient could get some rest.

"When you feel like it, I'll give you some meat to make your blood strong," she said to him.

"Thanks," he mumbled, more than ready to sleep, and it wasn't more than a few minutes time after they left him until he was out.

He slept through the evening, unaware of the quiet comings and goings of the family. When at last he woke up, inspired by a need to answer nature's call, he found himself surrounded by sleeping bodies. It was in the wee hours of the morning. He wasn't sure he was strong enough to get up and go out of the tipi to find his relief, but he was determined not to surrender to the alternative.

So with a great deal of effort, and a fair amount of stabbing pain, he got to his knees, and from there to his feet, where he stood reeling slightly until he felt steady enough to take the first step. Very carefully, he managed to make his way to the entrance flap, dragging his blanket behind him.

Outside in the cool night air, he stood for a moment, filling his lungs. There was not another soul stirring in the sleeping village as he made his way past the tipis, heading toward the spot on the riverbank where he had made his camp before. After relieving his impatient bladder, he decided it too much effort to return to his bed in the tipi. So he wrapped his blanket around himself and lay down next to the trunk of a large cottonwood. In a matter of minutes, he was asleep, and that was where they found him when the sun came up.

One of the old men of the village discovered the sleeping patient shortly after sunrise when he was on his way for his morning visit to the trees beyond the camp. Thinking the body lying beside the tree was dead, the old man went on to finish his business before returning to his tipi to tell his wife what he had seen. Suspecting who the dead man might be, his wife went at once to tell Red Basket.

"Did that white man's bullet put crazy things in your head?" Red Basket scolded when she came to stand over him. "What are you doing out here?"

She was as mad as he had ever seen her, so he attempted to derail her anger. "Good mornin'," he said, affecting as cheerful a tone as he could manage, considering the way he felt, and his usual stoic manner. "It's nice down here by the water, don't you think?"

Thinking he must be out of his head, she just stood glaring at him for a few moments longer while she let herself simmer down. After a long pause, she finally spoke. "You are too much like Teddy, I think. Are you hungry?"

"About to starve," he said.

"Good." She reached out to him. "Come, I will help you back to the fire and I'll get you some food. You must build your strength back."

Slater stayed two more days in Summer Rain's tipi before insisting that he was ready to move back to the side of the river. Finally when Red Basket realized that he was determined to go, no matter how hard she argued, she and Little Wren made a half shelter for him, using a large hide from a buffalo bull.

Using his old shirt as a pattern, and with Red Basket's help, Little Wren started sewing a new shirt for him out of a doeskin she had planned to use for her father. Broken Ax playfully teased Slater, telling him that he had stolen his new shirt. Slater insisted that his old shirt was sufficient. It had only the one bullet hole and would be fine when the bloodstained shoulder and sleeve faded out a little. But he learned that protesting to Little Wren was as useless as arguing with Red Basket.

When Slater was settled in his riverside camp, Broken Ax came to talk to him about the extra horses that had followed him to the village. "There were three good saddles and bridles on the horses," he said. "There was no place to put them, so I piled them behind the tipi and covered them with a hide."

Slater had not really thought about them until that moment, and chided himself for not having done anything about the horses. "I would like for you to look at the saddles and take the best one for yourself," he said. "To show my thanks for taking Red Basket and me in your lodge, and welcoming us, I would also like to give you the four horses that followed me here. That would make me feel better about the trouble I have caused you."

Broken Ax was astounded by Slater's generosity. "My sister and you are more than welcome. There is no need for such gifts."

"I want you to have them," Slater insisted. "Maybe you can give one of the other two saddles to Chief Lame Elk, and do what you want with the other one."

"I thank you, my friend," Broken Ax said. Then, with a sense of humor that was never far from the surface, he teased, "I thought you would bring me those horses for my daughter. She is already doing many things for you that are a wife's duty."

The somber expression that seldom left his face blanched only slightly. "I would not insult Little Wren," he said. "She would be worth more horses than four."

Broken Ax laughed. "That is what she would say." He remembered that Lame Elk's son, Running Fox, had offered ten and was refused.

His wound healed rapidly. There was no infection and he regained use of the shoulder within a week's time, although he could not yet put any strain on it. Although he protested that he was able, Red Basket would not permit him to help her cut poles for her own tipi. It was a woman's work anyway, she told him, and she needed no help. When she had finished it, it was a fine tipi, indeed. The time was right for him to abandon his makeshift camp and move into warmer quarters. The days were getting colder as fall warned of the winter to follow.

He was content to let his shoulder regain its strength at its own pace for a couple of weeks until he began to grow tired of tipi life and started thinking more of the mountains and forests.

Red Basket recognized the signs of restlessness. She had seen them often enough when Teddy was still with her. So when he announced one morning that it was time to ride to the mountains to hunt before the hard winter set in and the passes would be difficult to get through, she made no attempt to dissuade him.

"Do you think your shoulder is strong?" she merely asked.

"Yes," he answered. "It's almost back to full strength. I tested it with my bow yesterday. I've laid around your tipi too long. My body is gettin' lazy. If I don't get out pretty soon, I'll be too soft to ride. It's way past time when I shoulda been huntin' for the winter, but there's always game to find in the mountains, deer, elk, and bear. I've gotta get you enough meat to last you awhile."

She made no comment on it, but she noticed that he always talked about storing supplies and meat enough for *her*, and never for *them*. She suspected that he was thinking again about the offer he had had to scout for the soldiers. He had mentioned several times that he had to get back to Fort Ellis to get the money the army owed him for the days he scouted for them.

It disappointed her, for she had truly hoped that he would be content to stay in Lame Elk's village and eventually take Little Wren for his wife. She knew that Little Wren wanted it, even though the young girl had never confided that fact to Red Basket.

"Where will you go to hunt?" Red Basket asked. "Broken Ax said that the game is already getting scarce all along the river. The buffalo were not as many this past summer as before, but he felt that there was enough to see us through the winter. Even so, he said many of the people have been talking about moving closer to the government agency at Mission Creek at least for the winter, where the agent will give us food."

"Broken Ax is right," Slater said. "There ain't no antelope or deer on the prairie now, but I'm gonna go back to those mountains where I got shot. I saw plenty of sign up there in the little time I had to look for it. There's elk back up in those mountains, and bear. I think I can get you a good supply—for Broken Ax and Summer Rain, too. So you won't have to go to no agency."

"Why would you go back to the place where they tried to kill you?" Red Basket asked.

Slater shrugged. "'Cause them that tried to kill me are dead," he answered dryly.

"You said you did not kill the woman," she said.

"I didn't, but I expect she's long gone, most likely to some little settlement on the Yellowstone—especially if she really did know where some gold was hid in that camp."

Judging by what she would likely do if she was in Lola's shoes, she felt compelled to warn him, "Don't underestimate that woman. She sounds like a real bobcat, and she might be more dangerous than the two men that were with her. A woman can hold deeper evil than a man can. Why don't you ask Broken Ax to go with you?"

"I 'preciate what you're sayin', but I always did hunt better by myself. Those mountains cover a lot of territory. I ain't even goin' in the same place I was in when they jumped me."

"Those mountains are half a day's ride from here. You will have to smoke the meat there, or it will spoil," she said, trying to think of something to discourage him.

"That's what I plan to do," he said. "I ain't figurin' on comin' back till I've got my packhorse loaded down with smoked meat."

He was not aware of Little Wren standing behind him until she spoke. "You're getting ready to leave again," she stated simply.

He turned to face her. "Yep, I'm goin' to do some huntin'. I'll bring some meat for you and your folks. I figure I owe you that for makin' this shirt for me, since you wouldn't let me pay you any money for it. It's a mighty fine shirt. You did a good job on it."

"Red Basket did most of the hard part," she said. "But I'm glad you like it."

"If I'm lucky, maybe I can find enough game to help you through the winter."

"After you do that, then what will you do?" she asked.

"Whaddaya mean?"

"Are you going to stay with us, or are you planning to go to the fort and scout for the soldiers?"

It was the same question that Red Basket kept asking him, and he had always tried to evade answering. He knew that Red Basket earnestly wanted him to stay in the village, and he still felt some obligation to take care of her.

But he also felt the urge to be on the move, and scouting for the army would at least provide him the opportunity to ride against the Lakota, the people who had killed his friend. This was the reason he recited for himself, for deep down he did not like to admit that he simply had the urge to wander and was not ready to settle down.

When Little Wren asked the question, though, it somehow caused a different feeling. "Well," he finally answered, "right now I'm plannin' to come back here with some meat."

"And then what?" she asked again.

Why is she pressing for an answer? he thought. He felt confused and unsure of himself. Gazing into her deep inquiring eyes, he was suddenly aware of the girl's innocent beauty. Could she have any reason, beyond idle curiosity, to ask him his plans?

"I don't know," he finally answered, and turned back to continue loading his saddlebags, "just see what's what, I reckon."

"I think you are not sure what you want to do," she said.

"I reckon you got that right," he blurted in honesty, and he was getting more and more confused by the moment. "Course I know it don't make no difference to you whether I come back or not."

Certain now that he was unsure of his emotions, she said, "Maybe you don't know as much as you think." She turned then and walked away, leaving him to wonder.

"I'll be back," he blurted after her. She did not turn to look at him, satisfied that he could not see the smile on her face.

He knew he was naïve in many areas, simply because he had been forced into maturity with no role models or sage advisers. It was almost impossible for a man who had earned a warrior's reputation, as he had, to be so naïve. And now he had these new thoughts to confuse his mind, and he knew that they were going to be troubling to deal with.

"Damn," he muttered as he watched her graceful body and her confident walk.

Maybe in time, when she thought about it a little more, she would find someone who suited her more than he. The thought was verified when he stepped up into the saddle and saw Running Fox walking to intercept Little Wren. He gave the paint a little firmer kick than usual, telling himself that he needed to get away from this village where he could think clearly.

Once he left Lame Elk's village, he urged the paint to lope for about a mile before reining him back to a fast walk. It felt good to be back in the saddle and to feel the fresh prairie wind in his face. His shoulder was well on the mend and he looked forward to the hunt.

Half a day's journey brought him to the creek where he had made the fatal decision to ride into the mountains. As he had before, he stopped beside it to rest his horses and to eat some of the pemmican Red Basket had packed in his war bag that hung on his saddle. He stood gazing along the course of the creek as it disappeared into the hills that led up to the mountains.

He found he could not deny a curiosity to revisit the scene of his encounter with Slim Posey and Tom Leach—and Lola. What he had told Red Basket was true, he had seen signs of game back in that canyon, but there was bound to be as much in the other canyons in these mountains.

There was no use in going back to a bad luck canyon, so when his horses were rested, he rode farther south along the eastern side of the mountain range until he came to the entrance to a narrow valley leading into the heart of the mountains. There was a strong stream that split the valley floor, so it looked to be a good place to begin a search for his campsite.

Before the sun began to slide down toward the peaks of the high mountains, he had made his camp on the side of a lower hill beside a small stream that fed into a larger one that ran the length of the valley. It was a good choice, he decided, judging by the many tracks he discovered where the two streams joined. From his campsite, he could see the comings and goings of the animals when they came there for water. There was not a lot of grass for his horses, but enough to last for the few days he planned to spend there. If he had guessed right, and the fork below was a popular watering hole, he should have all the meat he could pack out of there in a few days.

Two days passed without the luck he had expected. It appeared that the spot he picked had been frequented by mule deer as well as an elk or two, but evidently they had moved back up farther in the mountains. The weather was getting colder, but no real winter storms had moved in yet, so he wouldn't ordinarily expect the animals to react that quickly. All he had to show for the two days wait was one mule deer he had killed with his bow.

The problem that plagued him the most was the empty time, time that allowed troublesome thoughts to enter his mind. Primary among these were thoughts about the precocious Crow maiden, Little Wren, and what he was going to do about her—if anything.

Sometimes he suspected that she might have an interest in him that was more than just a friend. But how could he tell? She had made a fine doeskin shirt for him, but she was very casual in the way she gave it to him, leaving it with Red Basket to pass on to him. Her air was always light and casual, it seemed. Maybe she thought of him like a brother, or a cousin. Even if she was more interested than that, she would most likely change her mind two or three times before she was actually mature enough to think about marriage.

I know for sure I'm not ready to think about taking a wife, he thought.

Wife. Just the sound of it terrified him. And in the Crow culture, when a man married, he moved into her tipi, and not the other way around. The thought of moving in with Broken Ax and Summer Rain until Little Wren built her own tipi did not appeal to him at all. If he married an Indian woman, he would have to choose—live like an Indian himself or leave her in her village when he rode off to scout for the army.

Teddy and Red Basket worked it out all right, he told himself. *But what if I get that wandering urge that comes over me from time to time?* It would be his guess that Little Wren would not want to leave her people and follow him to explore every mountain range he had not seen before. *It wouldn't be fair for me to marry her.*

"Wah!" he exclaimed in frustration. "All this thinkin' hurts my head!" He looked around him at his camp. The last of the one mule deer was smoking over the flames, ready to be wrapped and packed. His horses had grazed the little patch of grass down. It was time to move his camp. "To hell with it," he suddenly decided. "I'm goin' to Fort Ellis in the mornin' to get my money."

In the saddle early the next morning, Slater struck the crossing at Sweet Grass Creek where he and Red Basket had camped on their way to find her village. He had only ridden five miles, too early to stop to rest the horses, so he continued on, figuring to stop for breakfast closer to the southern slopes of the Crazy Mountains.

After a breakfast of deer meat and coffee, he was back in the saddle. After another stop to rest his horses later that day, he camped for the night beside a trickle of a stream south of the mountains. He would make it into Fort Ellis before sundown the next day.

Chapter 11

Leona Engels brushed a worrisome strand of gray hair from her forehead as she peeled the two small potatoes she was going to cut up to stew with the squirrels she was fixing for supper. Henry Weed was not much of a hunter. She had shot the squirrels herself with the small-gauge shotgun that Jace used to hunt with as a boy.

She couldn't help a derisive sniff when she recalled how Henry had so grandly presented the puny sack of potatoes to her after having been gone for two days. It was as if he were bringing her a precious gift to make up for his drinking spree. It made her sick to think of the food they could have bought with the small amount of gold dust he had squandered in some saloon in Helena.

His two-day absence was not unusual. It happened almost every time he and his partner, Jim Holloway, had a lucky day at the claim they worked together. She could not help feeling sorry for Jim. He never complained about Henry's binges. If she had done the right thing, she would have warned him not to accept Henry as a partner. But Jim had been swayed by Henry's glib claims of his vast experience and hardworking ethics when it came to mining for gold. It was Jim's claim. He had filed on it but somehow Henry convinced him to work it as partners. She laughed bitterly when that caused her to recall how she had been convinced that Henry was going to take care of her.

Her mind often went back to that ill-fated night in Daylight Gulch when her world went into a spin from which it had never recovered. And what now of Jace? She prayed for him every night, hoping that he had found a decent life somewhere. He had been right in his low opinion of Henry Weed, but she had no choice at the time. She was forced to trust Henry to take care of her as he promised.

It didn't take long, after they had left for Last Chance Gulch in Helena, for Henry's cruel colors to emerge. She had often thought about running away, but she had no place to go. And she was afraid, for he had threatened her, promising her what would happen if she ever tried to leave him. How could her life have gone so wrong? How could she have been so foolish as a young woman to have believed in a man like John Engels?

Noticing that it was beginning to get dark in the rough shack that was now her home, she paused to light the lantern on the table, the one piece of furniture in the shack. Darkness found this gulch buried deep in the mountains early in the afternoon. It was the part of the day she hated the most, for it meant that Henry and Jim would soon quit for the day. She walked to the door and looked down at the creek below, expecting to see the men making their way up to the cabin. They were still working away at the sluice box, however. They never worked this late unless they had unearthed a rich streak of color. She could only hope. Maybe it would be an upgrade in her life, if Henry had some real money. He had promised to take care of her, and his word was all she had to count on.

Finally, when it became too dark to see in the gulch, she went to the door again to see what was delaying them. They were coming up on the ledge to the cabin, and she could hear them talking excitedly as they climbed the layers of rock that served as steps.

"Yes, sir," she heard Jim say. "I knew it was there! I told you so, didn't I?"

"And I told you I could find it if it *was* there," Henry said, equally excited. "I'd say this calls for a drink of whiskey to celebrate."

That came as bad news to Leona, for that meant another night of Henry's mean drunks, which seemed to be the only kind he had anymore. She dreaded the prospect of his brutal pawing and the abuse that seemed to pleasure him. She went back to the table and waited for them to come in.

"Whaddaya lookin' so sour about, old lady?" Weed exclaimed. "You oughta be smilin' tonight, 'cause we finally struck it." He waited to watch her reaction.

She wasn't sure how big a strike he was talking about. She had heard him boast about big strikes before, but they were usually little more than enough for another binge in Helena, so she wasn't inclined to get too excited.

"Maybe we can pay Ike what we owe him," she said. Ike Bacon, who owned the store at the foot of the mountain, had been overly patient to extend them credit on the skimpy supplies they were always so desperate for.

"To hell with him," Henry replied. He gave Jim

Holloway a huge grin. "We'll buy his whole damn store. Right, Jim?"

Jim, a mild and respectful man, the opposite of his unlikely partner, gave Leona a little smile. "Henry's tellin' you the truth this time, ma'am. We'll see in the mornin' for sure, but I suspect we found that rich vein I knew was there all the time. If we did, I expect there'll be plenty of gold to suit everybody before it runs out. If we're lucky, maybe that won't be for a good while yet."

For the first time since coming to this remote gulch, Leona felt her spirits rise. "Oh, Jim, that's wonderful news." Maybe this was the beginning of a new life, out of the rough squalor she had come to know since pairing with Henry Weed. Maybe having a little money would change him from the brutal man she now knew. "I'm sorry I don't have a grander supper to serve you better than more squirrel stew."

Jim had been right. This time it was not simply a flash of the real thing. They finally struck a solid vein of gold. Leona's life almost immediately changed for the better. The men worked longer and more diligently than ever before, and she even noticed a decidedly different attitude in Henry. He assured her that when the gold finally played out, they would have enough to go wherever they wanted to live, with enough money to go worry-free. She would no longer have to worry about anything. God had answered her prayers.

The two men worked hard for the next few days. And then one night, after a long day's work, Henry came up from the claim to give her the shocking news that Jim had been killed. "We never saw it comin'," he explained, shaking his head as if still unable to believe the terrible accident. "We've been diggin' around that boulder for more'n a week. Jim was raking the last of a little bit of gravel out from the base of it, and all of a sudden it broke loose. I jumped aside just in time, or it woulda got me, too. Poor Jim didn't move fast enough and the boulder crushed him. I tried to do what I could to help him, but he was dead."

"Oh, my Lord in heaven!" Leona gasped. That this could happen to such a gentle soul seemed so unfair. "Are you sure he's dead? I'll go see if there's anything I can do."

"Ain't no use," Henry said, shaking his head sadly. "There warn't no doubt about it, and I've done buried him. He was crushed up pretty bad. I didn't want you to have to see him like that, so I went ahead and put him in the ground." He looked at her and sighed. "And right after we dug out the last of that vein. It don't seem fair, somehow."

"No, it doesn't," she said. "The poor man has worked so hard to get to that gold. I just feel so bad for him."

"That's just the way things work out, I reckon," he said. "Ain't nothin' me or you can do about it."

Supper was a sad affair that night, their conversation dominated by the tragedy and how disappointing it was not to be able to share the fortune they had taken from the mountain with the man who discovered the claim.

"It kills my desire to stay on here," Henry declared. "Like I said, we got the last of that vein this mornin', so there ain't really no use to keep diggin' here. So tomorrow mornin' I'm thinkin' about loadin' that gold up and takin' it in to be assayed, and maybe put it in that new bank in Helena—keep it safe for you and me, till we decide where we're goin'. When I get back, maybe we'll talk about it and decide. How's that sound to ya?"

"It sounds like the answer to my prayers," she replied.

When they retired to the pallet that served as their bed that night, it seemed that Jim's death had somehow transformed Henry into a more gentle soul. Leona anticipated a better day in the morning, after so many bitter ones.

"Well, look who's here," Lieutenant Russell called out when he saw the tall figure walking toward the headquarters office, leading two horses. "I was wondering when you would show up again—even if you were *gonna* show up." He flashed a wide smile of welcome. "Did you find Lame Elk's village all right—get Red Basket back to her people?"

"Yep," Slater replied. "She's with her brother and his wife."

"Well, I'll bet that takes a load off your mind. You got here just in time. You're just the man I need. You ready to go to work for the army now?"

Slater hesitated, remembering that he had told both Little Wren and Red Basket that he was going to go hunting and would return with meat for the village. "Well, I really came back to get that pay you said you would get for me. I reckon I can still collect it, can't I?"

"Sure you can," Russell said with a laugh. "You weren't here on payday, and you weren't assigned to any company or regiment, so we've just been holding on to it for you in Colonel Brackett's office. I'll go in with you to get it." He waited while Slater tied his horses out front, then went with him into the building.

Sergeant Millward glanced up from his desk when they walked in. "Well, Lieutenant Russell," he said, "I see you got your scout." He nodded at Slater then and asked, "How you doin', Slater?"

"All right, I reckon," Slater answered, somewhat surprised by the warm welcome he had received, almost as if they had been expecting him to arrive that afternoon.

Russell, still smiling, addressed the sergeant major then. "Slater would like to pick up some pay you've holding for him."

"Right," Millward responded. "I've got it right here." He opened a lower drawer in his desk, took out an envelope, and handed it to Slater.

"Much obliged," Slater said.

"All right, now that that's taken care of," Russell said, "let's go in and talk to Colonel Brackett."

"About what?" Slater asked.

"About why I'm damn glad you showed up here today," Russell said. "Come on." He turned and headed for Brackett's office.

Slater was left standing before the sergeant major's desk with only two choices. One of them seemed a bit rude, so he opted for the other one and followed the lieutenant in to the commanding officer's desk. Still surprised by his reception, he was rapidly getting the feeling that he was a part of something that he hadn't even known he'd committed to.

"Ah, Mr. Slater," Colonel Brackett greeted him, getting to his feet and extending his hand. "Glad you could make it in time. I expect Lieutenant Russell has filled you in on the objective." Seeing the puzzled look on Slater's face, he hesitated, "No? Well, let me bring you up-to-date." He sat down behind his desk again.

"There has been an increase in the Sioux raiding parties along the Yellowstone Valley," Brackett continued. "They're striking homesteads and any parties traveling along the river. So far, any patrols we've sent out to find them have been unsuccessful in locating their camps, although we're pretty sure they've established a base camp up in the Beartooth or Absaroka mountains. We just didn't know where to start looking." He paused. "Until yesterday—a trapper who's been working the upper Boulder River came in to sell some pelts, and he said he saw a party of about twenty hostiles following the river back up toward the mountains. So now we know what part of those mountains they're hiding in between their raids." He shook his head apologetically. "Frankly we'd ruled that area out, since they had suffered defeat on that river before, when Lieutenant Russell's patrol—led by you—chased them back up the Yellowstone. Jeb Sawyer, one of our scouts, said the hostiles would think that river was bad medicine, so they wouldn't go back there."

Brackett took a breath then before continuing. "The winter weather's starting to set in, so it's important that we find these hostiles as soon as possible, before they return to their villages to wait out the winter. Lieutenant Russell will lead a detachment of forty cavalry troopers into that area, since he has had success there before. He'll be leaving tomorrow morning, and that's why he and I are glad you showed up today. Sawyer will be going with the patrol, but Lieutenant Russell was hoping you'd get here in time to accompany him. Sawyer's a good scout, but he doesn't know those mountains like you do." Brackett concluded his lengthy briefing with a grateful smile. "We're glad to have you back."

Caught completely unprepared, Slater stood dumbfounded for a few moments, trying to decide how to respond. They had obviously assumed that he had come back ready to go to work, as that was the understanding he had left with. And at the time, he had to admit that was his intention. How could he now tell them that he had told Little Wren and Red Basket that he was going only to hunt—to provide meat for the village?

Looking at the expectant faces of the colonel and the lieutenant, he fully understood that the time left before winter to find these savage raiders was short. And he knew that no man knew those mountains as he did. So he made his decision and hoped that Little Wren and Red Basket would understand his predicament and forgive him. Also, Broken Ax had told Red Basket that there was enough buffalo meat to make it through winter, so it wasn't critical at this time. He would have time to hunt sometime before winter really had a chance to set in.

"I reckon I'll need to leave my packhorse and my packs of smoked meat somewhere," he said.

"You can leave the horse and the packs in the Second Cavalry stable, same place you took those horses you sold," Russell said. "Sergeant Bell is down there now, checking on the horses. He can help you, and show you where you can sleep tonight, and get you fixed up to eat in the mess hall with the men. You'll be issued rations and ammunition, just like the men." He paused. "You still carrying that Henry rifle?" Slater nodded. "We've got .44 cartridges for that, too. Need anything else?"

"Nope, that oughta do it," Slater replied.

"Good!" Colonel Brackett declared, ending the discussion. "Let's hope we can finally put a stop to that particular party of raiders."

Lieutenant Russell walked back outside with Slater. "I might as well walk over to the stable with you. I need to talk to Sergeant Bell about something anyway." Slater untied his horses and led the paint across the parade ground with Russell by his side.

When they reached the corral by the stable, they saw Bell examining the front hoof of a big Morgan gelding. When he looked up and saw Slater walking beside Russell, he dropped the horse's hoof and came over to the side of the corral to meet them.

"Well, I'll be . . . ," he declared. "Damned if you ain't got a habit of showin' up when you're needed. Ain't that right, Lieutenant?" He climbed over the rails to shake Slater's hand. "Glad you could make it to the party."

Even though he was still thinking over the possibility of backing out of the patrol while he was walking across the parade ground with Russell, there was no way he could do it now. He just hoped it wouldn't take long to find these Lakota raiders.

Chapter 12

Sergeant Bell took Slater in hand that evening, starting with finding him an empty cot in the cavalry barracks where he could leave his saddlebags and his
war bag. Bell also persuaded him to leave his rifle and
the .44 handgun he wore there as well. Slater was
reluctant to do so, for he always carried his weapons
wherever he went. The exception to this rule was his
bow, which he left with his saddle and packs in the
stable.

Feeling strangely vulnerable without the familiar
feel of the nine-pound Henry rifle in his right hand,
he went with Bell when mess call was sounded. He
declined the invitation, however, when Bell suggested
a round of drinks at a saloon between the fort and the
small settlement of Bozeman about three miles away.

"Last chance to get a shot of whiskey before we
head out tomorrow mornin'," he said. "No tellin' how
long we'll be gone."

"Thanks just the same," Slater said. "I reckon I ain't

got no taste for whiskey tonight. I'll see you in the mornin'."

He had never had a taste for the strong spirits that most men seemed to crave. He had seen what whiskey turned his father into, and he was determined not to let it do the same to him. So he thanked Bell for guiding him through all the bugle calls and telling him when the important one sounded, the one that told him it was time to eat supper. Then he went back to the cavalry barracks to sleep. He found that that was not a simple matter.

Some of the soldiers he saw in the barracks were in the patrol that he had scouted for, and they came to welcome him. They sat around his cot and talked until he said he was ready to sleep. They left him then and moved to the other end of the barracks, but the laughter and conversation continued.

Left alone, he paused to contemplate the cot. Since he was born, he had never slept in a bed of any kind. He remembered the bed that his parents shared, but ever since he could remember, he had always slept on a pallet of blankets on the floor. And since leaving his mother and Henry Weed, he had slept on the ground, or in a tipi, which was also on the ground. Now he stared at the contraption with the straw tick mattress, wondering if he would be able to sleep on it. At least there were a couple of blankets folded up on the foot of the cot. Evidently the soldiers did fine on them, so he figured he'd give it a try.

He unrolled the mattress and climbed onto the cot, pulling a blanket up over him. It felt as though the bed moved under his body weight, so he tried to hold very still, but it did not feel solid enough. He tried to turn on his side, but the springs of the cot sagged and swayed, seeming to discourage his every move. He felt as if he were suspended on a tree limb.

Finally, thinking he had to get some sleep, he got up, picked up his belongings, and went to the stable, where he rolled up in his blanket beside his saddle and promptly went to sleep.

When he heard the bugle calls start up again in the morning, he picked up his saddle and the things he thought he might need while on this patrol. Then he walked out of the stable to the complete surprise of the young private on guard duty.

"Where the hell did you come from?" the private asked.

"Back yonder in the stall with my possibles," Slater said.

"How'd you get in there without me seeing you?"

"I reckon you weren't lookin'," Slater answered, although he knew that he was already asleep in the stable when the guard changed, and this soldier relieved the one before him. He just didn't want to take the time to explain it, so he continued on to the corral where his horses were.

By the time the bugler blew stable and watering call, he was already saddled up and ready to ride, but he saw no signs of a patrol forming up on the parade ground. Instead the barracks emptied as the soldiers came to the stables to take care of the horses, but they didn't seem to be in any hurry to mount up and get started. Maybe, he thought, they decided to postpone the patrol, and if he had slept in the barracks, he would have known about it. Finally he stopped a soldier leading a horse back to the stable.

"Do you know if Lieutenant Russell's company is still goin' out this mornin'?"

"Sure is," the private said. "I'm goin' on that patrol."

"Well, when are we gonna get started?" Slater asked. "It's almost sunup now."

"After breakfast, when they blow assembly," the private said. Judging by the look on Slater's face, he could see that he was confused. "You don't remember me, but I was in the barracks with you last night. The next bugle you hear will be mess call. Then you can eat breakfast."

"Much obliged," Slater said.

I reckon the army's got a different idea of what first thing in the morning means, he thought.

It struck him as a mighty foolish way to run an army, or any kind of war party, if they ever wanted to get anything done. He thought back on the patrol he had led on the Boulder River, and recalled there was no such nonsense at that time, when the troopers were in the field. For that, he was thankful. Otherwise they would never catch up with any Sioux war party.

When the detachment was assembled and Lieutenant Russell arrived, he found Slater sitting on the ground, Indian fashion, and the paint Indian pony standing behind him, his reins on the ground. Slater got to his feet and climbed into the saddle, ready to ride, but the lieutenant inspected his troops before preparing to march. It was during this inspection that a civilian rode up beside Slater and introduced himself as Jeb Sawyer.

"You'd be Slater, I reckon," he said. "I expect I'll be the chief scout on this little shindig, since I've been scoutin' for a good while and you're still green."

"That so?" Slater responded, not really caring who was head scout.

"Yeah," Sawyer replied. "You just follow my lead and you'll do all right."

"Right," Slater said as he studied the man.

Sawyer was a lean, wiry-looking fellow with a dark bushy mustache and long stringy hair, almost to his shoulders, protruding out from under a sweat-stained hat with a single feather stuck in the crown. Like Slater, he wore a buckskin shirt, but unlike Slater, he wore cavalry trousers and boots. It was hard to tell how old he was, but he was certainly older than Slater. So Slater was already thinking, if Sawyer was as experienced and expert as he seemed to think he was, there might be no need for both of them.

I just might break off and return to Lame Elk's village after all.

This was in spite of the fact that he was confident that no man knew the Absarokas and the Beartooths better than he.

While they waited for Russell to give the order to march, Sawyer openly eyeballed the new scout, seeming to find something about Slater amusing. "Looks like you got yourself a new shirt," he finally commented. "Got them fancy little fringes on the sleeves. Cost you a pretty penny, I expect." Slater didn't answer, as it was not in the form of a question. But Sawyer was not ready to let it go. He was certain that Slater was trying to dress the part of an Indian, probably in hopes of impressing Russell. "You ever shoot that bow you got tied on your saddle? Or is that just for show—make you look more like an Injun?" He had not yet been told of the circumstances that brought Slater to be hired as a scout. Had he been, he might have saved himself from having to eat crow later on. "I've hunted with a bow a time or two," Sawyer went on. "Maybe we could have us a contest."

Having heard enough of the man's rambling nonsense, Slater gazed at him for a long moment with the stoic expression he usually wore. "You are a fool," he said, turned the paint's head away, and moved closer to the head of the column.

"What . . . ?" Sawyer sputtered incredulously, trying desperately to think of what to say in return, only to blurt after him, "You could learn a helluva lot about scoutin' from me, if you got sense enough to do like I tell ya."

Lieutenant Russell signaled for the scouts then, so he rode after Slater to the head of the column.

"That trapper said he saw a Sioux war party at that spot on the Boulder River where the rocks form a natural bridge," Russell said. He looked at Slater. "We were there before we had that skirmish with the war party we were following. This new bunch must have a camp somewhere in that same area, and according to the trapper, there was about twenty warriors. So that's where we'll start looking for them, at the natural bridge."

"Well, that ain't hard to find," Sawyer said. "I've seen that spot. We'd best ride straight east till we strike the Yellowstone. That's about twenty miles—be a good place to rest the horses. Then we'll cross the river and keep goin' east till we strike the Boulder. We can do it in a day."

Russell looked at Slater to see if he had anything to say about that. Slater shrugged and said, "That's as good a way as any to get to that spot."

Sawyer wasn't finished, however. "Like I said, any fool can find that spot, but you're wastin' your time lookin' for those Injuns up that river. I don't know what that trapper saw, but from what I heard from Colonel Brackett, you give them Sioux a pretty good lickin' on that river already. More'n likely, they found theirselves another spot to hole up between raids. Injuns don't like to go back to the same place they lost as many men as they did there. They think that place is bad medicine for 'em. Another thing, them mountains is too hard to get in and out of. They're most likely gonna find 'em a spot with a back door in case they're got to retreat in a hurry."

Russell listened attentively, as Sawyer was a seasoned scout. Then he asked, "Where would you look for them, if not up the Boulder River?"

"My guess would be farther east, over toward the Stillwater. The mountains are easier to get in and out of," Sawyer said.

Russell looked at Slater again. "Do you agree with that?"

"No," Slater said.

Impatient with the somber scout's reluctance to embellish on his answer, Russell asked, "Why not? What do you think?"

"First thing," Slater started, "I reckon that trapper musta known where he was when he saw that party of Lakota. And the Boulder is a lot closer than the Stillwater. There's a lot of places in the Absarokas— the Beartooths, too—to set up a camp that's hard to find. And there ain't no reason to think those Lakota don't know those mountains as well as anyone else." He could think of several places he had found while hunting that would offer the secrecy and the protection the war party would be looking for.

"I know some places," he said to Russell, "maybe save some time if I scout 'em out first."

Russell thought it over for a few moments only, remembering how Slater had saved their bacon when that Sioux war party had them pinned down on the riverbank.

"All right," he decided, "we'll head straight across and start our search on the Boulder."

Sawyer didn't say anything, but shook his head to show his exasperation for the lieutenant's decision.

While the cavalry detachment got under way, the Sioux war party they were hoping to find was celebrating another successful raid on an unfortunate settler's family in the Yellowstone Valley. The scalped bodies of a farmer and his two sons lay in the cornfield where they had been surprised by the sudden appearance of a screaming horde of painted demons.

The war chief, Man Looking Back, watched in smug satisfaction while many of his war party danced excitedly around the roaring fire that greedily consumed the newly built barn. The terrified screams of the milk cow trapped inside the burning barn added to the gleeful shouts of the warriors. Inside the log cabin, Iron Pony and Medicine Hat joined several others, ransacking the home for anything of value, no longer interested in the bodies of the woman and the small girl.

"Wah!" Iron Pony exclaimed, venting his disgust for the celebration of the others over the slaughter of the white farmer and his family. "We waste our time on these little raids when we should attack our enemies, the Crows, before the winter sets in. We know there is a village of Crows somewhere on the Musselshell. That is where we should be going now, instead of these meaningless raids so close to the soldier fort."

Medicine Hat knew the agony that plagued Iron Pony. He was haunted by the image of the one they called White Crow, and the death of his brother, Black Arrow. For it was White Crow who had killed Black Arrow. Striped Otter had seen him do it. More than that, because of White Crow, the other men of his village would no longer ride with Iron Pony as war chief, thinking his medicine was no longer strong. Iron Pony was a proud man, and a fierce warrior, but their losses had been so great when White Crow appeared to avenge the massacre of the village of old people deep in the mountains. But Iron Pony could not find peace within himself until he had severed the head of White Crow.

Still the cautious one, Medicine Hat said, "It's a long ride to the Musselshell. What if White Crow is not with that village?"

"Most of the Crow villages have gone to the white government's reservation," Iron Pony reasoned. "I don't think White Crow would go to the reservation, so a good place to look for him would be with this village on the Musselshell."

"Man Looking Back said we would return to our village on the Big Horn after another raid or two," Medicine Hat said. "I think all of our warriors will follow him. They are ready to go home now. It has been a good raid."

Iron Pony did not respond further, but the expression of frustration on his face was answer enough.

They followed the others out of the house after knocking the stove over and piling the table and chairs on top of it, feeding the fire that it started in the middle of the floor. Soon it, like the barn, began to blaze, and Man Looking Back came up to stand beside them.

"I think it would be a good thing to go back to our camp in the mountains," he said to them, "and tomorrow we will return to our village. There is more hunting to be done before the village is ready for the winter."

"What do the others say?" Iron Pony asked. "Maybe

we should scout farther to the north to see if there are
any more white settlers." There were twenty warriors
in the party. He hoped that perhaps not all of them
wanted to go home.

"Let them speak," Man Looking Back said. "It is
time to return to our people and prepare for the winter. Already it is late in the Moon of Colored Leaves.
That is what I say."

When all the warriors gathered around Man Looking Back and Iron Pony, the matter was discussed, but
everyone except Iron Pony was in favor of going back
with Man Looking Back.

Once again Iron Pony seethed with frustration
when he remembered times past when the warriors
would have followed him wherever he led them. He
made no protest, however, and followed the others
back to the Boulder River to return to their camp in
the hidden canyon. The others might be faint of heart,
but he was determined to go alone to find the Crow
village, even more certain that he would find White
Crow there.

When they started back tomorrow, he would head
north. He was confident of his ability to make his
way up through Crow territory without being seen.
He would find this village and he would wait until
he could find this evil spirit alone. Then he would
kill him.

And when he returned to his village with White
Crow's head, his medicine would be twice as strong
and they would never doubt him again.

It was late in the afternoon when the forty men of C
Company, Second Cavalry struck the Boulder River
and went into camp. A light snow, the first of the

season, had fallen during the last few hours of the march, but there was no accumulation. The horses were watered and fed a ration of grain, including Slater's horse.

"Don't go gettin' used to this," he said to the paint. "I don't want you to get spoiled."

Once the horses were taken care of, Lieutenant Russell called Sergeant Bell and the scouts up for a conference to decide the best way to begin the search for the reported Sioux raiders.

After Jeb Sawyer repeated his assertion that the raiders were nowhere near this side of the Absarokas, Slater suggested that he would like to scout a couple of canyons on the opposite side of the mountains that came down to the river.

"I got an arrow in a mule deer not far from here and I chased it through a narrow pass to a pocket I never knew was there before. It was like a little canyon formed on a saddle between two mountains, and a dandy place to camp, so I stayed right there to butcher the deer. There was water from a nice stream and grass for my horse. It'd make a good place for a war party to camp."

"Shit," Sawyer drawled, his tone thick with cynicism. "That'd be somethin', all right. We just march right up and find 'em at the first place we looked."

Ignoring the sarcasm, Slater continued. "I'd wanna go across the river before it gets dark, and see if I can pick up any tracks. Sawyer might be right, they might not be anywhere close to here. But I can find out for sure."

"That sounds like a good idea to me," Russell said. "Sawyer can go with you."

While the soldiers were building several fires to cook their supper, and Sergeant Bell was detailing the guards, the two scouts rode their horses up the river a short distance to an easier place to ford.

Once across, they dismounted and went the rest of the way on foot. The horses had been used only in order to keep their masters' feet dry. Slater found what he was looking for in a short time. There were many tracks of unshod horses, going in both directions on the trail that bordered the river, where it normally would have been unusual to find any tracks at all.

Interested now, Sawyer knelt down and felt the tracks, paying attention to the firmness of the edges and how easily they crumbled to his touch.

"Hard to say," he allowed. "We ain't really had no hard freezes yet, but we've had some nights that got pretty damn cold." He crawled over to examine some more tracks, forgetting his skepticism. "Lookee these over here. These tracks was left earlier today."

"That's what I figure," Slater said, without going over to confirm it.

"Ha," Sawyer snorted. "They might as well have left us a note and said, 'Here we are, fellers, we're headin' thisaway.'"

They followed the tracks for a couple hundred yards farther, where they came to a rocky area that went all the way to the water. It was impossible to see any tracks in the rocks.

"This is it," Slater said. "This is where they left the trail to go into that canyon." He stood erect and gazed at a solid rock wall about fifty feet high.

Sawyer took one quick look at the rock wall, dismissed that possibility, and kept walking. "Here they go," he called out when he crossed the rocky field. "Tracks over here. They're still on this trail."

Slater didn't move. "No, they ain't," he insisted calmly. "This is where they turned off."

"Ha," Sawyer blurted. "What'd they do, jump over that stone face? I'm tellin' you, their tracks lead on up this trail."

"Go ahead and follow it, then," Slater said. "I'm stayin' right here."

Sawyer hesitated. Slater seemed pretty sure of himself. "I expect it wouldn't be a very good idea to get too far up this trail. Might run right up on 'em."

"I doubt that," Slater said. "My guess is they left tracks on up that trail so nobody would think they turned into the mountains right here. I expect it'll disappear somewhere up ahead, maybe lead you in the water."

Sawyer considered that. It could be true. "How you figure they got over that rock cliff, if they went thattaway?"

"They didn't go over it," Slater said. "They went around it. Come on and I'll show you." He walked to the side of the massive stone face, with Sawyer right behind him. Almost to the outer edge, where the stone ended against a rocky cliff, he stepped inside the rock.

"Well, I'll be . . . ," Sawyer drawled. What appeared to be solid rock all the way to the edge was in fact a pocket, big enough for a man to lead a horse through. The illusion of a solid wall was made possible because of the stone inside the passage. Standing in front of it, only a few feet away, you would swear it was one solid piece.

"I expect we'd best be more careful from here," Slater cautioned. "When we get off this rock apron, we'll be on the ground again, and then we can see if they went in here or not."

They followed the narrow passage to the back side of the rock to step out onto a game trail that wound around the mountain. It suddenly became as dark as night when they found themselves in a tunnel of spruce trees that shut off the fading light of day. They stopped to listen.

Hearing nothing but the whisper of wind through the spruce needles, Sawyer whispered, "I've got a match. Maybe we can take a quick look at the ground for tracks." Slater nodded. Sawyer struck the match on his belt buckle and it burst into light that seemed as bright as a railroad flair in the dark tunnel. They both searched the ground quickly before the short life of the match ended.

"There," Slater said, and pointed to a hoofprint on the floor of the passage where a horse had slid a hoof in the thick needles.

"I reckon that's sign enough," Sawyer said, and blew out the match just before it burned down to his thumb. "How far does this trail go before you come to that canyon you said was back here?"

"About a quarter of a mile," Slater said.

"If they're in there, and it looks they might be," Sawyer speculated, "then we've got 'em trapped. They have to come outta there in single file."

"They've got a back door," Slater said. "It's the way I carried that deer outta there. At the other end of that canyon, there's a ravine that leads down to a creek at the foot of the mountain behind this one. So I reckon the lieutenant will wanna block both doors."

"Hot damn!" Sawyer whispered. "Let's get back and tell him. He oughta be tickled to find out he's got 'em boxed up like a birthday present."

"I expect we'd best move up this trail far enough to make sure they're in here first," Slater said.

"Yeah, I reckon," Sawyer said with some hesitation. "But I wouldn't wanna get too close. I don't cotton much to the idea of gettin' chased back down this little trail in the dark. I ain't that fast a runner."

Slater could not help noticing Sawyer's abrupt change of manner. Gone was the sarcastic attitude he previously displayed. In fact, he was downright civil.

"I'll just move up this trail a little bit," Slater said, "until I can see or hear 'em. Then I'll hustle back down here and we'll go back to tell the soldiers."

"Mind you don't let 'em see you," Sawyer said.

"They won't," Slater assured him, and started up the narrow trail at a trot.

Relying on his memory, he maintained that pace until reaching a place where the trail leveled off. Knowing it would drop down again into the canyon, he slowed to walk a few more yards before stopping when he heard the sound of voices. That was confirmation enough, but he inched his way a few yards more until he could see the campfires below to be doubly sure.

Satisfied, he returned the way he had come.

As they expected, Russell was excited to hear the news. "By God, they couldn't be in a better spot for us, could they? But we've got to strike 'em before they come outta there, and that means we've got to get into position tonight. We can't afford to lose this advantage." He looked anxiously at Slater. "Can you find their back door tonight, in the dark?"

"I can."

"Good, good," Russell proceeded excitedly, as he played out the ambush in his mind. "We'll split the company up to watch both entrances to that canyon and wait for them to come out in the morning. Sergeant Bell, you'll be in command of half the company, and I'll lead the other half."

"If you don't mind me sayin'," Slater said, "you won't need as many men to guard the entrance on this end. They'd have to come outta there one at a time. Two or three men with plenty of ammunition oughta be able to take care of it. It's the other end where you'll need most of your men, 'cause you'll have to place 'em on both sides of that ravine to stop those Injuns if they make a run for it."

"What if they don't make a run for it?" Russell asked.

"Then I reckon that's up to you," Slater replied. "You'll go in to get 'em, or set up outside and starve 'em out."

"Either way," Russell said, "the important thing is to get into position before morning so they don't have a chance to escape that box they're in." He turned to Sergeant Bell. "Pick five men to stay here with you to hold that entrance. Then give them all the word that we'll be moving out of here as soon as the horses are rested." He paused to consider. "And after the men have had supper," he added.

Campfires were smothered, and the troop prepared to mount amid the low grumbling of complaining voices. Lieutenant Russell held a last-minute briefing with Sergeant Bell and the scouts to coordinate the ambush.

The plan was very simple. If the Indians came out of the narrow stone entrance, Bell and his men were to turn them back with rifle fire. If the Indians came out by way of the ravine, Bell would hear the rifle fire and simply maintain his defense of the stone face.

Addressing the sergeant, Russell said, "Sawyer will go with you and show you where the hidden entrance is, so you can best position your men to stop anyone who tries to come out of it."

With nothing more to be said, the foray got under way.

Walking the horses as quietly as possible, Slater led the column of troopers north along the river trail for a distance of approximately three miles. A wide creek flowed into the river from the lower hills to the east at that point. There was no trail beside the creek, but the terrain was not so rugged here as that they had just left behind them. So it was possible to follow the creek through the trees and brush that bordered it.

After half a mile, the creek turned back toward the high mountains and their progress became a little more difficult. Slater could hear the occasional cursing of a trooper as his horse placed its foot wrong and almost stumbled. As they approached the first of the higher mountains, the going became difficult to the point where they had to take to the water and ride up the middle of the creek.

"Does it get any rougher than this?" Russell called to Slater in a loud whisper.

"Not much," Slater called back, "but we ain't gotta go much farther." True to his word, they had proceeded less than a hundred yards farther when he held up his hand to halt the column. Lieutenant Russell pulled up beside him.

"This is it," Slater said. "This is where that ravine spreads out from that ridge up there." He pointed to the top of the ravine. "That canyon closes on the point of the ravine, and I expect your Sioux war party is most likely camped thirty or forty yards shy of it."

The column of troopers climbed out of the water, guiding their horses carefully over the rocky creek bank and gathered in a small clearing in a belt of fir trees.

"If you don't want those warriors to know you're settin' up an ambush for 'em, you might wanna keep all your men right here till it gets closer to daylight. The wind ain't blowin' in our favor, and if you get too close, they might hear somebody say something, or a horse snort."

"Maybe you're right," Russell said. "I don't want to wait till they can see us moving up, though."

"You'll have plenty of time just before sunup," Slater assured him. "They ain't likely to head out anywhere before then. I know it's too dark to see much from back here. But if you want to, you and me can slip up the ravine a ways so you can get a better look at where you wanna place your men."

"Good idea," Russell said. He told a corporal what he was going to do, and instructed him to keep the men quiet and the horses calm. "If they want to, the men can catch a little sleep, as long as every other man stays awake. They can take turns, a couple of hours at a time."

Then Russell and Slater disappeared into the darkness to scout the ravine for firing positions.

They scouted the pine- and fir-lined ravine as thoroughly as possible for Russell to get a picture in his mind of the way he would position his men to sweep the floor of the ravine from both sides.

Satisfied, he signaled Slater and they returned to the clearing beyond the trees. Although the lieutenant had given his permission to do so, they found not a man asleep. Slater could almost feel the tension building among them. He walked over beside his horse, pulled a strip of smoked venison out of the saddlebag, and sat down to chew on it.

After a long and tense night, the faint light before dawn finally found the dark creek valley, and the men began to recheck their weapons and cartridges, moving about in an effort to ease the stiffness from the long wait.

On a signal from the corporal, they gathered closely around the lieutenant while he gave them their orders, stressing the point that this was not a police action. This was war, and in war the objective is to kill the enemy, but if the Sioux tried to surrender, they were to take captives.

That said, he detailed five men to stay with the horses. The remaining thirty were divided into two groups, fifteen on each side of the ravine. When everyone understood his responsibility, the company moved as quietly as possible up into the ravine with Russell indicating with hand signals where he wanted them positioned.

"Find yourself some cover to shoot from," he told them, leaving them pretty much on their own to select a place that suited them.

When Russell went with the men on the left side of the ravine, Slater decided to join those on the right, for no other reason than to make it even. With the ambush set, there was nothing to do then but wait.

The waiting was not over with the awakening of the hostile camp. More time crept by while the sounds of the Indians' preparations to move out of the canyon drifted over the ridge to those waiting in ambush below. And then, gradually, the sounds faded away and were gone.

"Hold your positions." The word was passed along both sides of the ravine.

Slater strained to look across to where Russell was. It was obvious that the hostiles had gone down the trail toward the Boulder River where Sergeant Bell's men were set to stop them. Slater wondered why Russell didn't order his men up the ravine to take new positions in the canyon, squeezing the Indians in even tighter. He tried to signal him with a wave of his hand, but it was too late, for he heard the first faraway rifle shot from Bell's group at the stone entrance. In a few minutes, there were more shots fired, as another hostile evidently tried to escape the trap. Then the firing stopped.

Here they come, Slater thought, picturing the Indians hurrying back up the narrow trail toward this end of the canyon.

"Hold your fire till they come down in the ravine!" Russell yelled.

His plan was to kill as many in the initial barrage as possible, because if the survivors retreated to hole up in the canyon, it was going to be tough to force them out. He knew there would be casualties if he had to charge up that ravine to smoke them out, for they would hold the high ground. There was no time to speculate further, for he saw the first of the hostiles appear at the top of the ravine. Leading their horses, they hurried over the lip and made their way down into the center of the ravine.

Concealed from sight, behind boulders and trees, the soldiers held their fire, as ordered. High up, near the top of the ravine, Slater counted the warriors as they came into sight. In a few minutes, all but a few of the hostiles were down in the ravine, each one leading his horse.

When they were almost to the bottom of the narrow gulch, Russell could not afford to wait longer. The leading warriors were getting close to the cavalry horses near the creek.

Up above, Iron Pony was startled by the sudden eruption of gunfire from the ravine below the camp.

It was a trap! The soldiers had closed off the escape route!

He had been one of the first behind Man Looking Back to lead the war party down through the trees to the secret stone entrance. Man Looking Back went out of the opening in the stone cliff and was shot down as soon as he stepped out into the open. Right behind him, Medicine Hat tried to get back inside the rocks but was also killed.

"Go back!" Iron Pony had shouted. "The soldiers are waiting for us! We must go out the other way!"

Even as he had said it, he hoped the soldiers didn't know about the back door to their camp. Lagging behind, he kept watch on the narrow trail, ready to fire on any soldiers that followed them. No one followed, and by the time he reached their campsite, all but a few of the warriors had led their ponies over the edge into the ravine.

Now, with the constant rattle of rifle fire coming to his ears from the ravine, he knew there was no way out of the trap, save one. He looked up the steep slope of the mountain that formed one side of the pocket they were trapped in.

Desperate to escape death or capture, he quickly considered the near-vertical climb it would take to go up the side of the mountain. There was no other choice, so he slung his rifle on his back and looped his extra cartridge belt over his shoulder. Then he selected what looked to him to be the best possible way up out of the pocket and started climbing up the rocky-faced slope.

His objective was to reach a tree-covered ledge, two hundred feet above. Using hands and feet, he pulled himself up the face of the cliff, trusting each hand- and foothold to support him. He climbed until he was about halfway up and paused to catch his breath between two rocks jutting out from the face of the cliff.

Looking back down at the canyon floor, he saw the last three warriors at the edge of the ravine, standing with their hands in the air. The sight of it made him more desperate to escape. He pushed himself to climb faster, the strain on his arms and legs causing his muscles to cramp. Still he forced himself to pull up, until finally he reached the ledge.

Near exhaustion, he managed to get his hand on a small pine near the lip and pull himself up on the ledge. He lay there on his belly for a few moments before pulling himself to the rim of the ledge, to look back down.

Anger flared in his brain when he saw the soldiers moving up from the ravine to take the three prisoners in hand. He couldn't help thinking that this defeat would not have happened if the others had listened to his pleas to ride north to attack the Crows.

Maybe Medicine Hat would sing a different song now, had he not been shot down, he thought, recalling that Medicine Hat had spoken against his plan. He put that aside. It was time to think about what he must do now.

He had started to push away from the edge when something he saw suddenly stopped him cold. It was as if he had stopped breathing for a few seconds.

It was him!

Standing near the soldier who looked like an officer, he stood, tall, holding the medicine rifle casually at his side.

White Crow! It could be no one else. Even at that distance, Iron Pony was sure. He almost cried out in frustration upon realizing the demon that had brought him such agony and humiliation was once again the cause of a devastating defeat.

Unable to release his anguish, he bit his lip until blood ran out of his mouth and down upon his chin, and he recited his vow to kill this demon that Wakan Tanka had permitted to torment him.

I must hunt him down and kill him, he vowed, *then put his head on a pole so my people will know my medicine is strong and I have taken his.*

The temptation to take a shot at White Crow from the ledge was almost overpowering; he wanted him dead so badly, but it was not a sure shot at this distance and this angle. But even if he didn't miss, he would be deprived of the trophy he was determined to have—White Crow's head. The demon's death at long range would not answer Iron Pony's passion to kill with his own hands. It had grown now from a passion almost to a sickness that knew only one cure.

He lay there for a long time, his eyes following every movement of the man responsible for his anguish, building the legend of the white Crow in his mind. Seeing how often the officer appeared to be consulting White Crow, Iron Pony assumed that, in itself, was evidence enough to prove he was no ordinary man. To kill such a medicine man would certainly allow him to take his medicine for himself.

I know where you are now, he thought. *You ride with the soldiers. I will track you until I have my chance to kill you. It makes no difference how long it takes. One day you will face me.*

He recalled thinking earlier that it had been bad luck when the others would not ride north to find the Crow village. But he now realized that it had been good luck disguised as bad luck, for it brought White Crow to him.

His despair lifted somewhat, for he saw the spirits favoring him, in spite of the deaths of his fellow tribesmen. After some time, he drew back from the cliff. He needed to find a horse right away if he was to follow the soldiers. Then he would wait for an opportunity to find White Crow alone.

The soldiers seemed in no hurry to leave. They lingered at the Sioux campsite for quite a while, their mission accomplished. Leaving the Sioux dead where they lay, the horse guard was called up from the ravine. Russell sent a soldier down the narrow trail to tell Sergeant Bell and his men to stay where they were, as he intended to exit the hostile camp that way. It was a shorter distance than the way back down the creek behind.

When the horses were brought up, the order was given to mount, the three Lakota prisoners were put on their ponies, and the column moved down the trail to the stone passage. When they reached the opening, they found the bodies of Man Looking Back and Medicine Hat, one on top of the other. They had been pulled out of the way by the soldiers left to guard that entrance.

When Striped Otter passed the bodies, he looked behind him to catch Angry Bear's eye. Angry Bear nodded solemnly. Like Striped Otter, he was saddened to see the war chief sprawled grotesquely in death. More than that, he felt dishonored for having surrendered, even though there had been no chance for escape.

As the company filed out of the entrance to the hidden trail, one at a time, each man leading his horse, they found Sergeant Bell, Jeb Sawyer, and the five privates of his detail seated around a fire on the rocky apron. They were drinking coffee and eating hardtack.

"Howdy, boys," Bell greeted them. "What have you fellers been up to? Sounded like you was havin' a little shindig back up the hill."

"We were at that," one of the older privates replied. "I sure as hell hope we didn't disturb your little tea party."

The japing stopped momentarily when the three Sioux prisoners filed out of the opening and stood beside their ponies. They were directed to the side of the trail by the two soldiers detailed to guard them. Seeing Bell and his men leisurely enjoying a cup of coffee, the two guards were moved to join the japing as well.

Seeing the guards relax their attention, Angry Bear decided it was his chance. He leaped on his horse's back and made a break for freedom. Whipping the pony relentlessly, he fled up the river trail at a reckless gallop toward the rugged mountains to the south. Several rifles were fired, almost at the same time, but none of the shots struck the fleeing hostile.

Jeb Sawyer unhurriedly laid the front sight of his Winchester '66 on the departing warrior's back and calmly squeezed the trigger. The Indian pony ran a dozen more yards before Angry Bear slid off to land beside the trail.

Relieved of its rider, the pony continued up the trail toward the high mountains. Sawyer extracted the empty shell, sat back down on his rock, and picked up the cup he had set down to avoid spilling any of the coffee it held.

The two troopers assigned to guard the prisoners reacted by immediately holding their carbines on the two remaining prisoners amid a chorus of gleeful shouts and exclamations of praise for Sawyer's marksmanship. Sergeant Bell told one of the soldiers to run up the trail to see if the Indian was dead.

"If he ain't, shoot him," he said.

Lieutenant Russell came through the opening then, immediately concerned about the shots he had just heard. When told of the circumstances that caused the Indian to be killed, he nodded, concerned no longer.

"One less to worry with," he said. He turned to Bell then. "Sergeant, I hate to break up your little party, but I would like to return to the post before dark. So get the men ready to ride, and we'll all stop for some coffee and something to eat when we strike the Yellowstone."

One of the last to come out of the passage, Slater led his horse over to the river to drink while the column was preparing to move out. While he stood there watching the paint drink, he was joined by Sawyer, who moved up to stand beside him.

"Russell's feelin' pretty smug right now," he said. "He's really feelin' good about not losin' a single man. I reckon that's a real feather in his cap. It was just like we expected on this end. First couple of Injuns out the door got shot full of holes—didn't no more try it after that."

"I expect not," Slater answered calmly. He sensed that Sawyer wanted to tell him something else. He didn't understand why he didn't come out with it, whatever it was.

"Yes, sir," Sawyer went on, "wasn't much to do on this end." He said nothing more for a long moment until Slater took the paint's reins, thinking the horse had had enough to drink. "Listen, Slater," Sawyer said. "I reckon I owe you an apology."

Surprised, Slater asked, "For what?"

Finding it difficult, but knowing he owed the young man, Sawyer pressed on. "For actin' like a damn jackass before I knew if you was green or not. Sometimes I let my mouth run loose when my brain's shut down." He stood looking at Slater for a few seconds more, waiting for his response, but Slater was too astonished to reply. "Anyway, I apologize, and I hope you won't hold it against me."

Still surprised, Slater looked him square in the eye for a moment. Then he finally replied, "Was it the new shirt?"

Sawyer burst out with a loud guffaw. "Yeah, reckon it was. Where'd you get that fancy shirt, anyway?"

"A Crow woman made it for me," Slater said. "My old one had a bullet hole in it."

A short while after C Company departed the banks of the Boulder River, Iron Pony made his way down through the trees that grew thick near the base of the mountain. He stopped suddenly when he caught a movement beyond the fir trees that bordered the river.

Moving cautiously then, his rifle ready to fire, he descended a few more yards to a better position to see the trail that ran beside the river. He saw it then, an Indian pony, but without a rider. It was walking aimlessly along the trail, grazing on the small patches of grass it found among the rocks. Iron Pony immediately worked his way down to the river path and approached the horse, speaking calmly in an effort to prevent the pony from retreating. The pony merely stood still, watching the approaching warrior with curiosity, and made no move to draw away as Iron Pony took hold of the reins.

No longer on foot, Iron Pony turned back toward the north. He estimated that he was approximately a mile south of the stone entrance to the camp between the mountains. More determined than ever to follow the soldiers, in hopes of an opportunity to get to White Crow, he guided the pony carefully along the rocky riverbank.

He had not gone far when he came to a body in the middle of the path. He dismounted and turned it over to discover that it was Angry Bear, shot in the back. The sight of it caused the anger to rise in his blood once again, and he fought to contain the urge to cry out in frustration. It was one more reminder of the pain that White Crow had brought to his people.

With no thought of taking care of Angry Bear's body, or any of the other dead left in that fatal ravine, he jumped on Angry Bear's pony and hurried to pick up the trail of the departing soldiers.

Chapter 13

Slater discovered that he had a new friend, from a source he'd least expected. When Lieutenant Russell halted his company upon reaching the Yellowstone River again, it was to rest the horses. Since the company had not taken time for breakfast before leaving the Boulder River, he told his men they could build fires to make coffee and cook food. That meant hardtack and bacon for the troopers, but Slater passed it up, choosing his own smoked deer meat instead.

When he sat down beside one of the fires, Jeb Sawyer sat down beside him. Slater couldn't help noticing that, except when the column was on the march, and the scouts were out ahead, left and right, any time there was a rest called, Sawyer was always at his elbow. Slater wondered if the wiry scout was still trying to atone for his cynical attitude toward him at first.

What he wasn't aware of was that Sawyer had questioned Sergeant Bell about him while they were waiting in ambush by the stone entrance to the Sioux camp. After Bell had raved about Slater's actions during the original encounter on the Boulder, Sawyer realized how much he had misjudged him. He was now intent upon making the young man his friend. As far as Slater was concerned, he held no hard feelings for his original treatment by Sawyer, since it was evident that he had changed his attitude. And that was on top of an apology.

The gain of one friend, however, was offset by a mortal enemy, intent upon ending his life. Slater remained unaware of his standing with the near-crazed, bloodthirsty savage—and also of the fact that, even now, he was being hunted. His thoughts had returned to dwell on the promise he had made to Red Basket and Little Wren. He didn't like the idea of giving his word to someone, then not living up to it. He would make up for his tardiness with a packhorse loaded down with meat before the winter was over. This he vowed, unaware of the man lurking roughly a mile behind the column. His thoughts were interrupted then by a question from Sawyer.

"Where are you hangin' your hat when the company ain't in the field?" Sawyer asked.

Slater couldn't answer right away. He had not had occasion to think about where he would bed down when the soldiers were in garrison. It occurred to him then that he could not live in the stable with his horses. And one experience in the cavalry barracks had been enough to convince him that he didn't want to stay there, even if that was a permanent option.

"I don't know," he answered after a long pause. "I'll fix me up a camp somewhere close, I reckon, like I always do."

"Man, you can't do that," Sawyer responded. "I mean, there ain't no need to. You can bunk in with me. I've got a little cabin right outside the fort. It's just a one-room log house, but it's a good-sized room, plenty big enough for both of us. Got a warm fireplace—I built it myself—and it's nice and snug, tighter than a schoolteacher's fanny. Whaddaya say? I'd be right glad to have some company for a change. Matter of fact, I've got half a shed built for my horse. I bet the two of us could get some lumber from the fort sawmill and build us a regular barn."

Slater had to admit that the proposition deserved some consideration. It would be better than living in a tent or a makeshift camp down by the creek. He was almost ready to accept the invitation when he considered that Red Basket—and Little Wren, too—expected him to return to the Crow village soon. It threw him into an instant dilemma. He regretted the fact that there was no way he could get word to them that he would not likely be back any time soon. He was going to scout for the army. He had told Red Basket that was what he would most likely do, told her before he even took her to find her brother. And he realized that he had been simply swaying in the wind of indecision up to that point.

"I've gotta go back to Lame Elk's village on the Musselshell sometime before a hard winter sets in," Slater finally thought aloud.

"Whaddaya gotta go up there for?" Sawyer asked, never having heard Slater mention Lame Elk before.

Slater shrugged, realizing then that he had spoken out loud, and not really caring to share his reasons and what he felt were his obligations. "I made a promise that I'd help supply them with some meat for the winter," he said. "And I don't wanna break my promise."

Sawyer removed his hat so he could scratch his head while he thought about what Slater had just said. "You know, when the army put you on the payroll to scout, I'm thinkin' they would expect you to be where they can use you any time they need a scout for one detail or another. Have you thought about that?"

He had really not. "Not till just now," he said. Colonel Brackett and Lieutenant Russell had been understanding the last time, when he left to take Red Basket home. But a second time they might not be so accommodating—and he had decided that he wanted to scout for the army. It was a job, a steady job that he would be paid for every month, and that sounded good to him.

If Little Wren had any sense, she'd know she'd be better off married to a man with a steady job.

He surprised himself when the thought popped into his head and wondered why he had even thought it. He immediately countered it with a thought of the lithesome Indian girl staying alone while he was off somewhere with a cavalry patrol.

No, she would be better off with her people, he told himself. "I reckon I'll know what I'm gonna do by the time we get back to Fort Ellis," he said to Sawyer. He was spared further explanation by the lieutenant's order to mount.

Slater and Sawyer rode out ahead of the column, and C Company moved out behind them. The solitary figure on the other side of the river rose to his feet and got on his pony, watching the departing column for a long while before urging the pony into the river to cross over. He continued to follow the column of soldiers, almost choking on the bitter frustration of his situation, knowing the poor odds of ever finding White Crow alone.

In spite of this, he was driven by his desire for revenge and the need to regain the respect of his brother warriors for his medicine and his ability to

lead them in battle. He continued to follow the soldiers, because he could not go back to his village until
he returned with the head of the demon who had
caused the death of so many of his people.

As the column drew closer to Fort Ellis, Iron Pony
was forced to become more cautious, as they were now
passing close to several farms. As determined as he was
to try to stay as close as possible, he could not afford to
be seen. A lone Lakota warrior, he would likely be shot
on sight, by soldier or farmer, but he continued to follow
until the buildings of the fort came into view.

After a short distance, he was forced to stop when
the column rode onto the parade ground. Finding a
brace of cottonwoods next to the creek bank, he guided
his pony over to stand between them. From there, he
watched the lieutenant dismiss his troops to take their
horses to the stables. He felt the intense anger rising
once more when he saw the two scouts leisurely ride
over to a building on one corner of the parade ground
and dismount to stand beside their horses. It appeared
to be the headquarters building, for the officer came to
join them after he had dismissed his men. Then all
three men went inside the building.

None of the soldiers walking back and forth across
the parade ground, or moving between the buildings, noticed the lone individual standing beside his
pony between the cottonwoods.

After a while, the two scouts came out of the building and got on their horses again. Instead of riding
them to the stables, however, they loped across the
parade ground and turned onto a road that led away
from the fort.

Iron Pony hurriedly jumped on his pony. Leaving
the brace of cottonwoods, he rode a wide circle around
the buildings facing the parade ground to strike the

road taken by the scouts. When he came to it, he could see the two scouts about half a mile ahead of him. He turned onto the road and followed, being careful to maintain the distance between them and himself. He could feel the excitement building up inside him for the opportunity presented to him: White Crow and his companion were riding away from the protection of the soldiers.

A wagon, pulled by a team of two horses, appeared on the road far ahead, coming toward him. He could see the driver and some people in the wagon wave to the two scouts as they passed.

Lost in his desperate passion to kill, Iron Pony did not veer off the road, to avoid the wagon, but maintained his pony's steady pace. When the wagon approached him, the driver started to wave but stopped short when he got a good look at the fierce warrior, painted for war, as was the horse he rode.

Stunned, the man gaped, astonished. Another man and two young boys in the back of the wagon were equally dumbfounded, staring in disbelief, as the wagon rolled slowly by the lone savage, his head and eyes looking straight ahead of him, as if not seeing them at all.

When some distance past, their heads still turned, and all eyes still fixed on the Sioux warrior, the wagon driver found his voice again. "Well, I'll be. . . ," he stammered. "What in the world. . . ? Am I seein' things?"

"I'm seein' 'em, too," his friend said. "Just as big as life . . . and he was comin' from the fort."

"I ain't sure but what I need a drink of whiskey," the driver exclaimed. "I ain't sure I saw what I just saw."

"I'm damn sure I need a drink," his friend replied. "I coulda almost reached out and touched him."

"We saw him, too," one of the boys said. "Can we have a drink, too?"

"In about ten years," the driver said.

When they came to a creek running across the road, Sawyer said, "We turn off here." He left the road and followed a narrow path beside the creek. After a short ride of about a hundred yards, they came to a log cabin with a shelter enclosed on three sides beside it. "This is it," Sawyer said, "home, sweet home, everything you need but a woman to do the cookin'."

Slater pulled the paint to a stop beside Sawyer's horse and remained seated in the saddle for a few minutes while he took in the scene. It was a rustic enough cabin, but it was better than he had expected, with a shingled roof and a short stone chimney. There were a few spots on the side wall where the chinking needed replacing, but overall, the cabin looked fairly tight, just as Sawyer had claimed.

"Whaddaya think?" Sawyer asked. "Just like I told you, right?"

"I reckon," Slater said, and dismounted. "I ain't seen the inside, though."

Sawyer remained in the saddle, watching Slater inspect his handiwork, proud of his efforts. Slater walked over beside the makeshift stable, then looked up and down the creek. There was a thick stand of trees, mostly cottonwoods, that bordered both sides of the creek, and plenty of grass for the horses beyond them. It was a good spot for a cabin. He walked back to the front of the cabin and stood for a moment looking at a sign made of several narrow boards with a message scrawled in big letters.

"What does the sign say?" he asked. He had never spent a day in school, and his mother had never deemed it important that he should learn to read. And up to this point in his life, he had never known a need for it.

Amused, but not overly surprised, Sawyer recited, "Anybody found in this cabin when I get back will be shot on sight."

"That's a lot of words," Slater said thoughtfully. He stood aside while Sawyer got down off his horse and pulled a key from his pocket to unlock the large padlock on the door. After opening the door, Sawyer stood aside and invited his guest in.

"Mind your head on them roof beams," Sawyer cautioned, since he had not planned for anyone of Slater's height when he built his walls. There were not but two beams bracing the front and back walls, but they were of massive timbers and could likely cause a man a headache if he carelessly snagged his head on one of them.

Slater nodded in reply while he looked over the inside. As Sawyer had boasted, there was plenty of room for two men to share and a deep stone fireplace on a side wall. Slater was happy to see that Sawyer had not gotten too grandiose and installed a wooden floor. He would be much more comfortable unrolling his blankets on the dirt floor. In fact, the cabin, other than being much sturdier, was not unlike a tipi—except for the stone fireplace on one wall. He decided it would be a great deal better than the temporary camp he would otherwise build for himself—depending on what kind of cabin mate Sawyer turned out to be. He decided that he was glad that Sawyer had offered his hospitality, thinking he would be content here.

"Whaddaya think?" Sawyer asked again.

"Oughta do just fine," Slater said, unaware of the sinister welcome lurking in the cottonwoods a short distance down the creek.

"Fine and dandy," Sawyer said, happy to have some company for a change, even if it was with a near mute. "Let's turn the horses out to graze and I'll build us a fire in the fireplace. Then we'll get some coffee goin' and cook something to eat. I don't know 'bout you, but I'm hungry enough to eat the blind side of a bear."

"Have you got bear meat?" Slater asked naïvely.

"No, wish I did," Sawyer answered, shaking his head, amazed by his new friend's candor. "You really have been livin' with the Injuns for a long time, ain't you?"

"I reckon," Slater answered, curious as to why the question was asked. He pulled his saddle off the paint and led it past the line of cottonwoods by the creek to release the horse to graze in the grass beyond. Sawyer followed along behind.

"Makes a nice pasture, don't it?" Sawyer asked as they watched the horses' reaction to the open grass prairie. "And they'll stay pretty close to the creek," he added, "at least mine always does."

"Mine will stay close," Slater said, knowing the paint never strayed very far from him. He turned to go back to the cabin, just as the rifle slug passed by him, striking Sawyer in the back. Slater heard the crack of the rifle at almost the same time Sawyer dropped to the ground.

He spun around quickly and dropped to one knee to discover a horse charging him at a full gallop, with an Indian riding low on the horse's neck trying to reload his single-shot rifle as fast as he could. There was no time to wonder how this could be happening so close to the fort, or if there were others about to attack. He could only react to the danger of the moment. His natural reflex, to quickly bring his rifle up to fire, was useless, for his rifle was on his saddle left by the door of the cabin. Still wearing the .44 Colt, however, he drew the weapon and braced himself for the attack that was almost upon him.

In the fading evening light, it was difficult to see the crazed face, twisted with angry determination, as the galloping pony bore down on him. In an effort to thwart the attacking savage's efforts to take dead aim at him, Slater jumped up from his knee and sprang from side to side, back and forth, in a deadly game of hide-and-seek, trying to keep the horse's head between him and the savage. It was enough to spoil Iron Pony's efforts to get a clear shot at him before the horse was inches away from knocking him to the ground.

Grasping for any hold he could get on the rider's body as he passed by, Slater was able to get a hand on Iron Pony's ankle, causing him to squeeze the trigger and send a wasted shot into the ground. Slater clamped down hard, pulling the hostile off as his speeding pony ran out from under him. The force of it sent both combatants tumbling to the ground, which caused Slater to lose his pistol when he collided with the hard creek bank.

On their feet at once, they faced each other, ready to do mortal combat. With no time to speculate on where the savage had come from, or how he had happened upon Sawyer and him, Slater crouched slightly in a defensive stance, wondering why Iron Pony hesitated. The fury that had twisted the Lakota warrior's face into a mask of hatred transformed into a smirk of open contempt. Seeing his hated adversary's hands empty of weapons, he raised his rifle to aim at Slater's chest but paused again to torment him.

"You have killed many of my people, White Crow, and now it is time for you to die. When I have killed you,

I will cut off your head and put it on a pole in my village."

A quick glance over the creek bank, where his .44 had fallen, told Slater that he had no chance to get to it before the hostile fired. He had no defense other than his determination to defy death until he could attack.

"Why do you call me White Crow?" he asked, speaking in the Crow tongue, thinking that the Sioux would understand him. He hoped the question would distract the savage from hurrying the execution.

"Because that is your name," Iron Pony snarled, "and now you die."

He pulled the trigger, only to be startled by the metallic click of the hammer striking an empty cartridge. In the violent collision minutes before, neither man realized that the rifle had fired. Slater did not hesitate further. He charged the confused savage, knocking him over backward, and they rolled over and over down the creek bank to stop at the water's edge.

Springing to their feet simultaneously, they stood face-to-face once again for a brief instant before both men drew their skinning knives and clashed in desperate combat. It soon turned into a deadly test of power as each man grasped the wrist of the other, straining to overpower him.

For long seconds, the contest seemed a standoff, for the combatants seemed equal in strength, and the penalty for losing was too severe for either to give in. It soon became apparent that the struggle was to become one of endurance, as they both strained to gain the advantage.

Suddenly they were startled by the sharp report of a .44 Colt, and Iron Pony's hand went slack when a bullet ripped into his side. Quick to take the opportunity handed him, Slater wrenched his knife hand free of Iron Pony's grip and drove the blade deep into his stomach. Their eyes locked briefly as the stunned savage stared in disbelief before sagging helplessly, supported solely by Slater's right arm, until he withdrew the knife and let him collapse at his feet.

Almost physically spent, Slater took only a quick glance to make sure the warrior was finished before turning to look in the direction from which the shot had come. Sawyer was lying on his stomach, his arm still stretched out with his pistol in his hand, his face resting on the hard dirt. Slater went to him at once, certain that he was dead, for the back of his shirt was soaked with blood. He knelt beside him and rolled him onto his side. Sawyer's eyes fluttered slightly, then opened halfway. "Did I get him?" he asked feebly.

"You did," Slater answered, "and you damn sure saved my life."

"Are there any more of 'em?"

"I reckon not," Slater said, "or we wouldn't be talkin'." He tried to get a better look at the wound in Sawyer's back, not sure if he was dying or not. There was so much blood that he couldn't tell. "I gotta get you back to the fort, to the hospital. Think you can stay on a horse?"

"I don't know," Sawyer said, laboring with every word. "I can try."

"Let me make sure of our friend over there. Then we'll see," Slater said. He took the .44 from Sawyer's hand and returned to the dying hostile by the edge of the water. With no hesitation, he held the pistol to Iron Pony's forehead and pulled the trigger. Then he went back to see if Sawyer could be put on his horse.

He managed to get the wounded man on his feet, but Sawyer was already too weak to stand, even with

Slater's help. So Slater picked him up in his arms and carried him to the cabin and laid him down on his bedroll by the fireplace. He looked around the cabin until he found some ragged cloth to stuff against the wound to slow the bleeding.

"Ain't nothing more I know to do for you," he said. "But it looks to me like you can make it. So I'm gonna build a fire in the fireplace so you stay warm. Then I'm gonna saddle my horse and ride back to the fort and find the doctor, and I'll bring him out here to take care of you." He paused to make sure Sawyer understood that he wasn't leaving him for good. "You just lay there, and don't die after I go to all the trouble of findin' the doctor."

"I ain't makin' no promises," Sawyer replied weakly.

"You damn sure better not die before I get back. If you do, I'll throw your body in the same hole with that son of a bitch you just shot."

When Sawyer nodded in response, Slater hurried out the door and ran to get his horse. He didn't take time to saddle the paint, just grabbed his rifle from the sling and jumped on the horse's back.

With a brilliant full moon rising over the treetops, he followed the trail back down beside the creek, scanning the creek banks carefully to make sure the crazed savage had acted alone. When he reached the road, he nudged the paint into a full gallop and held him to it all the way to the post, which was a good mile away. While he rode, many thoughts filled his mind. Sarcastic when they first met, Sawyer had transformed into a solid friend, and he had fired the shot that might have saved Slater's life. It was a new experience for him. He had never been beholden to any man before. It was hard to say whether or not Sawyer had actually saved his life, because he wasn't sure who might have overpowered who. The savage was a powerful man, and while Slater was determined to prevail, he had to admit that it was dead even when Sawyer decided the outcome. And for that, he owed him.

He knew which building was the post hospital, so he rode straight to it, slid off his horse, and ran inside, startling a soldier on duty at the desk. "I need the doctor!" he exclaimed.

"What for?" the surprised corporal replied. "What's wrong?" He was obviously dumbfounded by the sudden appearance of the obvious civilian, dressed like an Indian, and no idea who he was. "This is a military hospital."

"I know that," Slater responded impatiently, then hurriedly explained what the emergency was.

"Damn!" the corporal exclaimed when he realized it was one of the scouts who had been shot. "But the doctor ain't here now."

Before Slater could demand where he was, they were interrupted by the sergeant of the guard coming through the door, having heard unexplained gunshots before. He had subsequently been alerted by one of the men on guard duty that he had seen a man on horseback gallop onto the post and head straight for the hospital. By a stroke of good fortune, it was Sergeant Bell.

"Slater!" he blurted. "What the hell's goin' on?" Slater hurriedly repeated the story and told him that Sawyer was unable to stay on a horse, or he would have brought him to the hospital. As soon as Bell heard it, he turned to the corporal.

"Dr. Davis has already gone home," the corporal blurted right away before Bell could speak.

"Who have you got here now?" Bell asked. When told that there were two hospital orderlies in the ward

area, Bell continued. "Send one of 'em to the post sur-
geon's house to get Dr. Davis. The other one can go
with me to the stable to hitch up the ambulance. Then
he can follow Slater here to pick up Jeb Sawyer. And
let's get it done quick."

"But who's gonna watch the patients if you take
my orderlies?" the corporal asked.

"I reckon you are," Bell said. "Now don't waste
any more time. The man could die while you're settin' here frettin' about it."

Things happened quickly after that. Sergeant Bell
helped the orderly hitch a team of horses to the ambulance and gave him orders to get back in all possible
speed. "Slater will take you there," he said to him.
Then he turned to Slater. "I'd go with you to give a
hand with Sawyer," he said. "But I'm pullin' sergeant
of the guard, so I can't leave the post." As an after-
thought, he asked, "And you're sure there weren't no
more Injuns with that one that jumped you?" When
Slater said he was, Bell commented, "If that ain't the
dangedest thing I ever heard. Just gone loco, I reckon."

"I reckon," Slater agreed, and jumped on the paint's
back when the orderly said he was ready to go.

They found Sawyer in pretty much the same shape
he was in when Slater left. The orderly took a moment
to take a look at the wound to see if there was anything more he could do before they moved him. The
only problem they had run into was that the trail back
into Sawyer's cabin was too narrow to allow the team
of horses to pull the ambulance all the way. They
made it halfway back before almost getting it jammed
permanently between two trees, so they left it there
and Slater and the orderly carried Sawyer to the ambulance.

When they made it back to the hospital, they found

the doctor waiting for them. He examined the wound and decided there was no reason to wait.

"We might as well go in and get it," he decided. "Let's get him cleaned up." He turned to Slater and Sergeant Bell, who had joined them. "You men can clear out of here now. I don't see any reason why he won't make it all right. It's a good thing you didn't wait any longer to get him here, though." Slater took one last look at the patient, and couldn't help noticing the pitiful look on Sawyer's face. He was obviously not as confident as the doctor.

Slater and Bell walked outside and stood by the steps of the building while Slater related the details of the attack at the cabin. "What did you say he called you?" Bell asked.

"White Crow," Slater said.

"And that don't mean nothin' to you?"

"Nope," Slater said. "He told me that was my name, but it don't mean anything to me."

"Maybe he was goin' after somebody named White Crow," Bell suggested, "and he got you mixed up with him."

"Maybe," Slater said.

Chapter 14

As the doctor promised, the patient came through the surgery in fine fashion, although he complained of extreme discomfort when Slater came to visit him the next day.

"I don't mind tellin' you I was not likin' my chances when you left me here last night. That's a mighty scary thing to me, a doctor with one of them sharp knives comin' after me. I ain't never had but one bullet took outta me before—took a .44 slug in my leg one time—and a Flathead medicine man dug that out—like to kilt me. So I figured diggin' one outta my back might be more'n I could stand. But it warn't bad atall, at least not as bad as that medicine man. They soaked a rag with some of that . . ." He paused, trying to remember, then asked the orderly who was changing his dressing, "What did they call that stuff?"

"Chloroform," the orderly said.

"Yeah, that stuff," Sawyer went on. "They poured some of that on a rag and held it under my nose and told me to breathe it in. Hell, I tried not to at first, but before I knew what was what, I'd done gone to sleep. When I woke up, he was already done. Only thing is I've got a helluva pain back there now. And I'm drinkin' all the laudanum they'll gimme."

Seeing a chance to finally slip in a word when the excited scout paused to take a drink of water, Slater was inspired to comment dryly, "'Pears they musta cut out your vocal cords."

"Cut out my vocal cords?" Sawyer asked, confused. "Whaddaya mean?"

"So you can't talk," Slater deadpanned.

"Can't talk. . . ?" he started, then, "Oh, so I can't talk." Then it occurred to him. "You're japin' me. You made a joke!" He looked at the orderly and exclaimed, "He made a joke!" The orderly merely shrugged, unable to appreciate the significance of Sawyer's remark, with no prior knowledge of the somber young man's history of no sense of humor. Sawyer couldn't help chuckling, even though it pained him. "I reckon I have been runnin' on, ain't I? Well, I'll shut up a little while so you can tell me about that visitor we had last night."

"There ain't much to tell," Slater said. "He was a Lakota Sioux, I can tell you that for sure. But I ain't got no idea how he stumbled on us, or what in the world he was doin' there all by himself. Looks like he was just out to kill some white men, and right in the middle of a bunch of soldiers, too. Maybe he was just out to do something brave to show his people he had big medicine."

Sawyer didn't say so, but he wondered if that was entirely true. He thought about what Sergeant Bell had told him about Slater killing an entire Lakota war party—and his actions against a second war party on the Boulder River. It struck him that maybe that Lakota warrior knew exactly who he was attacking. Maybe Slater had earned himself a special name for himself, White Crow, and there might be more Sioux warriors coming after him to make big medicine for themselves. It was a sobering thought.

"I dragged him off on the other side of the trees this mornin'," Slater went on. "I figured we didn't need to smell him when he started to get ripe, so I dug a hole and dumped him in it. We picked up a pretty good Injun pony, a speckled gray. A single-shot rifle, some cartridges for it, a good knife, that's about all he had that was worth anything. I reckon I'll go by the cavalry stable and pick up my packhorse and go on back to the cabin. When they say it's all right, I'll take you home."

"I 'preciate it," Sawyer said, seemingly quiet now.

Slater spent the next few days getting acquainted with his new home base. With the coming of colder weather, reported incidents of Sioux raiding parties declined to the point where army troops were not called upon to respond but once. This was a one-day patrol the day after Sawyer went into the hospital. Slater was assigned to act as scout, but the report turned out to be an incident in which a small rancher in the valley lost one cow, killed and eaten by some hungry Indians. They were long gone by the time the patrol arrived, so the troopers returned to the fort that night.

Slater had the time to fulfill his promise to return to Lame Elk's village, but he felt he should not leave while Sawyer was indisposed. So he spent his time working to improve the cabin and to do a little work on the barn that Sawyer had started but never completed. Sawyer was released from the hospital four days after his sur-

gery, primarily because the doctor and his staff grew
weary of the patient's constant complaining.

Once he was back in his cabin, he seemed content
to take his time healing, for it would be some time
before he was back on his feet again. Slater was satisfied that it had been a good move to share Sawyer's
cabin.

Situated near the fort, he had mountains to the
north, south, east, and west, with many canyons and
hollows to hunt. And for a brief while, he was even
busy enough to keep thoughts of Little Wren and Red
Basket in the back of his mind. There was a little town
about three miles west of the fort, still in the early
stages of birth. He had not been there, but Sawyer said
it was growing steadily, and already boasted a saloon,
a blacksmith and stable, and a general store. He said
they were calling it Bozeman, after the feller that cut
the trail through Sioux territory to get to the gold
strikes. Slater had not visited it because he had no
need of the services the town offered. The general supplies he needed, he found in the post sutler's store. He
was in a good place, at peace in his mind, as long as he
smothered occasional thoughts about the Crow village
on the Musselshell.

Unknown to him, or Sawyer, there was already a
new saloon going up in Bozeman. Carpenters were hurrying to finish it before the real hard winter set in. The
new establishment was to be operated by a man and
woman, as equal partners. The woman was reported to
be a wealthy widow, who gained her wealth in the gold
fields, and her partner likewise had struck it rich on
a claim in Last Chance Gulch near Helena. Both parties had come to Bozeman to look over the potential
for growth in the new town. They met by chance and
decided they could build a much finer saloon if they

pooled their resources. The result was to be the opening of the Golden Chance, the finest drinking establishment in town. A rumor was also circulating among some of the soldiers who visited the town that the widow wasn't half-bad-looking, and she might be offering additional services to the troops.

When Sawyer got wind of it, the news seemed to stimulate his healing process, for he could hardly wait to see for himself. Taking advantage of the infrequent patrols, Slater had made several trips into the Big Belt Mountains to the north to hunt elk. He knew where to find the great animals in their valleys and pockets where they went in the winter, and he had been able to cure a fair quantity of meat for both Sawyer and him as well as for Red Basket and her brother. One evening he found Sawyer eagerly awaiting his return from one of those trips.

"Damn!" Sawyer exclaimed, standing in the doorway of the cabin to greet Slater as he rode in, leading his packhorse, loaded with meat. "I've been waitin' for you. I thought for a while there that you was gonna stay up in those mountains overnight."

"I told you I wasn't," Slater replied.

"I know, I know," Sawyer answered hurriedly. "But Corporal Jarvis came by here this mornin' to see how I was doin'. He said the Golden Chance is finally done, they've already got their whiskey brought in, and they're open for business. He said it's as fine a place as you'd likely find in Omaha or St. Louis."

"Is that so?" Slater responded dryly, not really interested, as he started unloading his horses.

"I was thinkin' me and you could ride in to Bozeman and take a look at the new place. I swear, I think a little drink of whiskey would start me to gettin' well quicker."

Slater stopped untying his pack strap and turned to fix Sawyer with an incredulous gaze. "Is that a fact?" he replied. "It's a little late, ain't it?" He turned back and continued loosening his pack straps.

"I swear, Slater," Sawyer complained to his ever-stoic partner, "if sometimes you ain't the dimmest candle in the box. It's a damn saloon! They'll most likely be open all night."

"I need to do something with this meat I brought back," Slater protested. "How 'bout we ride over there tomorrow?"

"I need a drink tonight," Sawyer pleaded. "I got my mind worked up to it, waitin' all day for you to get back."

"What were you waitin' for me for? Why didn't you just go on over there by yourself? You can sit a horse now."

"Damn, partner," Sawyer drawled, "I thought about doin' that, but I thought you might wanna little drink yourself, seein' as how it's a brand-new place and all. So I thought it was the right thing to do to wait for you."

Slater turned to face him again. He thought he could guess the real reason Sawyer waited for him. Sawyer knew he had no interest in the new saloon, or any other one. He suspected Sawyer was a little hesitant to go there by himself. He was on his feet, but he still wasn't back to full strength. It took a while to recover from a wound like his, and it was a natural feeling to be physically cautious and unsure of yourself. He wanted Slater with him in case he ran into any trouble. And that was always a possibility whenever alcohol and rough men were stirred together.

"I've still got this meat to take care of," he said, hesitating.

"Hell, cold as it is, that meat'll keep," Sawyer insisted. "It'll be fine. I'll help you cure it tomorrow. Whaddaya say? We won't stay long, just long enough to have a couple of belts."

Releasing a weary sigh, Slater gave in. "All right. Let me get finished unloadin' it."

"I knew I could count on you," Sawyer said, a wide grin across his face. "My horse is in the barn, already saddled."

Corporal Jarvis had not exaggerated. The Golden Chance was a fine-looking building, especially when compared to the rough structures there before it. Slater imagined that the owner of the competition was not too happy about the grand opening.

It was well past the supper hour, and there were several horses tied to a new hitching rail. Off to the side of the building, a horse and wagon stood that had no doubt brought a load of soldiers from the fort. Slater and Sawyer pulled up to one end of the rail and dismounted.

After tying their horses, they walked inside, Sawyer in the lead. He headed straight for the bar, which a buxom woman, with long hair the color of a carrot, stood behind, helping the bartender pour drinks for the men crowded there. Slater stopped, dead still, to stare at the woman, scarcely believing his eyes. Lola Leach glanced up at the tall man in buckskins casually holding a rifle in his hand. Startled, she instantly opened her eyes wide in shock and spilled whiskey on the counter when she overfilled the shot glass she had aimed at.

"Hey!" the customer exclaimed. "Don't waste that precious stuff." She shifted her eyes toward him for just a second before setting the bottle on the counter and returning her gaze to the man coldly watching her every move.

After a long moment more, during which both parties seemed to be frozen with indecision, her look of alarm suddenly broke into a smile, and she greeted him. "Well, hello, sweetie, fancy seein' you here. Come on over and I'll pour you a drink," she said, and reached under the counter.

He quickly pulled his rifle up before him, but relaxed when her hand came back with a glass. He nodded when he understood how she was choosing to deal with their short history. He walked up to the bar and slid the shot glass of whiskey over to Sawyer, who accepted it without hesitation while staring in astonishment.

"Slater," she said softly, and unconsciously rubbed her jaw while continuing to smile at him.

"Lola, ain't it?" Slater responded. "I see you used that knife."

"All that stuff don't matter anymore," she said. "That's done and over with." She seemed to be stating her position as far as revenge was concerned. "I told you that ol' boy had found gold in that crick." She made a sweeping motion with her hand, indicating the busy saloon. "You shoulda listened to me. You coulda had a part of this."

"Wouldn'ta done me much good if I was dead," he reminded her.

"I'm willin' to let it lie, if you are," she said. "Matter of fact, I reckon I'm beholdin' to you for gettin' rid of that trash I was stuck with. I've got a new partner now, and I'm doin' a legitimate business here. Whaddaya say? Are you gonna be a problem for me?"

He thought about what she said for a few moments before responding, not really sure how he felt about the situation. Maybe she was right. Finally he said, "I've got no reason to cause you trouble. I figured we settled all the trouble back up in the mountains. When I rode down outta there, I left it all back there."

"Glad you feel that way. There ain't no sense in stirrin' up a pot of stew that's done gone rancid." She grinned big and said, "I'll let you meet my partner. He's in the kitchen, eatin' a late supper."

"Some other time," he said, having no interest in getting downright friendly with her and her partner. He turned abruptly and walked out the door, leaving Jeb Sawyer standing there speechless.

When Slater had gone, Sawyer turned back to face the smiling woman. "You know Slater?" he asked, recovering his ability to speak.

"We had occasion to bump into each other a while back," she said casually. "I didn't expect to see him again so soon." That was all she cared to offer. "What's he doin' around here, anyway?"

"Me and him are scouts for the army," Sawyer said.

"Well, he oughta make a good one," she said, then moved down the bar to refill an empty glass.

Sawyer tossed his third shot down and slammed the glass down hard on the counter while he endured the burn. He paused a few moments to consider his need for a fourth one before reluctantly turning to go after Slater. Outside, he found the quiet man standing by the hitching rail, gazing at a three-quarter moon that had just shown through a break in the heavy clouds overhead. He appeared to be deep in thought.

"I'm ready to go," Sawyer sang out, "just like I told you I would." Slater answered with no more than a grunt. They untied their horses and climbed aboard before Sawyer asked, "How do you know the lady in there? What was her name?"

"Lola," Slater answered. "I shot her husband and his partner." He pulled the paint's head around and started toward the end of the short street.

Sawyer gave his horse a kick and caught up beside Slater. "No, you don't, dad-gum it!" he said, exasperated with his stoic partner's tendency to keep things to himself. "Not this time, you don't," he insisted. "Whaddaya mean, you shot her husband and his partner?"

"They tried to kill me, so I shot 'em," Slater answered.

"That don't make no sense," Sawyer pressed. "She acted like she was glad to see ya. Looks to me like she woulda been thinkin' more about shootin' ya."

"I thought about that," Slater admitted, still offering no elaboration.

Sawyer was not to be ignored, however, and kept questioning until he wore the silent man down. And eventually Slater related the whole incident that had taken place in the Crazy Mountains, and the situation that he'd left Lola in.

"Damn!" Sawyer exclaimed. "She was a regular wildcat, weren't she? I'd say you was lucky to get outta that alive, instead of nothin' but a bullet in the shoulder." He said nothing more for a few minutes while he thought about the story he had just heard. Then he said, "She sure came out of it all right, though." He rode on in silence a few minutes longer. "And all her money is blood money."

"I reckon," Slater said.

Another conversation took place behind them in the Golden Chance that would have been of equal interest to Slater, had he known about it. After the two scouts had left the saloon, Lola went into the kitchen to see why her partner had taken so long to eat his supper. She found him standing just inside the kitchen door where he could peek into the barroom without being seen himself.

"What the hell are you doin'?" she asked.

"Who was that man you were talkin' to?" he asked, instead of answering her.

"Which one? I've been talkin' to a lot of men," she replied.

"The tall one, wearin' animal skins, like an Indian," he said, "the one you were talkin' to for about fifteen minutes."

"Him? He's one of the army scouts, over at Fort Ellis. Why? Is he somebody you know?" It was obvious from his behavior that it might have been somebody he didn't especially want to see. "If you wanna know the truth, he's the reason I'm a widow," she chortled, amused by the thought, considering how she had landed on her feet afterward. "Is he somebody you know?" she repeated.

"I don't know," he said. "I ain't sure. It's been a helluva long time if it is who I think it is. He weren't much more'n a boy when I last saw him, but he sure favors him, even in that Indian getup he's wearin'. Walks like him—I don't know, he just looks like him." He shook his head, perplexed. "It probably ain't him. What did you say his name was?"

"I didn't," she said. "His name's Slater."

That didn't mean anything to him right away, but it struck him after he said it over a few times in his mind. "Slater!" he exclaimed then. "It's him!" Staring at her with eyes wide with alarm, he blurted, "That's his middle name. His name is John Slater Engels Jr. That's his whole name! It's him, all right! I knew I'd seen that man before!"

Sharing his alarm now, Lola demanded, "Well, who in the hell is he?"

"He's the son of the woman I left up in Last Chance Gulch."

"He's your son?" Lola asked, astonished.

"No, he ain't *my* son," Henry said. "He's John Engels' son, the man his mother was married to before I moved in with her."

"Your widow," Lola said.

"Well, no," he said. "I never married her, and I reckon I did tell you she was dead. But the fact of the matter is, after I struck it rich up there, I didn't really have no use for her. So I just lit out for better diggin's."

Lola was not happy with the news at first, but the thought occurred to her soon after that it was Henry Weed's problem and not hers. Her first concern had naturally been for any circumstance that might endanger her new enterprise, but on second thought, why would it? If Slater should find out about Henry Weed, and decide to seek him out, the worst that could happen would be for one of them to kill the other. Either way, she wouldn't stand to lose. If Weed killed Slater, nothing changed. If Slater got Weed, she would be left with sole ownership of the Golden Chance and any money Weed had left.

"So you dumped his mama, did you?" She chuckled, amused that he had held that back, since they had both supposedly confessed that they were conscienceless scoundrels who would stoop to anything. "What are you thinkin' about doin'? You can't hide in the kitchen every time he comes in the saloon. I reckon you could try to catch him somewhere by himself and put a bullet in his back."

As appealing as that sounded to him, Weed was not a man with guts enough to do his own dirty work. He was too fearful to stalk a man as dangerous as Slater appeared to be. Then the solution to his problem struck him.

"Maybe I won't have to worry about takin' care of ol' Jace," he said with a smirk, referring to Slater by the name he had known. "Maybe the army will take care of him for me."

He told her then what he was going to do. After she heard his plan, she was impressed, and curious to see if it would work. It had a chance, she allowed.

Colonel A. G. Brackett looked up from his desk when Sergeant Major Millward rapped lightly on the open door. "Sir, there's a Mr. Henry Weed here to see you."

"Who's Henry Weed?" Brackett asked.

"He says he's one of the owners of that new waterin' hole in Bozeman, the Golden Chance," Millward answered.

"What's he want?" Brackett asked, expecting to hear some complaints about some rough behavior by some of his soldiers.

"I don't know, sir. He just said it's important that he talks to you."

"All right," Brackett said with a weary sigh. "Send him in." He put the report he had been studying aside and got to his feet, remembering to present a cordial front for the local civilian businessmen. "Mr. Weed," he greeted Henry when he walked in. "What can the army do for you?" he asked while motioning toward a chair in front of his desk.

"Yes, sir, thank you, sir," Henry responded nervously, and sat down. He was not at all comfortable in the presence of any form of authority, having usually been on the wrong side of the law. "Well, sir," he started, trying to recite the speech he had rehearsed. "I figured it was my duty as a law-abidin' citizen of this territory to let the army know about a fugitive from the law that's workin' right here under another name." This seemed to pique the colonel's interest a bit, so Weed continued. "There's a feller you hired to ride scout for you who's wanted in Virginia City for murder. He goes by the name of Slater, but that ain't his whole name. He's John Slater Engels Jr. and he killed a feller named Arlen Tucker. He was a blacksmith."

Brackett's attention was fully aroused at this point. He immediately called a picture of Slater to mind, and the way Lieutenant Russell had described him as a killer as lethal and as stealthy as a mountain lion. Still, he had to question the accusation, for the man had not struck him as a murderer.

"How do you know this?" he asked. "What proof do you have to support such a charge?" Slater was an excellent scout. Brackett didn't want to lose him.

"It was back a few years," Weed said. "I was there. I knew the boy. He's an outlaw, just like his daddy was. His daddy killed a man in Virginia City, and the vigilance committee hung him. The boy went into town to get the body and killed the man that tried to stop him. That'd be Tucker."

"You saw him do it?" Brackett asked.

"Well, I warn't right there when he shot Tucker, but I was workin' a claim right next to his daddy's, and his mother came to me for help when the boy came home. He admitted in front of me that he shot Tucker, cut him down with that Henry rifle of his daddy's. He threatened to kill me if I tried to stop him from runnin'. Then he packed up some things and lit out. I reckon he's been on the run ever since."

He sat back then to judge how the colonel took his story. Judging by the grave expression on Brackett's face, he was satisfied that it had given him reason for concern. "I don't know, but I reckon there's still a warrant for his arrest, even after this long a time," Weed said.

Brackett hesitated. This was serious news, indeed, and hardly welcome at this time, but he would have to act on it. "Well, Mr. Weed," he said, "these are very serious charges. And we can't arrest a man on nothing but an accusation by someone. All I can tell you right now is that I will investigate these charges and see if we can verify what you have told me today."

"You gonna let him run loose?" Weed asked. He was hoping for an immediate arrest. "If he finds out I told on him, he's liable to take off again. Matter of fact, I'm hopin' you ain't gonna tell nobody it was me that told on him, 'cause he's liable to come after me."

Brackett was still hesitant. Slater just didn't seem like the kind of man who would do that. He had little choice, however; he would have to investigate the complaint.

"I expect we'll have to take him in custody until we can find out more about the crime." He got to his feet and extended his hand to Weed. "Thank you, Mr. Weed, for bringing this to our attention. I assure you we'll look into it and do whatever the law calls for. I'm sure you understand that it's necessary to verify your testimony."

Weed got up and shook the colonel's hand, but he was not entirely happy with the outcome of the meeting. He had hoped the colonel would send some soldiers immediately to arrest Slater, but at least he had promised not to let him run free while they telegraphed around trying to verify his story.

After Weed left his office, Brackett remained at his desk, considering what he had just learned. "You heard?" he asked Sergeant Millward when the sergeant major stepped just inside the door. Brackett knew that Millward listened to everything that might be interesting going on in the colonel's office.

"Yes, sir," Millward replied. "I guess I couldn't help overhearin'."

Especially with your ear stuck against the wall, Brackett thought.

"You want me to detail some men to go out to that cabin and bring him in?" Millward asked.

Brackett hesitated, and then said, "No. Just send one man out there and tell him that I want to see him. I don't want to arrest him before we hear his side of the story."

"I swear," Private Bostic declared when he rode up to the cabin, "you boys are gonna clean them mountains outta any critter that's fit to eat."

"Talk to him," Sawyer said, nodding toward Slater, who was turning a side of venison over on the racks he had built for the purpose of smoking the meat. "I'm just helpin' with the curin'."

"Looks like you're fixin' a helluva lot more than two men can eat in one winter," Bostic said.

"Ha!" Sawyer grunted. "He ain't lettin' me keep but a little portion of it. He's thinkin' on feedin' a whole village of Injuns."

"This wouldn't hardly be enough to feed 'em the whole winter," Slater said. "But it'll help save a little of their buffalo meat."

"Whaddaya doin' out this way, Bostic?" Sawyer asked. "Get lost tryin' to find your way back to the fort?"

"Colonel Brackett wants to see Slater—Millward sent me to fetch him," Bostic replied.

"What's he wanna see me for?" Slater asked.

"I don't know. Millward didn't say—just told me to ride out here to tell you."

"Right away?" Slater asked. "I ain't halfway done with this meat."

"I reckon," Bostic said with a shrug. "When the colonel says he wants something, it usually means right now."

"Go on, Slater," Sawyer said. "I'll finish that up for you."

"All right," Slater said, "soon as I wash some of the deer off my hands and throw a saddle on my horse." He went to the creek to rinse his hands.

When they reached the fort, Bostic wheeled his horse toward the stable while Slater continued on to the headquarters building. He dismounted, looped the paint's reins over the hitching rail, and went inside.

"Sergeant," Slater greeted Millward.

Millward didn't return the greeting but instead pointed toward the office door. "Go right on in. The colonel's waitin' for you."

Slater couldn't help thinking that the sergeant major appeared to be a little stiff, not at all typical. His attitude seemed to be official-like, instead of the good-natured manner of a favorite uncle, as was his usual state. Likewise, he was met with a very grave expression on the face of Colonel Brackett when he walked into his office.

"You wanted to talk to me, Colonel?"

"Yes, I did, Slater," Brackett replied. "Slater," he repeated, as if considering the name. "You know, you've never told us your full name. We don't even have it on the pay vouchers when you get paid. That's not the way we usually keep records in the army. So tell me, what should we put on your pay vouchers for the rest of your name?"

Slater had hoped this subject would never come up. And until now it had never been a problem. "It's just Slater, sir. That's my whole name."

"Come, now, man," Brackett charged, "you've only got one name? When you were born, your mother and father didn't see fit to give you a proper name?"

"Reckon not," Slater replied stoically, suddenly feeling uncomfortable with the interview.

"Well, we've got to have a proper name for the army payroll records," Brackett went on, warming up to the game. "So how about we just write in a name just to make it official?"

Slater shrugged indifferently.

"Fine," Brackett continued. "How about John? That's a good common name. John Slater, you like it?"

"I reckon," Slater said, certain now that he didn't like where this was going.

"Hell," Brackett declared, "we might as well give you a full official name. I like Engels. Would that suit you? John Slater Engels Jr., does that sound like it would be a good name for you?"

So this is what this meeting is all about, Slater thought. His secret was out, but how? "Well, looks like you know my name," he said. "Why didn't you just ask me if that was my name, instead of makin' a little game out of it?"

"If I had, would you have denied it?" Brackett asked.

"Most likely," Slater replied truthfully. "I don't like that name." He had a feeling that there was a bigger issue to come, so he decided to find out. "Well, if that's all settled, I'll be on my way."

"I'm truly sorry to say that there's a more serious problem we have to address," Brackett said. "Now that you've admitted that you are John Slater Engels Jr., there is a matter of the murder of a man in Virginia City named Arlen Tucker." He paused to watch Slater's face. "And I'd like to hear what you have to say about that."

Slater went cold inside and every muscle in his body seemed to tense up like steel springs.

It had happened! The very thing he had hoped never to have to face was now laid out in front of him like a bloodstained shroud.

He glanced at Sergeant Major Millward standing in the doorway and noticed that the burly sergeant was wearing a sidearm. He was certain he had not been wearing it when he greeted him at the door. His initial impulse was to run, but he didn't see the possibility for success in the attempt without causing injury or death to anyone in his way. And he could not bring himself to do harm to the colonel or Millward.

Finally he made a simple statement. "He shot at me, so I shot him."

"Are you telling me that this man shot at you first?"

"That's a fact," Slater replied.

"And you killed him, but it was in self-defense?" Brackett shook his head, puzzled. "If that was the case, why did you run? Weed said you ran." He dropped the name before he caught himself. It was like throwing kerosene on a fire.

"Weed!" Slater exploded. "Henry Weed!" The somber facade that had always been presented to friends and enemies alike was transformed into a mask of pure fury, causing Brackett to recoil and Millward to drop his hand on his revolver.

"Easy, boy, easy." Millward attempted to calm the violent outburst. "Don't make me do somethin' I don't wanna do. You just stay calm, and we'll talk this thing out and get to the truth."

As suddenly as he had erupted, Slater's usual deadpan expression returned to hide the fury burning inside him, and he sat back in his chair, much to the relief of both of the soldiers. The hated name had registered in his mind, however, and if the slimy hoodlum was nearby, he would find him and see that he was amply compensated for exposing him.

Very calmly, he asked, "Where is Henry Weed?"

"I'm not at liberty to tell you that," Brackett answered. "It was careless of me to even mention the name. I had not meant to. It would do no good to tell you how I happened to talk to Mr. Weed." He released a long sigh, as if frustrated. "I'd like to keep you from committing another murder."

"I didn't murder anybody," Slater insisted. "I told you, he shot at me, so I shot back. I don't even know if I killed him. I didn't wait around to see."

"Did anybody see you shoot him?" Millward asked.

"Yeah, one ol' drunk settin' beside the buildin', but I don't know if he was too drunk to see what happened. I was just a kid. I was scared, and I ran. That's the whole story." He looked from one face to the other, then asked, "What are you plannin' to do with me?"

Both the colonel and the sergeant wanted to believe him. Lieutenant Russell and Sergeant Bell as well had expressed great admiration for his courage and his grit. Brackett was caught in a dilemma. He knew he should put him in the guardhouse until he had checked with the authorities in Virginia City. There was supposed to be a U.S. Marshal headquartered there. Maybe he could wire the marshal for confirmation of Slater's guilt.

He wished that he could let Slater remain free while that was being done, but he couldn't let the man go, trusting his word not to flee. His decision was made for him when he remembered how intimately Slater knew the mountains that surrounded this valley. If he fled to the mountains, he would never be seen again.

Reluctantly he ruled. "I'm going to have to sentence you to the guardhouse until we can verify your story. I'm sorry, but I've got no choice."

There was no change in the somber expression, but inside, the colonel's decision fell like a great boulder upon Slater's spirit. He could not bear the thought of being locked up in a small place with walls around him, shutting him off from the mountains and valleys.

Many thoughts bombarded his brain. What of Little Wren and Red Basket? Once again, a barrier had been placed in his way, keeping him from making good on his promise to them. These worries became entangled with thoughts of Henry Weed and the possibility that he had somehow landed here. And what of his mother? Was she alive or dead? Or was she here somewhere close? If that was so, it could only mean Bozeman. He had to find out, and how could he when he was locked away in the guardhouse?

"Are you going peacefully?" Brackett asked, breaking into his desperate thoughts. He knew he'd be faced with a problem if Slater decided not to. In hindsight, he would have had a squad of men there to escort the prisoner to the guardhouse.

"I reckon," Slater said, much to their relief. "I don't wanna cause no harm to you or Sergeant Millward."

The colonel was cursing himself mentally for not having that squad of escorts. He had not handled this interrogation very well, and now Millward was going to have to take Slater to the guardhouse by himself.

It was obvious to Slater that the colonel was reluctant to lock him up, and might have released him on his word to remain near the fort until something final was resolved. But he couldn't very well do that, because truth of the matter was Slater knew that he would not have waited for the army to check anything. He would have headed for the mountains straightaway, there or the Musselshell. That was Slater's way. If things were not good where he happened to be, then he'd go somewhere where they might be better.

Well, he thought, *I ain't gonna make things hard for the colonel.*

"Will you let Jeb Sawyer know what happened to me?"

"Sure will," Millward said.

"Let's go, then," Slater said, and got to his feet. Sergeant Millward stood aside to let him pass through the door. When they got outside, Slater asked, "Will you take care of my horse and things?"

Millward assured him that he would personally take the paint to the stable, and put his saddle in the tack room. That settled, they walked past the ammunition storehouse toward the guardhouse.

Chapter 15

"You can talk to him through the bars," Sergeant Fred Welch told Sawyer when he went to visit Slater in the guardhouse.

Then he opened the door leading to the cell room, which was actually one large room with no individual cells. Half of the room was occupied by two rows of cots. There were five prisoners in addition to Slater incarcerated at present, and they were all lounging on their beds, except Slater. He was standing at one of the small barred windows at the end of the cell room, staring at the hills in the distance.

"Hey, Slater," Welch called out, "you got a visitor."

"Hey, Sarge," one of the inmates japed, "you comin' to let me outta here?"

"Yeah, Price," Welch returned, "just as soon as I find that key I lost." He turned to Sawyer and said, "Take as long as you want."

"How's he doin'?" Sawyer asked, knowing Slater wouldn't be doing very well confined to a small space with a group of loud-mouthed drunks and petty thieves.

"All right, I guess," Welch said. "He don't cause no trouble. Most of the time he just stands there and stares out that window."

He turned then and went back to his desk in the outer office, leaving the door open.

"Jeb," Slater acknowledged when he walked over to the cell door.

"How you doin, Slater?" Sawyer asked.

"All right, I reckon," Slater replied.

Knowing that was a lie, Sawyer pressed him for information. He was stunned when he was told that Slater had been put under arrest on murder charges. In the short time he had known Slater, he felt confident that he knew the man well, and in his mind, he couldn't believe him to be a murderer without good reason. But he also knew that Slater did not share a great deal of his thoughts, especially when they related to his past.

"Tell me what this is all about," Sawyer insisted. "You look as edgy as a mountain lion."

In his typical simple and concise way, Slater answered, "When I was fifteen, I shot a man."

Sawyer continued to press him until he was finally able to hear the whole story. When he had heard it, he was not surprised to learn there was justification for the young boy to have shot the man.

"So this feller, Henry Weed," Sawyer asked, "he's the son of a bitch that went to the colonel about it?"

"What I wanna know is, what is Henry Weed doin' at Fort Ellis?" Slater said. "And where is he now, just passin' through, or settled somewhere near here?"

"You think he might have some money?" Sawyer asked when a thought popped into his head. "I mean like money to put in a business, like a saloon?"

The thought struck home with Slater as well. "You

mean like the Golden Chance?" He paused while that possibility took form in his mind. "Henry Weed wasn't nothin' but a two-bit outlaw. If he has any money, it's because he stole it, or he mighta struck it rich up near Helena."

"He might be the rich partner that woman at the Golden Chance is in business with," Sawyer said. "I don't recall hearin' his name."

It was enough to cause Slater's mind to spin wildly, and he knew he had to find out before it drove him crazy. Then it occurred to him that, if it was Weed, then his mother was in Bozeman, too. "His wife!" he blurted. "Did you hear anything about this man's wife?"

"He ain't married," Sawyer said. "I do recall hearin' that woman say he was a widower. She joked about them teamin' up, a widow and a widower."

Slater's eyes seemed to go blank, like those of a dead man, and his face appeared to turn to solid granite, hardened by the fury burning inside him. If this man was Henry Weed, and he was a widower, then his mother was dead, and in all likelihood, by Henry Weed's hand.

"I've got to get out of here," Slater stated softly, but with deadly conviction.

His desperation was not lost on Sawyer. He could see that his friend was just about to explode. "I know, I know!" Sawyer quickly tried to calm him. "I'll go see Lieutenant Russell and ask him if he'll help you. He thinks a lot of you, and when I tell him the whole story, I know he'll hurry things up to get you outta here." He could see that Slater was not placated by that. "For Pete's sake, Slater, don't go and do somethin' crazy and get yourself shot. Russell will help. I know he will. Just sit tight for a little while, and give 'em a chance. Brackett will do what he can, too. They know better'n to think you'd just up and murder somebody."

After a few moments, the stone-cold face softened to regain the normal somber expression Sawyer was accustomed to seeing, and Slater reassured him. "All right, I'll sit tight, but do me a favor, will you?"

"Sure," Sawyer replied right away.

"Pick up my horse and saddle at the stable and take him home with you. I ain't too happy lettin' those soldiers take care of him. They ain't used to workin' with an Indian pony like my paint, and I'm liable to be in here for a few days before they find out anything from Virginia City."

"Well, you're right about that," Sawyer said. "They're liable to try to shoe him or somethin'. I'll go get him right now."

"Don't forget my saddle," Slater said, "and make sure my rifle's still in the sling."

"I'll do 'er," Sawyer replied cheerfully. "I'm goin' right now, soon as I go find Lieutenant Russell. I reckon I'll see you tomorrow."

"Right," Slater said. He remained at the cell door until Sawyer left. Then he turned about and went back to the window.

"Go back to lookin' out that window," Private Price needled him when he walked by his cot. "Whaddaya see when you're starin' outta that window?"

"Mountains," Slater answered, and went to the window, where he stood up close to the small opening. He slipped the large spoon, which had come with his supper, out of his pocket and resumed his efforts to loosen the heavy spikes that held the bottom of the iron bars in place, being careful to shield his motions with his body.

"Shut up, Price," one of the other prisoners said.

* * *

As the evening hours passed slowly by, he remained at the window, working diligently on the three spikes, ignoring the occasional derisive remarks from the other prisoners. Had the window been any higher off the floor, or had he been a shorter man, he might not have been able to hide his determined efforts.

While Price and one or two others figured he might be "touched in the head," the rest of the inmates felt a modicum of sympathy for the near Indian who fought desperately to hold on to his beloved mountains. He remained at the window until the bugler blew taps and Corporal Johnson came with the changing of the guard and told him to go to bed.

"Those mountains will still be there in the mornin'," Johnson said.

It was a long night as he lay waiting for his fellow prisoners to fall asleep. He had no trouble staying awake, for he could not come to terms with the saggy cot, just as it had been with his first night in the cavalry barracks.

When finally the steady drone of snoring convinced him that he could go back to the window without being observed, he got up from the cot and walked silently to resume his work. The progress made during the afternoon and evening had been enough to convince him that he could force two of the three crucial spikes out of the sill.

The question he was not certain of was, could he work the final spike loose before sunrise? If not, it would mean another day and night before he could attempt to escape. His spoon was already bent almost double, and every time he straightened it again, he feared he weakened it so that it might eventually break in two. He had no choice other than to continue worry-ing the spike back and forth in an effort to force it to loosen.

Finally, in the early hours of the morning, what he feared might happen did. His spoon broke into two pieces.

He cursed silently as he held the two useless halves. Frustrated, he threw them out the window, but he was not ready to give up. There were still sev-eral hours of darkness left before sunup, so he tried another method. Since the first two spikes were loose, he pulled them out, and using one as a lever and the other as a fulcrum, he tried to pry the remaining spike up. To his surprise, the spike had been loosened enough with his spoon, so that it began to slowly back out of the sill. He immediately felt an increase in his heartbeat.

It was going to work!

He continued to work away at it, until it was free.

The next problem to be solved was whether or not he could squeeze his body through the small open-ing, and that was provided he was able to force the bars to hinge outward enough. There were no spikes through the sides of the iron frame, but there were spikes holding the top firm. He was gambling on the possibility that he could loosen the top spikes by using the iron frame itself as leverage. It was by no means a sure bet, but he was desperate to the point of taking the bet.

He braced himself for the moment of truth, took a deep breath, then strained against the frame with all the strength he could summon. There was just a little give in the spikes as the heavy frame moved outward a few inches. Encouraged by his initial effort, he continued again and again, gaining inches at a time. Soon he had forced the frame halfway, and he needed no incentive to continue.

Finally he succeeded in creating an opening that he felt he could force himself through. With one last look over the sleeping prisoners, he pulled himself up into the opening. For a brief moment, he feared it had all been in vain, but when he finally worked his shoulders through, he knew the rest of his body would make it with less effort.

Once he had cleared the window, he dropped to the ground, remaining in a squatting position while he listened and looked around him.

When he was sure there was no one to witness his escape, he stood up and pushed the iron frame back in place. He hoped no one would notice that the window bars had been forced up, at least long enough to keep them from immediately figuring out where he had gone. He dropped the spikes he had taken out on the ground, knowing he would be unable to force them all the way back down with his fingers.

Moving quickly along the back of the guardhouse, he knelt at the corner and waited until he spotted the sentry walking this guard post.

Once he had passed, Slater set out along the back of the stable at a trot, heading for the road to Bozeman.

Jeb Sawyer scrambled up from his bedroll and grabbed his rifle when he heard a loud knock on the cabin door. "Who the hell is it?" he roared.

"It's me, Slater. I'm comin' in, so don't shoot me." He opened the door partway cautiously. "Are you awake? I'm comin' in."

"I'm awake," Sawyer answered, although he wasn't

entirely sure. He stood there by the fireplace, still holding the rifle until he could see that it was really Slater. "What in the hell are you doin' here?" he asked, amazed. "What are you doin' out?"

"I couldn't stay in that guardhouse," Slater said. "I've got things I've gotta do."

"Like what?" Sawyer responded. "You're goin' after that Henry Weed feller, ain'tcha? Doggone it, Slater, I talked to Lieutenant Russell, and he said he'd make sure they got word to Virginia City right away. How'd you break outta the guardhouse, anyway?"

"Went out the window," Slater answered. "I 'preciate Lieutenant Russell tryin' to help me, but I might not have time to wait for word from those folks. Even then, it might not be good news, so I've gotta find out some things for myself."

"Damned if you ain't somethin'. You're gonna have the whole dang army after you—you know that? You want me to go with you? Went out the window?"

"No," Slater said. "I don't want you to go with me. I can't have you mixed up in this. Did you pick up my horse and saddle?"

"He's out back with the other horses," Sawyer said. "I shoulda known you was fixin' to do somethin' like this. Lemme pull my boots on, and I'll help you saddle up."

"I 'preciate it, Jeb."

They worked as quickly as possible, knowing that dawn was not far away and the first place the soldiers would look for Slater would be at the cabin. They saddled the paint and rigged his red sorrel packhorse with a small pack of meat and ammunition, coffee, and a few other essentials. It was not yet daylight when Slater was ready to ride.

"Well," Sawyer said as Slater stepped up into the saddle, "I reckon I'll see ya when I see ya. Try not to get yourself kilt."

"I'll try," Slater said, wheeled the paint around and splashed through the creek, and set out through the rolling prairie to intercept the road to Bozeman, instead of going back on the usual path.

It was not very long past reveille on the post when a hastily mounted detail of six troopers, led by a young second lieutenant, named James McGuire, turned onto the path by the creek that led to Jeb Sawyer's cabin. They pulled up before the cabin and Lieutenant McGuire called out, "You there, in the cabin, come out and show yourselves!"

In a few seconds, the door opened and Sawyer came out wearing nothing more than his long underwear and his boots. "What's goin' on, Lieutenant? What are you boys doin' up here?"

"We're looking for Slater," McGuire informed him. "Is he inside? If he is, he'd best get himself out here right now."

"Slater?" Sawyer asked innocently. "Why, no, he ain't here. He's in the guardhouse back at the fort."

"He escaped from the guardhouse, and I expect he came straight here," McGuire insisted.

"Escaped?" Sawyer exclaimed, excited. "Well, I'll be go to hell! How'd he do that, somebody forget to lock the door?"

"He went out the window," McGuire said, rapidly losing his patience, for he suspected that Sawyer might be stalling him. "Look, Sawyer, we're pretty sure Slater would come straight to your cabin to get his horse and saddle. Are they gone?" He directed his men to dismount.

"No, sir. Come on in and look around—cabin ain't hardly big enough for him to be here and me not know it. Course, I was doin' a little drinkin' last night, so I just got outta the bed." He stepped aside when a couple of soldiers went inside.

"Ain't nobody in here, Lieutenant," one of them called out.

"Where's his horse and saddle?" McGuire asked. "He usually rides a paint horse, doesn't he?"

"In the shed, yonder," Sawyer said, pointing to the half-finished barn. "I picked his horses up myself yesterday."

Two troopers ran to check and promptly hollered back, "His horse ain't here, but there is one saddle."

"Ain't there?" Sawyer asked, as if astonished. "Let me see myself." He hustled out to the shed and made a show of looking right and left. "Well, forevermore," he exclaimed. "It is gone—and his saddle, too. That's my saddle there." He stood there seemingly perplexed, scratching his head. "When did he get 'em? He musta slipped in here while I was asleep." He turned to face McGuire. "He's sure as hell gone now, ain't he?"

"I don't suppose you know where he might have gone," McGuire said, suspecting that Sawyer was simply wasting his time.

"Well, no, sir, but knowin' Slater, and the kinda feller he is, I expect he lit out straight north to the mountains."

McGuire, perplexed, said nothing for a long moment before finally commenting, "Since you're supposed to be employed as a scout, I could ask you to put on some clothes and find his trail for me. But I have an idea that might be just another waste of my time." He fixed Sawyer with a knowing smile.

"Why, no, sir," Sawyer replied eagerly. "I can get ready to ride right quick, and we'll see if we can pick up his tracks. Course, he's damn nigh an Injun, so he knows how to cover a trail."

"Don't bother," McGuire replied sarcastically. Addressing his men then, he said, "Mount up. We'll go on back to the post and see what the colonel wants to do."

"Lemme know if there's anything I can do to help," Sawyer called after them.

He stood near the cabin door and watched them until he could no longer see through the trees along the creek.

Well, boy, he thought, *I hope that'll give you a little more time to do whatever you're aiming to.*

Slater paused by the double doors of the Golden Chance. He pushed one of them open far enough to give him a view of the room he was about to enter, and he was pleased to see Lola Leach and Henry Weed sitting at a table near the kitchen door, eating breakfast. Weed was partially facing him, enough so that he could readily identify the villainous features of the conniving miscreant Slater had known when a boy. Other than having aged considerably, Weed looked the same. Slater stepped inside the empty saloon.

Engaged in an oft-repeated attempt to convince Lola that, as her business partner, he shouldn't have to pay for her bedroom services, Weed took no notice of the tall man who had just stepped inside the door.

Frustrated with the usual turndown from Lola, he glanced toward the door as he took another sip from his coffee cup. The specter that met his eye caused him to spill his coffee down the front of his shirt.

"Jace!" he almost screamed as the cup dropped noisily on the table.

Lola pushed back from the table trying to avoid getting splashed, startled by Weed's sudden spasm. Seeing the cause then, she got out of her chair and backed away from the table.

"Henry Weed," Slater proclaimed slowly. His tone, laden with contempt, sounded like an accusation instead of the simple statement of a name. Frozen by the spectacle that had suddenly appeared, Weed recovered somewhat and dropped his hand on the handle of the .44 he always wore. Slater's rifle came up immediately to cover him. "Go ahead, Weed, pull it. I'll oblige you."

"Whoa, Jace!" Weed blurted fearfully. "I wasn't goin' for my gun. I was just surprised, that's all. I didn't know it was you, boy." He attempted to fake a chuckle. "I mean, it's been a helluva lotta years, and you all dressed up in that Injun outfit. I just didn't recognize you," he said, forgetting that he had screamed out his name. "Yes, sir, you're a sight for sore eyes, all right. Ain't that right, Lola?"

For her part, Lola, having recovered from her initial fright, was more inclined to find the situation amusing. She moved a little farther away toward the kitchen door.

"I've got no part in this," she declared, smiling when she noted the sick expression on Weed's face.

Slater walked slowly toward the table, his rifle still aimed at Weed.

"Yes, sir," Weed said weakly, "it's good to see you again. Set down and have some breakfast. We've got us a good cook. She'll fix you up some eggs and bacon. I'll bet you ain't had no eggs in a long time."

Ignoring Weed's pathetic attempt to defuse the approaching disaster, Slater walked up to stand directly before him. "Talk I've heard says you're a widower," he said softly, his words measured and deadly. "I'd like to know a little more about that."

"No, no!" Weed quickly blurted. "That ain't true! That ain't true atall! You know I wouldn't never do no harm to your mama."

"I don't know that atall," Slater said, his tone still deadly calm as he raised the rifle up to aim it directly at Weed's forehead.

Weed shrank back in cold fear, knowing he was about to die. "No, wait!" he cried out. "Your ma ain't dead! I swear it! She's alive and well, got herself a fine cabin on a little stream called Beaver Run near Helena." When Slater didn't pull the trigger, Weed pleaded further. "Me and her decided we'd split up, that's all."

"What you mean is you ran off and left her to try to make it on her own," Slater said.

"No, sir, Jace, I wouldn'ta never done a thing like that," Weed said, "not to your ma." Thinking that maybe Slater was beginning to buy the story, Weed sought to add more. "Why, I loved your mama—like to broke my heart when she run me off."

That was too much for Slater to tolerate. Maybe he had scared the truth out of the cowering weasel. Maybe his mother was alive. He knew he was going to have to find out for himself, as he glared down at the terrified man.

He had come looking for him with the intention to kill him. As he looked upon him with such loathing disgust, he decided he wasn't worth the cost of a cartridge. He reached over the table and grabbed a handful of Weed's coffee-stained shirt. With one powerful tug, he dragged the frightened man across the table-top and onto the floor.

"If I don't find my mother alive," he threatened, "you're a dead man. There ain't no place on earth or hell I won't find you."

"She's alive! I swear it!" Weed cried.

Slater shoved the pathetic man flat on the floor, and took one quick glance in Lola's direction to find her still with a half grin on her painted face. It was then that Weed saw his chance. He dropped his hand down to pull the .44 from his holster, only to be slammed beside his head with the butt of Slater's rifle.

Knocked senseless, he collapsed back on the floor and lay still. Slater took the pistol from his hand and tossed it across the room, took another look at the smiling Lola, and walked toward the door.

"It's always a pleasure to see you, Slater," Lola called after him as he stepped outside.

Chapter 16

After two and a half hard days' ride, Slater had reached the town of Helena, which had been built almost overnight right along Last Chance Gulch. That was three days ago, and he was still searching for a stream called Beaver Run. He had asked in every saloon and store he could find, but no one had ever heard of the stream, and he was beginning to believe that there never was such a stream. Or maybe, he thought, it was known by some other name, which left him just as lost as before.

Discouraged, he had almost decided to return to Bozeman for another meeting with Henry Weed when he happened upon a small trading post beside a wide creek in the mountains south of the town of Helena. Running low on some supplies, he rode down to the creek and the weathered log building there with the handcrafted sign. He pulled up by a short hitching rail and dismounted.

After looping his reins over the rail, he ducked his head to enter the dark interior of the store. There was no sign of anyone, so he stood for a moment, looking around at the half-empty shelves. It didn't appear to be a very thriving business.

"Hello," he called out. "Anybody home?" There was no answer.

There was an open door to another room at the back of the store, and while he stood there waiting for some sign of life, a large yellow dog padded lazily out of the room and walked up to him to be petted. Slater scratched behind the hound's ears for a few seconds, then walked to the door and called out again, still with no answer.

I guess I'll wait and pick up what I need in town, he thought, and went back outside. He walked back to the rail to untie his horses.

"Some way to run a business," he said to the paint. "I reckon a man could just take what he wanted and ride off."

"A man could try," a voice overhead said, "if he don't mind ridin' off with a double load of buckshot in his hind end."

Startled, Slater spun around to look up and find a gnarly-looking, elflike old man standing on the roof, holding a double-barreled shotgun. "Damn!" Slater swore. "Why didn't you sing out when I called you?"

"I was on the back part of the roof, tryin' to patch a hole. Hell, I couldn't hear anybody inside the store at first. I'm hard of hearin' as it is, and when I did hear you, you was already out front. I'da come down to see what you wanted, but I kicked my ladder over when I swung my leg over to get on it—caught the side of the ladder with my foot—dang near fell off the roof."

Astonished, Slater shook his head. "No higher'n that roof is, you coulda just jumped off."

"Twenty years ago, maybe," the old man said. "I'd be obliged if you'd walk around back and set my ladder back up."

"Have you got any coffee beans?" Slater asked.

"Sure do. If you'll set my ladder up, I'll fetch some for you."

Slater walked around the log building and found a rickety ladder on the ground. He set it up against the edge of the roof and held it steady while the old man climbed down.

Once he was on the ground, the little man looked up at the formidable man towering over him and said, "I ain't got no coffee beans—ain't had any for over a month. I'm 'bout to starve for a cup of coffee myself."

Surprised, Slater said, "You just told me you had some coffee beans."

"Well, I was on the roof then. I didn't have no way of knowin' if you'd set my ladder up if I didn't have no coffee."

"If that don't beat all. . . ," Slater started impatiently. "Why would I do that?"

"I don't know. Tell you the truth, you kinda looked like an Injun, and I thought you might take a notion to clean me out and set the place on fire. And I just wanted to have my feet on the ground, in case you did."

"Do you have a lotta trouble like that around here?" Slater asked.

"Not for the last five or six years," the old man replied. "But you can't never be too careful." His heavy gray beard parted just enough to display a smile. "Glad to make your acquaintance. My name's Ike Bacon. I ain't never seen you in these parts before, and I've had this store here for fifteen years. I'm sorry I ain't got no coffee. Like I said, I got a helluva cravin' for a cup myself. Anythin' else I can help you with?"

"You ever heard of Beaver Run?" Slater asked, just on the chance, since Ike had been here so long.

"Sure, everybody knows where Beaver Run is," Ike said.

"Can you tell me how to find it?"

"Sure can," Ike said. "Take a half turn around. You're lookin' at it."

Almost stunned, Slater found himself gaping at the busy creek running behind the trading post, he whipped back around immediately. "I'm lookin' for a woman—"

"Me, too," Ike interrupted with a chuckle.

"I'm lookin' for a woman that was livin' with a man on a mining claim somewhere on this creek," Slater continued, ignoring Ike's attempt at humor. "The man ran off and left her. His name is Henry Weed." He needed to go no further.

"Henry Weed," Ike echoed at once, "that sorry piece of dung. I know him." He turned his head and spat in disgust. "He moved in on Jim Holloway's claim a few years back. Him and Jim was gonna work it as partners, and they did for a while. Jim came in here one day, struttin' like a rooster, said him and Weed had struck that rich vein he knew was there from the first day he put a pick in the ground. Wasn't a week later when ol' Weed came in here and told me Jim got kilt by a boulder he loosened, said it ran right over Jim. Weed said that vein had run out and he was leavin' the valley. That woman wasn't with him."

Concerned anew for his mother's safety, Slater pressed. "Tell me how to find that claim."

"Follow that crick right up the mountain for about half a mile, till you come to a cabin settin' on a rocky ledge above it," Ike said. "That's it."

"Much obliged," Slater said, and went immediately

to his horses. Before stepping up into the saddle, he went to his packhorse, opened one of the packs, and took out a sack. "I ain't got many of these left," he said, "but I'll share what I have." He hesitated a moment, then said, "Take off your hat." When Ike did, Slater poured half of his dwindling supply of coffee beans into the hat.

The heavy gray beard opened again, this time even wider than before. "Why, God bless you, partner. I 'preciate that—a whole bunch."

He stood back then, holding his gift in his two hands and watching Slater ride off up the mountain.

Leona opened the cabin door after another long and troubled night, anxiously listening for any sound that might mean Henry had returned from Helena. He had taken all four horses with him, his and Jim's two. His reasoning was that it would look less tempting to any would-be outlaw. That way, he would look like a typical trapper. It would be safer than leading one heavily packed horse, as he carried all their fortune to the bank to be assayed. She stared long and hard for as far as she could down the creek, hoping to see his horse suddenly appear. Like every day before, however, there was nothing.

At first, when he hadn't returned, she thought he was simply celebrating his newfound riches and when he finally sobered up, he would make his way back home—just as he had promised her. There was no way for her to know if he had been attacked or suffered an accident. She couldn't face the thought that he had left her behind, so she waited, barely able to survive, day after day.

In her anguish, she sat down on the ground in front of the cabin to continue to watch the trail leading up from below—praying he would appear, at the same time, fearing it would be a stranger.

Without invitation, a stray thought of her son entered her despair, and she cried out silently, *Oh, Jace, now I'm lost, too.* She hung her head and sobbed uncontrollably.

Suddenly she paused and listened, much as would a frightened rabbit. She thought she heard something down the mountain and she strained to hear it more clearly. *There!* She heard it again, closer, like horses coming up the trail beside the creek. *He came back!* she thought. But what if it was not him, but some drifter or claim jumper? She ran back into the cabin and sank on her knees to peek out the one window.

In a few minutes, she saw him, a tall man riding a paint horse and leading a packhorse. She could barely breathe as her heart began to pound with fear. Dressed in animal skins, he looked to be an Indian, and he stopped to look at the cabin. She trembled uncontrollably and almost gasped aloud when he urged his horse into the water and started across.

Oh, God, please help me, she prayed silently. He rode up from the water to stop his horse before the ledge, staring at the cabin above him, as if trying to determine if the cabin was empty. *He's looking for a place to take over,* she thought.

Helpless to defend herself, no weapons except a shotgun with no shells and a small kitchen knife, she decided her only hope was to bluff him.

"This cabin ain't available," she cried out as forcefully as she could manage. "I've got a rifle aimed at you right now, so you'd best just move on before my husband gets back. And he'll be back any minute now."

Slater was shocked for a moment. It had been so many years, yet he recognized his mother's voice. "Mama, it's me, Jace!" he called back. "I've come to get you." There was no answer from within the cabin, so he called out again, "Ma, it's Jace. Did you hear me?"

There was still no answer. He stepped down from his horse, then paused when he saw the cabin door open a few inches. He climbed up the layers of rock that served as steps and approached the door, stopping a few feet from it so she could look at him. The door opened wider, and a withered gray-haired woman stood, holding the latch.

"Jace?" she asked weakly, not trusting her eyes as she studied his face. "Is that really you?"

"Yes, ma'am, it's me," he said.

Suddenly she was overcome with the magnitude of the moment. The sight of him after so many years was almost too much for her. He quickly stepped up and caught her as her knees began to fail her, lifted her up in his arms, and carried her back inside the cabin.

Inside, he looked around him for a bed. There was none. In fact, the cabin was little more than a rough shack, this hovel that Weed had described as a fine cabin. The air in the shack was heavy and foul-smelling, so much so that he decided she would be better off outside. So he carried her back out of the cabin and laid her gently down beside the creek. She was so thin and emaciated that it was more as if he had carried a child in his arms.

He went back inside and pulled some blankets out of the cabin. Using them to make a mattress, he spread them on the ground, then wrapped her in one he carried in his packs before placing her on the mattress.

After checking again to make sure she was breathing, he went about building a fire to keep her warm. The next item was to cook something for her to eat, because it was apparent that she hadn't had anything for some time. He had what was left of his coffee beans and plenty of smoked venison, so he put that on the fire to give her something right away. When he came looking for her, he hadn't thought about the possibility that she might be approaching starvation.

In a few minutes, she regained consciousness, and her eyes opened wide, staring at him as if expecting him to suddenly disappear, not sure if she was dreaming or not.

When his image failed to fade away, she saw that he was real, and she began to sob uncontrollably, realizing that her prayers had been answered. She was not going to die in this wilderness.

"Jace?" she asked again to be sure.

"Yes, ma'am," he answered. She took the strip of roasted meat he offered, and began to chew on it gratefully. "I'll have you a little coffee in a minute or two," he said.

He stayed close by her side for the rest of that day. She seemed to need him close, afraid that if she closed her eyes, he might be gone when she opened them again. Gradually she regained some strength, and by the time nightfall descended upon the mountain, she drifted off into a sound sleep.

The next morning, she was secure in the knowledge that her lost son had come to save her, and her long ordeal with Henry Weed was at last over. After another day and night, she felt she was strong enough to ride, so Slater made a saddle for her, Indian-style, with blankets and straps from his packsaddle. They descended the mountain to stop at Ike Bacon's store, where Slater bought dried beans, bacon, flour, salt, and sugar, in order to provide his mother with something other than jerky to eat. Ike was very generous in his prices and even tried to return Slater's coffee beans.

"If I'da knowed you was still up there in that camp, I'da sure come up there to help you," he claimed.

"I'm sure you woulda," Slater said as he turned the paint's head toward the valley.

They began a journey that would take four days to reach the only place he could think of where his mother could be cared for, and he might escape an army patrol.

"It's Slater!" Little Wren exclaimed excitedly.

Red Basket turned to look in the direction Little Wren indicated. It was Slater. That much she could tell by the paint pony and the way he sat the saddle. There was someone behind him on the red sorrel. It looked like a woman, and as they came a little closer, she could clearly confirm it.

Without thinking, she turned to look at Little Wren, whose joyful face had turned into a frown. A few minutes later, when the riders approached the outer ring of tipis, the young girl's face relaxed into a smile again when it was clearly an older woman riding the sorrel. By then, others in the village saw the riders and came to greet them.

As Slater had anticipated, his mother was warmly welcomed by the Crow camp, especially Red Basket, for she saw it as a sign that Slater would be even more closely bound to the village.

"Leona," she repeated when Slater introduced his mother. "You are welcome here. I think you will make this your home." She turned and smiled at Slater. "While you have been away, I have been helping Little Wren build her tipi. I think she has decided it is time to prepare her lodge for her husband."

The news caused Slater to look quickly at Little

Wren, an expression of distress displacing his usual stoic demeanor. He felt himself a fool for being too occupied with so many other issues that he'd let her slip away. There was no one to blame but himself, but even if he had made his feelings known, he might have misinterpreted her regard for him. He looked at the lovely young maiden smiling so warmly at him and made an effort not to show his disappointment.

"Who's the lucky man?" he asked, knowing the answer would be Running Fox.

"You," she said, still smiling. "Red Basket told me you want me for your wife. You just don't know how to ask." She poked her lips out in a pretend pout. "I'm tired of waiting. You ask me now."

He was totally stunned, not certain this was really happening, but he knew if he missed this opportunity, there would probably not be a second chance. So he blurted, "Will you be my wife?"

"I'll think about it," she said, and giggled delightedly while the small crowd that had gathered around them burst into laughter. "You have to talk to my father."

Broken Ax beamed proudly.

It was supposed to be a happy time for the man who simply called himself Slater, and in many important ways, it was. There were still problems that plagued his mind, however, issues that had not been resolved—the desire to extract vengeance from Henry Weed for what he had done to his mother—and the threat that any day a cavalry patrol might show up in the village. Red Basket had extended an invitation to his mother—insisted, in fact—that she move into her lodge.

"I need the company of a woman closer to my age," she said.

Slater was happy that his mother was obviously very pleased to be received so warmly by the village. Still, these other things troubled his mind.

Then one day, a rider was spotted approaching the village. He was leading a string of three heavily loaded packhorses.

"Sawyer," Slater murmured softly, and put the bridle he had been repairing aside. He rose to his feet and walked to the center of the village to greet his friend.

"I figured you'd eventually make your way back here to Lame Elk's village," Sawyer said when Slater walked forth to meet him. He dismounted and looked around him. "Thought you might appreciate it if I brought all this meat you been curin'. Figured you warn't expectin' me to eat it."

"I was thinkin' you might show up here one day," Slater said. He looked over the string of packhorses, already drawing the interest of the others in the village. "This'll sure help with the meat these folks have cured so far."

"Some of the other villages are havin' a hard time of it this winter, and they're movin' in closer to the Crow Agency where they can get a little help from the government," Sawyer said.

"Yeah, that's what I hear," Slater said. "Lame Elk and the elders have been talkin' about that, even though they had a decent buffalo hunt this past summer. Course, that don't set too well with me, seein' as how the agency is so close to Fort Ellis."

"That might not be as big a problem as you think," Sawyer said. "Colonel Brackett sent me to find you."

"That so?" Slater replied, immediately wary.

Sawyer couldn't help chuckling at his friend's reaction. "Yeah, that's so. He thought maybe you're ready to surrender." Then before Slater could respond, he went on. "I'm just joshin' you, partner. Fact is, Lieutenant Russell finally got somethin' done with those folks over in Virginia City. You didn't kill nobody. That feller, Tucker, is still alive and kickin', although he's got a big scar next to his belly. The reason there warn't no sheriff or deputy marshal lookin' for you is because of what the barber told 'em. He said he drank too much, made him sick, and he sat down outside the side door of the saloon to get some fresh air. He was drunk, he said, but sober enough to see that Tucker drew on you and you shot in self-defense." He paused then to let Slater absorb what he had just told him.

Slater was speechless. It was almost too incredible to believe. He looked at once to Little Wren, then found his voice.

"I won't have to run, or hide, anymore." He felt as if a heavy weight had been lifted from his soul, and he could now live as a free man. There remained only the thought of Henry Weed that would not let his mind rest completely.

"That's a fact, partner," Sawyer went on. "And Colonel Brackett sent me to find you to tell you that. He also said he'd sure like to have you back as a scout come spring. So that'll give you somethin' to think about." A thought struck him then. "Come to think of it, if Lame Elk does move the village in close to the agency, it'd make it a lot easier for you to ride with the cavalry from time to time." He was aware of the pretty young Crow girl who had moved up close beside Slater.

"Tell you one more thing that might interest you," Sawyer continued. "That feller that caused all the trouble in the first place, that Henry Weed, well, he passed away last week."

"What?" Slater recoiled, startled. He looked immediately to his mother standing nearby. Her expression told him that she had heard Sawyer.

There was a definite twinkle in Sawyer's eye when he explained, "Seems he'd been actin' loco ever since he got knocked in the head. Maybe a horse kicked him, or somethin', I don't really know. Anyway, that lady partner of his—you remember Lola—she found him in his room, lyin' on the floor, with the side of his head blowed away, and a pistol in his right hand. Clear case of suicide, everybody said. Anyway, I thought you'd be interested."

Slater thought about it for a few moments. Sawyer said the pistol was in his right hand, which was kind of unusual, since Henry Weed was left-handed. It didn't take much imagination to conclude that Lola took care of the Henry Weed problem for him and got Weed's half of the business as well.

He looked around to see his mother's smiling face as she stood next to Red Basket. The only one missing now was Teddy Lightfoot, but Slater had a feeling Teddy was happy that all his troubles were over—all except one. He put his arm around Little Wren and gave her a big squeeze.

"Come on, Sawyer," he said with a wide smile, "and meet my wife and my mother, and then we'll have us a feast of some of that meat you brought. I ain't ever felt this good before."

Gazing happily at the smile on Slater's face, Red Basket nodded contentedly. Speaking in her heart, she thought, *See, Teddy, he has finally learned to smile. It looks good on him.*

Read on for a preview of
another thrilling adventure
from Charles G. West

WRATH OF THE SAVAGE

Available now from Signet in print
and e-book.

Second Lieutenant Bret Hollister swallowed the last of his coffee and got to his feet. He took a few seconds to stretch his long, lean body before walking unhurriedly over to the water's edge, where he knelt down to rinse out his cup. When he stood up again, he glanced over to catch the question in Sergeant Johnny Duncan's expression. Knowing what the sergeant was silently asking, Hollister said, "Let's get 'em mounted, Sergeant. We need to find this fellow before nightfall."

"Yes, sir," Duncan answered, anticipating the order and turning to address the troopers who were taking their ease beside the stream. "All right, boys, you heard the lieutenant. Mount up."

He stood there, holding his horse's reins, and watched while the eight-man detail reluctantly climbed back into the saddle. When the last of the green recruits was mounted, Duncan climbed aboard and looked to the lieutenant to give the order to march. *A sore-assed bunch of recruits,* he thought, although not without a modicum of sympathy for their discomfort. Not one of the eight men had ever ridden a horse before being assigned to the Second Cavalry just three months before. Duncan knew that the reason they had been assigned to this detail today was primarily because of their greenness. He also knew that the reason he had caught the assignment was that Captain Greer felt confident he could nursemaid the raw troopers, and maybe the lieutenant in charge of the patrol as well.

Bret Hollister might make a good officer one day, Duncan speculated, depending upon whether or not he stayed alive long enough to wear off some of the polish associated with all new lieutenants coming out of West Point. He had only been with the regiment a year and a half, right out of the academy, and as far as Duncan knew, he hadn't distinguished himself one way or the other. This rescue detail would be the first time the sergeant would report directly to Hollister, so in all fairness he supposed he should give the young officer a chance to prove himself.

Hollister had been posted to Fort Ellis in time to participate in the three-prong campaign to run Sitting Bull and Crazy Horse to ground. That campaign resulted in the annihilation of General George Custer's Seventh Cavalry at the Little Big Horn. By the time the four hundred troopers from Fort Ellis made the two-hundred-mile march to the Little Big Horn, they were too late to reinforce General Custer. So the only combat experience Lieutenant Bret Hollister had was in the burying of slaughtered troopers of the Seventh and relief of the survivors under Major Marcus Reno. It was hardly enough to test the steel in the young officer.

Duncan's thoughts were interrupted briefly by the order to march, but his mind soon drifted back to his dissatisfaction at being assigned to nursemaid a green patrol, commanded by a green officer. It was especially irritating when the rest of the regiment was preparing to move out to intercept a band of Nez Perce intent upon escaping the reservation. He didn't like being left behind by his company and regiment, the men he had soldiered with for more than two years.

"Damn it," he muttered, "orders are orders."

"Did you say something, Sergeant?" Bret asked, reining his horse back a bit.

"Ah, no, sir," Duncan replied. "I was just talkin' to myself."

Bret smiled. "Better be careful. Talking to yourself might be a sign of battle fatigue."

"Yes, sir," Duncan said. *Don't know what the hell you'd know about battle fatigue,* he thought. Then he reprimanded himself for his attitude. *Best forget about my bad luck and think about why this patrol was ordered out.*

The admonishment made him feel a little guilty, for the patrol was an important one. Reports of two separate raids on homesteaders along the Yellowstone River by renegade Sioux and Cheyenne had come in to the post just hours before the regiment was prepared to march to intercept the Nez Perce. From the report of the young man who had ridden to Fort Ellis with the news of the attack, both families were massacred. Duncan figured the Indians had too great a head start for there to be any reasonable chance of overtaking them. He supposed the real purpose of the patrol was to show some response from the army, even with only an undersized patrol of eight privates, one sergeant, and one officer.

Because of the nature of the mission, and the need to travel light, the men had been ordered to leave all personal items and clothing behind at Fort Ellis. Each man was issued four days' rations and told to take only one blanket, one rubber ground cloth, one hundred rounds of ammunition, no cooking utensils except one tin cup, and four days' horse feed. Those marching orders told the sergeant that they were expected to return to base as soon as they confirmed that the hostiles were no longer in the area.

Duncan had persuaded Captain Greer to let them seek out Nate Coldiron to help track the Indians responsible for the raids, just in case the trail was hotter than the young man reported. One day of their rations would already be gone in the time it would take to find Coldiron, but it couldn't hurt to have the old trapper along. He was a hell of a hunter, and Duncan thought the patrol might be out longer than four days in spite of their orders. If that was the case, he was confident that they wouldn't go without food.

Coldiron, a cantankerous old trapper and former army scout, had a cabin on the east side of the Gallatin River at a point where a wide stream emptied into it. Duncan had been to the cabin once before when Coldiron had agreed to lead a scouting mission a year earlier. Duncan knew he could find it again, so he led the small patrol west from Bozeman to intercept the Gallatin River, the point from which they were now departing. As best he could determine, the stream that flowed by Coldiron's cabin was about twelve miles south, so the patrol set out to follow the river.

The farther south they traveled, the rougher the country became as they approached the rugged mountains that hovered over the narrow river. Along the way, they passed many streams that fed down into the river, all looking enough alike to make it difficult to identify one particular one, especially after a year's time. "Are you sure you'll recognize the stream we're looking for?" Bret felt compelled to ask Duncan. "It's not easy to tell one of these from all the others."

"Oh, I'll know it when I see it," Duncan assured him. "We ain't gone far enough to strike it yet."

It was toward the later part of the afternoon when they finally reached what Duncan referred to as Coldiron Creek. "This is it," he proclaimed, and pointed toward the top of the mountain. "It goes straight up that mountain. Coldiron's cabin is about half a mile up."

Bret could see why Duncan had been so confident in his ability to identify the proper stream. It emptied into the Gallatin between two big rocks. He followed the winding stream up the slope with his eyes until it disappeared into the thick foliage of the tall trees. Above the tree line the steep mountain peaks stood defiantly discouraging the casual climber. "It looks pretty rough. Maybe we'd better dismount and lead the horses up there."

"It looks rough," Duncan replied, "but there's a game trail followin' the stream up the hill, and we can ride it if we take it slow. It's just hard to see it from here. I'll lead the way."

He didn't wait for the lieutenant's order, but started up through a thick stand of fir trees that bordered the river. Bret fell in behind him with eight unenthusiastic troopers following him, complaining about the occasional branches that slapped at their faces.

"Quit your bellyachin' and keep up," Duncan called back over his shoulder, admonishing his men.

As Duncan had said, they soon struck a game trail that circled around from the north side of the mountain and started up the slope beside the stream. Bret couldn't help thinking how far removed he was from the cavalry combat training he'd been drilled in at the academy. There had been very little time spent on the basics of Indian fighting. He was convinced that it was certainly a worthwhile patrol. But what were the odds of tracking a war party of Indian raiders that had a two-day head start? Not very high, in his estimation. Then he reminded himself not to question orders. He didn't want to start complaining like the privates following him. His thoughts were interrupted then by the sound of a rifle cocking, and a booming voice. "Somethin' I can help you soldier boys with?" The question was followed almost immediately by an exclamation. "Well, damn me—Sergeant Johnny Duncan! I thought you was dead."

"Not by a long shot," Duncan replied. "Where the hell are you?"

"I'm right here," Nathaniel Coldiron replied, stepping out from between two boulders on the other side of the stream.

Bret Hollister would never forget his first sight of the old scout. From behind the boulder, a man more closely resembling a grizzly bear pushed through a thicket of berry bushes and crossed the stream, oblivious of the water. Clad entirely in animal skins, he wore no hat. His long gray hair, tied in a single braid, hung down his back almost to his belt. A full beard, more gray than black, covered the bottom half of his broad face—so thick that, until he opened his mouth to speak, there appeared to be no hole there at all.

"What you doin' up here, Duncan?" he asked as he eased the hammer down on his rifle—a Henry that looked unusually small in his oversized paw.

"Lookin' for you," Duncan answered.

"What fer?" Coldiron asked, all the while casting a critical eye on the officer and enlisted men behind the sergeant.

"Got a little job for you," Duncan said. "That is, if you ain't got too old to do some trackin'."

Coldiron snorted scornfully. "If you thought I was,

I don't reckon you'da drug your tired old ass up here lookin' fer me." He nodded toward Bret then. "Who you brung with you?"

Standing patiently by while the two old acquaintances greeted each other, Bret spoke up before Duncan could answer. "I'm Lieutenant Hollister. We came looking for you in hopes you might be able to track an Indian war party that massacred two white families over on the Yellowstone near Benson's Landing."

Coldiron nodded thoughtfully, openly distrustful of most army officers and all officers as young and green as this one appeared to be. "I heared about that raid," he said after a pause. "Two families got burned out. That was two nights ago. And you're lookin' to track 'em?"

"We're looking to try," Bret replied. "Those are my orders."

"Orders is orders. Ain't that right, Duncan?" Coldiron glanced at the sergeant and laughed as if he had made a joke. "That's a mighty cold trail you're lookin' to follow."

Bret began to lose his patience with the seemingly sarcastic brute. "That's the only trail there is. If you don't think you can help us, then I expect we'd best not waste any more of your time."

Coldiron chuckled and winked at Duncan. "Don't get your fur up, sonny. I didn't say I wouldn't help. I'll go over there with you and take a look around— see what's what."

"Fine," Bret replied. "That's all we're asking, but let's get one thing straight from the start. My name is Bret Hollister. I'll answer to Lieutenant, Hollister, or Bret, but don't ever call me sonny again. Is that understood?"

Coldiron jerked his head back, surprised by the young officer's spunk. It was only for a moment, however, before he chuckled heartily. "All right, *Lieutenant*, that's understood."

Also amused by the lieutenant's defiant attitude, Duncan said, "I reckon we'd best get started as soon as possible—cold as that trail is, and it's a pretty long ride if we have to go back the way we came." He looked up, trying to find the sun through the treetops. "It ain't gonna be long before dark in these mountains."

"I expect you're right about that," Coldiron said. "Ain't no use to start out till mornin', anyway. We ain't goin' back the way you came up the Gallatin. We'll cut across through the mountains, and if we try to make it in the dark, we're liable to break a leg or somethin'. Besides, I got things to take care of before I can go. I gotta check my traps for certain." He turned to start up the slope. "You boys follow me and I'll carve off some deer haunch to cook for supper, unless you druther have that salt pork and hardtack the army gave you." His remark stirred a quiet murmur of anticipation among the eight troopers as they followed up through the steep path to Coldiron's cabin.

Afraid the horses might stumble as the path steepened even more, Bret had the men dismount and lead them the last fifty yards to the small clearing where the cabin sat, backed up against the slope. Coldiron had obviously built his small abode using logs from the trees he had cleared. Bret wondered if he had had help in the construction, but from the look of the man, he seemed capable of doing the job by himself. A short distance beyond the cabin was a sizable meadow where the huge man's two horses were grazing. Sergeant Duncan and the men took the horses there to graze overnight while Bret volunteered to help their host build a fire. "Them Injuns take anybody alive?" Coldiron asked when Bret brought an armload of wood from a pile near the cabin.

"Not according to the report by the thirteen-year-old boy who rode to Fort Ellis," Bret answered. "They killed everybody and set fire to the homes."

"Like I said," Coldiron replied, "I heard about the raid. I didn't hear about nobody bein' took alive, either."

"That's what I was told," Bret repeated.

"That kinda surprises me," Coldiron said. "Sometimes they'll carry off a young woman."

"The Sioux and Cheyenne have been known to take women hostages plenty of times before," Johnny Duncan commented as he walked up, having overheard the last remarks. "I don't see why these Sioux would be any different."

"Blackfoot," Coldiron said. "They was Blackfoot. They ain't Sioux or Cheyenne. They most likely were movin' too fast to bother with captives."

"Huh," Duncan grunted. "How do you know they were Blackfoot? We were told they were Sioux. Them and some Cheyenne renegades have been attackin' some farms along the Yellowstone for the last two months."

"The Injuns that hit Benson's Landing was Blackfoot," Coldiron stated matter-of-factly. "I seen 'em when they came down the river last week. I figured they was lookin' to steal horses or raid homesteaders, but there ain't no homesteaders on the Gallatin, so I reckon they moved on. They was a long way from home, if they were from that bunch up near the Judith. I thought that mighta been them comin' back when you soldier boys came ridin' up my trail."

"Maybe so," Duncan allowed. "Don't make much difference, though. Injuns is Injuns. Where's that haunch of deer meat you was braggin' about?"

Coldiron chuckled again. "Still on the deer," he said and pointed to a tree by the stream on the far side of the cabin, where a carcass was hanging from a limb. "I was just fixin' to butcher it when I heard you boys comin' up my trail soundin' like a freight train. I hadn't kilt it more'n fifteen minutes before that."

His comment surprised Bret. "We didn't hear a shot," he said. "If we were that close, I woulda thought we'd have heard the shot."

"Most likely because you boys was makin' so much noise comin' up through them bushes," Coldiron said, then waited for a few moments before explaining. "Coulda been 'cause I shot it with my bow, though." He looked at Duncan and laughed heartily. "If one of your boys can give me a hand, I'll go saw us off a haunch. Wouldn't be a bad idea if we smoked a supply of meat to take with us. We don't know how long it'll take to catch up to that raidin' party."

Duncan nodded toward Private Tom Weaver, motioning for him to follow Coldiron.

National bestselling author
RALPH COMPTON

"A writer in the tradition of Louis L'Amour and Zane Grey!" —*Huntsville Times*

Available wherever books are sold or at
penguin.com

S543